Ruthless Spirits

by

Sandy Wolters

Spirit Voices, Book Two

Ruthless Spirits

Cover Art by *RJ Morris*

The Wild Rose Press, Inc.
PO Box 708
Adams Basin, NY 14410-0708
Visit us at www.thewildrosepress.com

Publishing History
First Fantasy Rose Edition, 2018
Print ISBN 978-1-5092-2101-1
Digital ISBN 978-1-5092-2102-8

Spirit Voices, Book Two
Published in the United States of America

The sound of Rainy's voice

floated on the breeze and nudged him out of his thoughtful deliberations. Glued to his hiding place, Terry was transfixed as her arms lifted to the sky. The ritual athame glinted in the dusky light like a beacon calling to him. She used the dagger to bury some little trinket at the base of the altar where a few short minutes ago Jody and Jared had stood to pledge their love.

Each movement flowed from one to the next and appeared choreographed like a beautiful dance. Enthralled, Terry couldn't take his eyes off Rainy as she rose and slowly turned in circles. The ceremonial knife, now carefully wiped clean on her robes, pointed away from her body and toward the ground.

Sinking further into the shadows, he continued to watch the spectacle of Rainy's ritualistic duties. The hypnotic effect persisted and strengthened. Terry's temples started throbbing to the percussive beat of her almost silent voice. His vision blurred. Images became obscured, and colors took their place. A bright purple light now encased Rainy's body. The intense glow radiated outward and arched through the athame. The luminous purple lightning sliced through the air from the tip of the ceremonial knife—creating dazzling orange flames that circled the wedding altar. Terry's mind's eye captured the brilliance of the blaze as the phantom fire steadily built and extended out to where the guests had sat just a short time ago.

Dedication

To my beloved Grandma
for showing me the way of things.

Prologue

The past several weeks had been pure hell. Anxiety, a constant companion, currently ruled every aspect of Rainy's mind, body, and soul. Being a Wiccan High Priestess, she was fully aware that this extreme level of unfounded turmoil signaled that a life-altering change was barreling toward her at breakneck speed. The agonizing weight of the unknown settled squarely on Rainy's shoulders. As of yet, no amount of meditation or quiet contemplation offered answers to the disposition of the impending transformation. She'd have to be vigilant and keep her wits about her. Good or bad, something significant was about to rock her world.

On a shaky breath she declared, "Mother Goddess, I promise to accept whatever challenges and opportunities you bring my way with grace and dignity. I will keep my eyes open and do my best to act on those experiences so that I may learn and grow as one of your children. I ask that you bless me and provide the strength and courage needed to do your work.

"Blessed be."

****

The inky black mist slithered through the boxes biding its time. Rage had festered to a fevered pitch over the decades spent in captivity. But something changed. The atmosphere in the glass building that had served as a cage for far too long pulsated with anticipation. The vibration so dense, tremors shimmered on the air, gently shifting the blackout curtains to and fro. The chosen one had reached adulthood and was coming. Soon the beast would prowl, free to roam and take back everything it desired. This time, there would be no stopping until the entity had full reign over those daring to occupy what belonged to him.

"*S-o-o-o-n*," the phantom hissed as it slid back into the depths of the mirror. "*S-o-o-o-n*."

Chapter One

Heavy footsteps rushed up the stairs behind Terry. Before he could be stopped, he softly rapped on the door.

"What do you think you're doing?" Nathan whispered in a menacing tone.

Terry whipped around to face his friend. "I know you think I'm blowing this out of proportion, but I'd do the same thing for you." He had known Nathan his entire life and loved him like a brother, but the *you're-an-idiot* glare he currently touted pissed him off.

"Don't look at me like that. Our best friend is in there, and I'm her man-of-honor. I promised her all traditions would be followed, and I'm keeping my word."

Nathan wasn't budging. Terry was forced to continue pleading his case. "Don't you remember when we were kids and Jody would talk for hours about her dream wedding? We *both* promised her come hell or high water that we would make that dream come true. That means *all* the traditions must be respected no matter how silly they seem. *You* may want to renege on that promise, but for Jody's sake I'm going to follow through."

"Terry, their ceremony is going to be a handfasting. It's not a traditional wedding."

"I know that. Even with a handfasting, it's still bad

luck to see the bride before the wedding. I looked it up." Terry defiantly raised his hand to knock again, but Nathan grabbed him before he could touch the door.

"You do realize that Jared is in there with her, right?"

"Of course I do."

"Are you willing to have him take your head off over this?"

Trying to be brave, Terry pursed his lips. "I'm doing this for Jody. And besides, Jared knows what our plans are for tonight. How mad could he get?"

Nathan rolled his eyes as he harrumphed. "*Fine.* If you're going to be a stickler about this, move aside and let me handle it. I wouldn't want you getting hurt the night before we walk Jody down the aisle."

Three sharp raps thundered on the door. Nathan covered his eyes and strolled in like he owned the place. "You two lovebirds better be dressed because I'm about ready to remove my hand from my eyes."

Burying her head into Jared's shoulder, Jody snorted. "It's okay, Nathan. You can look. We're still decent." Jody's hair was tousled, and her shirt only had one button holding it together.

At the sight of Jared's bared teeth, Terry momentarily questioned the sanity of bursting in on the couple. The groom snapped, "Damn. I knew I should have locked that door."

Straightening his spine and digging deep to find the needed courage for his girl, Terry continued into the room. Laying blame as if two children had been caught necking in the backseat of a car, he exhaled an exaggerated "tsk tsk." Wanting to lighten the mood and never being known to miss an opportunity for a little good-natured witticism, he pointed at Jody and Jared and scoffed. "Well, Nathan, what did I tell you? It looks like we made it just in the nick of time."

The two men gleefully chuckled as the groom pulled the bride into a tight embrace. Looking as though he were ready for a fight, Jared's face turned beet red while he spoke through clenched teeth. "That's it, Monkey. Say your goodbyes. I'm going to kill them."

"Hey. That's not very nice." Terry's thumb motioned toward Nathan with the precision of an experienced hitchhiker. "I'll have you know that Nathan and I have just saved you from dooming your marriage. You know just as well as I do that a groom can't see the bride before the wedding. *I'd* think you'd be grateful to us. Besides, we have pizza getting cold and beer getting hot in the guest house. So *you* can say *your* goodbyes. Come on. Let's get moving. Tut tut." Two sharp claps of the hands emphasized his point.

Jody's voice took on a high-pitched squeak to refrain from laughing. "A-h-h, Terry, it warms the cockles of my heart that you're taking your man-of-honor duties so seriously."

Feeling vindicated Terry elbowed Nathan. "See? What did I tell you?"

Not so warmed, Jared zeroed a steely gaze on Terry. "Well then, *Runt*, I hate to be the one to burst your bubble, but Jody and I have decided to buck tradition and spend the night together."

The use of Terry's nickname almost knocked him over. The childhood moniker Nathan had given him wasn't meant as a slight. Standing at an average height of five-foot, ten inches tall, he wasn't short in stature by any stretch of the imagination. But with Nathan having a good seven inches on Terry and Jared more than six, he was by far the smallest in this testosterone heavy crowd.

Jared wasn't the type of man to use nicknames or let new people into his life. After their rocky start, Terry had begun to doubt the possibility of ever having an amicable relationship with the man his best friend loved. But Jody was too important to both Terry and Jared for either of them to walk away. The use of his nickname was a gift from the groom even if it had been presented with an angry lilt.

"Oh no, you don't." Terry marched forward with mock anger and poked Jared in the chest—an action that never would have occurred before the use of his nickname. "As the bride's man-of-honor, one of my duties is to make sure that my girl, here, is taken care of. I *insist* that the traditions are followed." Cocky now, Terry tilted his head and pinched his lips to keep from smiling.

Nathan's posture stiffened, and his laughter died out before Jared could respond. "Wait a minute. Did anyone hear that?" With narrowed eyes, his attention shifted to the bedroom door. Walking purposely across the room, he poked his head into the hallway and called out, "Hello? Is someone there?"

A moment later his bearing relaxed, and a broad smile lit his face. "We'll be right down.

"Rainy is downstairs. Come on." He snapped his fingers several times to urge everyone to get moving. "Let's go. I'm dying to meet her."

Jody rushed to the bed and grabbed Jared's duffle bag. Handing it off to Terry, she offered her softest apologetic expression to the man she planned on spending the rest of her life with. "Sweetheart, it looks like we're outnumbered. Tradition won out. Beer and pizza are in your near future."

Resigning himself to the night's sleeping arrangements, Jared only grunted.

****

Rainy didn't have long to wait until the foursome made their entrance down the massive log staircase. Raucous laughter preceded them. The atmosphere around the beautiful bride sparkled with joy as she clung to her groom's arm.

"Rainy! I'm so glad you could make it tonight."

"I hope you don't mind that I let myself in. I kicked the door, but no one answered. My arms were full, and I was afraid I'd drop my present."

"Of course not." Head bobbing in the direction of the men standing behind her, Jody offered a devilish grin. "These three were just leaving. We'll have the whole place to ourselves."

Releasing Jared, Jody moved forward to embrace Rainy. Certain people in this world knew how to hug. They offered up a piece of themselves when doing so which made the gesture even more tender and authentic. Jody was one of those people.

"Are you kidding? I wouldn't have missed this girl's night for anything in the world."

"Let me introduce you to my friends before they scurry off and do whatever it is that men do the night before a wedding." Bubbling with excitement, Jody clamped onto Rainy's arm and maneuvered her forward. "I can't believe this is the first time I've had all of my favorite people in the same room."

Until this moment, Jared had been the largest and,

Rainy admitted to herself, the most extremely well-built specimen of a man she'd ever had the pleasure of meeting—definite drool worthy. But Jody currently tugged at the arm of an enormous barrel of a man, pulling him forward with ease. *This guy is a freaking wall.*

"I'd like you to meet Nathan. He's Jared's best man and will also be walking me down the aisle."

The gigantic man acknowledged Rainy with a nod and surprised her with a hundred-watt smile. Reaching out, he cupped her offered hand in both of his with more tenderness than she would have ever thought possible. It didn't take long for Nathan's shimmering aura to surround Rainy, filling her with personal tidbits about himself—everything from his life history to personality traits were revealed in a split second. This man was the living definition and spirit of the term *'never judge a book by its cover.'* For one so large, Nathan had a heart of gold. She almost swooned. *He's a gentle giant.* It was a rare occasion to come across someone so giving and compassionate, especially considering his tremendously intimidating bulk.

"Nathan, this is Rainy. Since Jared and I moved to the Flagstaff area, we've become close friends. She's been mentoring me with my psychic gifts and has been kind enough to agree to officiate our handfasting ceremony tomorrow."

"Pleasure, ma'am. It's nice to finally put a name to a face. Every time I talk with Jody, she mentions you and how much you've helped with keeping her abilities in check. As someone who loves her, I'm eternally grateful for everything you've done."

"Please, call me Rainy. It's nice to meet you too,

Nathan. I've heard so much about you that I feel as if we already know each other. Jody's an exceptionally gifted person and a quick study. All the credit for her growth goes to her."

After exchanging pleasantries with Nathan, Rainy's attention shifted to the smallest man in the group. Her heartbeat started to stampede in her chest as he cautiously stepped forward. Trying to school her features so the others wouldn't notice anything amiss, she forced a smile. Just as she did, the man tripped over his own feet and landed on his hands and knees directly in front of her. The duffle bag he carried flew from his grasp and hit Rainy squarely in the midsection. With a loud *oomph*, she toppled to the floor. *Talk about being knocked off your feet.* She had a difficult time keeping a straight face.

Jody rushed to Rainy's side and helped her up. With one fist, Jared took a tight hold on the scruff of the man's neck, easily pulling him to his feet.

"Rainy, are you all right? I'm so sorry."

Laughter at the absurd introduction bubbled up as she dusted herself off. "I'm fine. Don't worry yourself about it."

On a deep exhale, Jody introduced the klutz who'd stolen Rainy's breath. "This is Terry. He's my man-of-honor. He's going to be pulling double duty at the wedding too. Along with Nathan, he'll also be walking me down the aisle. Let's hope he's a little more agile tomorrow."

The close proximity with this man resulted in an unfathomable effect on Rainy's body—one she'd never experienced before. Trying to keep the raging emotions in check, she analyzed the sensations while doing her level best not to expose any uncertainty to the others in the room.

This man sparked a sense of déjà vu. Momentarily rendered dumbstruck from the rampaging emotion, she was unable to mentally grasp the meaning behind her soul's apparent recognition of this person. The life-altering change she'd been expecting crept into her mind. *Could this man be behind the transformation I've been preparing for?* Rainy allowed her extrasensory abilities to take over and curl on the air between herself and the man standing in front of her.

Instead of gaining insight into *his* thoughts and feelings, a bizarre sensation of being awakened from a deep winter hibernation caused Rainy's body to hum with the renewal of spring. *What the hell does that even mean?* She had to restrain herself from shaking her head to loosen the cobwebs that had suddenly clouded her brain.

Exasperated by the strange circumstance of this meeting and lacking her usual self-assurance, Rainy timidly offered her hand. When their eyes finally met, his gaze bore into hers and filled with what she could only perceive as utter confusion. As if unsure how to react, Terry's attention quickly turned downward to stare at her extended palm.

For the first time in Rainy's life, she stood across from someone and didn't have the slightest idea what was going through his mind or how he felt. None of his life's stories breezed into her awareness. His wants, his needs, not a single thing about this man came to her psychically.

While it was never her intent to intrude on other people's privacy, her extrasensory abilities always revealed people's innermost secrets within moments of meeting them. Not with this man. He was the first person she'd ever met that was a complete mystery. *Terry.* His name rolled on a loop through her head while she tried to get a feel for him.

Before either one of them could figure out how to proceed, Jared bopped Terry on the head none too gently. "Hey, Runt. Watch your manners."

"I'm s-sorry," he stuttered without looking back up. The instant Terry took Rainy's hand, a mixture of intense emotion bombarded her senses. Not his, but hers which left her even more rattled. Bliss blended with sorrow. Hope mixed with disbelief—all of which were neatly tied together in a great big bow of anticipation. While they'd never met in this lifetime, her soul recognized him. Terry must have felt it too because he finally raised his head. A penetrating gaze searched for answers in her eyes.

Before Rainy had a chance to catch her breath, Nathan came up behind Terry and punched him in the arm. "Well, ladies, I hate to cut this short, but it's time for the men-folk to take their leave. We better get out of here before Terry does any further damage. He looked down at the man-of-honor. "Hey, numb nuts, if you think you can handle it without knocking any more people down, why don't you grab the bag? I may have to cart Jared out of here in a fireman's hold."

Rainy could see what she thought was irritation flicker over Terry's face, turning his features crimson, as he grabbed the overnight bag and fled from the room.

In the blink of an eye, the extraordinary moment was broken but far from forgotten.

****

"Teach me something else!" Jody poured the remaining sparkling wine from the second bottle of the evening into the special chalices Rainy had given the couple as a wedding present.

"Okay. H-m-m. Let me think." Rainy tapped her chin. "Try this one. *Cá bhfuil an leithreas, le do thoil?"*

Dreamy eyed, Jody sighed from the beauty of the language and took the time to write it phonetically on the pad in front of her. "That's beautiful. I can't wait to whisper these sweet little nothings in Jared's ear on our wedding night." Turning her attention toward the notepad, Jody spoke the phrase to the best of her ability. Adding a sultry lilt, she cooed, *"Caw wil on leh-riss, leh duh hul."* Pen in hand, she looked expectantly toward Rainy over the brim of her goblet. "What does that phrase mean?"

Grinning, Rainy took a sip of wine. "Where is the toilet, please?"

With a mouth full of champagne, Jody could either spit the bubbly beverage all over the counter or choke on it. Being polite she choked. A few moments later, she got her breath back. "Well, maybe I'll keep that little nugget in the wings for when we go to Scotland where toilet phrases will be more useful."

"Actually, this is Irish Gaelic. From what I understand, it's a bit different than the Gaelic spoken in Scotland. People in Ireland call the language *Irish.*

"We've pretty much covered the extent of my vocabulary. Cheryl, my assistant, is fluent. She's been trying to teach me but not having much luck, I'm afraid. The poor girl's been patient, but my attention span only seems to extend to the romantic phrases."

Rainy tossed a bit of cheese to Wilma, Jody's beagle. Fred, Wilma's brother, piped up and howled a demand for the same treatment.

Jody began thumping the countertop with her newly manicured fingernails. When Rainy glanced up, her friend sported a quirky drunken smirk. One eyebrow rose as her chin came to rest on a tightly clenched fist. "I'm hoping I've plied you with enough wine that you're ready to spill the beans. I've been waiting for the last three hours for you to mention Terry. You've been very cool about what happened when you met him."

She should have figured her star pupil and friend would have recognized the world tilting on its axes during the introductions. Jody was perceptive. Opening another bottle of wine and topping off her goblet, the corners of Rainy's mouth curled. "Why, Jody, I don't know what you're talking about."

"Pfft. Don't give me that. I saw those sparks flying. What gives?"

"Your friend, Terry, he's charming. I'll give you that." The evening's champagne intake had Rainy relaxed and more openly curious about the man than she'd intended to be. Her lips, now slightly numb, puckered while trying to figure out the best way to approach all her questions. They'd been rolling around in her mind from the first moment she laid eyes on Terry.

"I noticed when you introduced me to Nathan, neither one of you mentioned my profession." Nervous tension started to creep up, but she wasn't exactly sure why. To gather courage, Rainy bit the inside of her lip. "Does Nathan and Terry know about me—about what I am? Who I am?"

"H-m-m." Jody pondered the question. Rainy could almost see the wheels spinning in her friend's mind as she reflected on past conversations with her friends. "You know, I don't think I ever mentioned your profession." Jody tilted her head to the side while biting her fingernail. "Nope. I think the only thing I told them was that you had become a close friend and together we've been working to get my psychic abilities under control. Why? Is that a problem?"

Rainy clinked her goblet against Jody's. "No. No problem. I guess they'll find out tomorrow."

She was compelled to learn more about *him*. Who better to ask than his best friend? "Getting back to Terry, now that you mention it, I was wondering…" A vision of that sweet face flitted through Rainy's brain serving to derail her train of thought. Acutely aware of the broad smile she currently touted, she'd relayed more information than intended without even speaking a word. *Who cares?* Jody wasn't a busybody. Any and all secrets were safe with her.

A loud snort brought Rainy back into the conversation. "*Yes?* You were *wondering?* I may be able to talk to spirits, but I'm not a mind reader," her friend goaded.

"Sorry. I had a momentary loss of brain function. It must be the wine."

"Uh-huh. Sure it is."

"Is Terry always so…well, what I mean to say is he always so…"

"Goofy? The word you're looking for is goofy."

Rainy snickered and was happy she hadn't picked that moment to sip more wine.

"Well, actually, I was going to say shy or maybe klutzy but goofy works." After thinking it over, Rainy nodded her head with purpose. "Yes. That term does suit him better."

"As easy as it would have been for you to misunderstand Terry's initial response to you, I hope you can look past that. If you were to ask me— someone who's known and loved him a lifetime—you had quite an effect on him. I've never seen that man so out of sorts."

Jody hiccupped and crinkled her nose. After a bout of the giggles, she schooled her features to look serious but couldn't maintain the façade and broke out into another fit of laughter. "Oh hell. I guess I've had my limit. What I meant to say was that I've never seen Terry so skittish around a woman. He's a confident and self-assured man when it comes to other people. He's always the life of the party. That is if he's even paying attention. Typically the artist side of his brain takes over. He turns that gaze on a person and broods until he figures out the perfect way to immortalize them on canvas. I wouldn't be a bit surprised if he weren't sketching you at this very minute. Which—if you don't mind my saying so—is not a good thing. He's supposed to be working on our handfasting cord for the service tomorrow."

Unable to contain her giddiness, Rainy's heart rate sped up. Leaning forward, she clasped Jody's hand. "Do you really think he's interested?"

Jody held her goblet high. "Oh, hell, yeah."

"Well, that *is* news."

"I can't believe he fell at your feet and knocked you down in the process. The poor guy must be so

15

embarrassed."

"He shouldn't be. Terry had the same effect on me, but I was able to keep my balance—well, at least until the moment he knocked me to the ground." The memory had them sharing another chuckle at the goofball's expense.

Jody's demeanor suddenly shifted and softened. She stared into her goblet, a sure sign there would be a topic change. *Thank goodness.* Rainy needed time to process her feelings when it came to Terry. Getting romantically involved with a good friend of a friend might not be the best decision. *What if it didn't work out? Would she lose Jody too?*

With a chalice tightly clutched in one hand, Jody pulled Rainy close for a quick embrace. "I didn't want to get serious tonight, but I've had one glass too many and feel the need to be mushy.

"As you know, by design, my entire life has been lived as close to a hermit or shut in as possible. Because of the constant spirit encounters, I've never been chummy with anyone but Nathan and Terry. Since our childhood, we've protected each other and loved one another. We've always made a point of being there for the others through thick and thin. We were the three musketeers. My entire life, those two men were the only people that I could count on and who truly knew me.

"Don't get me wrong. I've always been fulfilled. While Nathan, Terry, and I are still tight and will remain so, *you* have been responsible for giving me my life back. Because of you, I'm not afraid to open my world up to new people and experiences.

"I got lucky and found Jared, the love of my life.

He accepted me and my abilities for what they were, even though it was a difficult road. Can you believe what a scared little kitten I was when you and I first met? Do you remember how jumpy I was when you came to check on the protection wards you'd placed around our home? With your tutoring and help, I've taken control over my abilities and feel empowered. My life has improved by leaps and bounds because of you. I'm blessed to have you in my life."

Touched, Rainy opened her mouth to speak, but an unsteady slash of her friend's hand cut her off. "No. Please, let me finish.

"I've never been close to another woman. The extent of my interpersonal relationships with any female has come down to nothing more than a work associate. It's a sad fact but true. Every relationship I've ever had with a woman was a one-way street. I could never trust anyone enough to divulge anything about myself or my abilities.

"I've never had the experience of a true female friend until now. Nothing like what you and I have shared. You've opened my life up to a kinship between us, a sisterhood if you will. I guess what I'm trying to tell you—and doing a poor job of it—is that I'm grateful to you for accepting me as I am. I love you.

"My fears are slowly fading away. You've made it possible for Jared and me to have some semblance of a normal life together outside of the boundaries of this cabin's walls."

Jody took a moment to dab at her eyes.

"Ever since Jared and I helped little Mikala escape from the kidnappers, I've been living my life like a scared little rabbit. You are the only person alive that knows just how close to death I was during that tragic affair.

"When we found each other, you were patient and mentored me through my abilities. You offered tools to keep me safe. I am in control of my life for the first time. And on the eve of my wedding, I can't thank you enough because I wouldn't have been strong enough to continue on this journey without your help.

"Because of your mentorship and friendship, I feel confident that Jared and I can withstand anything supernatural that comes our way. But if something happens and we find ourselves in trouble, I know you'll have our backs."

Rainy was so moved she pulled Jody into her arms. Both women shed tears of joy for the blessings of the other. "I'm proud of you, Jody. You and Jared have come a long way since we've met. I'll always be here for you and willing to help in any way I can. That's what friends and family are for."

Chapter Two

Rainy made her way to the altar and signaled her readiness to begin the ritual. She lived for joyous occasions such as this, especially when held outdoors amidst the towering ponderosa pines. While the weather in the Flagstaff area could be sketchy in the late summer months, it currently held the promise of mild temperatures, dazzling sunshine, and light breezes.

Jared joined Rainy at the altar and looked beyond dashing in his impeccable suit. The radiant smile he brandished all but screamed his innermost dreams and secret wishes were about to come true. The love for his bride sparkled in his eyes for all to see.

"Welcome, everyone, to Jared and Jody's handfasting celebration. If you would all please rise and welcome the bride into our ceremonial circle."

A collective gasp of approval filled the meadow as everyone's attention turned toward Jody. Her dress was magnificent and the perfect choice for an outdoor wedding in the pines. Reminiscent of wispy clouds lazily floating through the sky, the white A-line made of tulle wafted around her body leaving the impression that she glided down the aisle rather than walked. The gown sported delicate flowered lace, tinged with a subtle pink that had been appliquéd on the bodice. Exquisite filigree petals made their way up into cap sleeves and worked their way around to expose the backless cut of the dress.

Jody's bouquet was a beautiful display of miniature Fairy roses instead of the usual blood red flowers everyone seemed so fond of these days. If a person were in the right frame of mind, they could easily imagine the flower's namesake nymphs handpicking every one of the charming little rose buds for this bride. While stunning, the elegant pink flowers couldn't hold a candle to the woman carrying them.

More striking, though, was the raw power between bride and groom as Jody made her way toward Jared. Every wedding Rainey performed was special, but being in the presence of these two at this moment in time felt nothing short of epic. Her psychic vision didn't miss how the air sparkled and shifted as if the proximity between them created their own unique power. They may not know it yet, but their magic was stronger than anything she'd ever seen or felt before. Mother Goddess had big plans in store for these two. Of that, she was certain.

Walking on either side of Jody were her best friends, Terry and Nathan. Rainy had to stifle a giggle as both men proudly promenaded the bride to her groom. The two grinned their fool heads off just like any proud father would.

Nathan, the big brute of a man, wore an elegant navy blue suit that must have set him back thousands. While not a handsome man in any sense of the word, she was certain his strength of character and tenderness drew women to him like a moth to flame. He'd make quite a catch for some lucky lady.

The sight of Terry, however, had Rainy licking her lips to keep her mouth from going dry. The firm pull of desire struck her hard in the gut and left her breathless. After their initial introduction last night, she'd been curious to see if the man's effect had been all in her head. Since he was the only person Rainy had ever met in which her psychic abilities couldn't decipher, he was a fascination, to say the least. Without the security of her life-long extrasensory perceptions, she forced herself to look at Terry in an all new way.

Rainy garnered from his appearance that the shy man she'd met last night certainly marched to the beat of his own drummer. Being a Wiccan High Priestess and forging her own unique way helped her see the strength in Terry's choices. She wondered if that trait extended beyond his clothing style. She hoped so. He wore a sad looking vintage brown suit that, by her estimation, had probably seen better days a century ago. His disheveled wavy hair reached out in all directions under the brown felt bowler hat making her want to lean in and tease those locks back into place. The distinctive early 1800's dapper storekeeper look was topped off with a scruffy three-day beard. With all of that, she still found him irresistible and wouldn't change a thing. The tousled look, while unique, added character and worked for him in all the right ways.

The three life-long friends made their way within the protected ceremonial circle and came to a stop in front of the altar. To keep all unwanted negativity out, Cheryl, Rainy's assistant, closed the circle behind them.

"Welcome, one and all. We have come together today to rejoice with Jody and Jared as their love for each other binds them together in this handfasting ceremony.

"Jody, have you entered into this handfasting circle

of your own free will?"

Standing tall and proud, the bride beamed. Love for Jared flushed her cheeks as her gaze never wavered from his. "I have entered into this circle and joined my love at this altar of my own free will and accord."

"Who is it that accompanies and stands with you at the altar?"

Nathan thrust his chest out with pride and took another step closer to the altar. "I, Nathan Gordon, stand with Jody and Jared and offer my blessings on this union." He turned, kissed Jody, hugged her, and moved to Jared's side to take his place as best man.

Terry threw his shoulders back and made direct eye contact with Rainy. "I, Terry Anderson, also stand with Jody and Jared to offer my blessings on this union." He turned, kissed Jody, whispered reverently 'I love you' and stood beside her as the man-of-honor.

"Jared, have you entered into this handfasting circle of your own free will?"

The look of yearning and intensity of love the tall, dark groom displayed for his bride made Rainy weak in the knees. She sneaked a curious sideway glance at Terry. *One day, someone will love me like that. Are you the one?*

"I have entered into this circle and joined the love of my life—the woman who saved me from a life of misery and loneliness, at this altar of my own free will and accord." Jared's deep baritone voice served to pull Rainy's wandering mind back into the ceremony.

"Blessed be. As a special offering, Mr. Anderson has made the binding rope for the handfasting ceremony. Terry, if you would please hand me the cord."

Jody and Jared eagerly joined hands as Rainy proceeded to bind them symbolically.

"As I bind your hands, so shall your lives be bound. Your duty to the other shall be to love, comfort, support, and embrace. You are obliged to be gentle with one another, share in all good and all bad, and treat the other above your own needs.

"Jared, if you agree to the binding, please speak to your love now."

"Jody, my bride, my love, I promise to love, comfort, support, and embrace you. I will always be gentle with you and treat your needs above my own."

"Blessed be. Jody, if you agree to the binding, please speak to your love now."

"Jared, my groom, my love, I promise to love, comfort, support, and embrace you for the rest of my life. I will always be gentle and treat your needs above my own."

"Blessed be. I call on the Goddess of the East to offer the gift of opening your hearts to one another. During those times anger intrudes and breaks communication from the heart, I ask the Goddess to provide a fresh start with each rise of the sun. I call on the Goddess of the South to offer the gift of warmth drawn from your heart's passion for lighting dark times and encouraging them to pass quickly. I call on the Goddess of the West to offer the gift to deepen the commitment between you as the tide is committed to the sea and the steady flow of water is committed to the rivers. I call on the Goddess of the North to offer the gift of a sturdy foundation and the strength of home no matter where you may be.

"Look into each other's eyes and affirm your

answers to these questions to the one you love. With each answer, I shall encircle your joined hands with this precious cord.

"Will you share in each other's heartache and pain?"

"We will."

"Will you share in joyous times and laughter?"

"We will."

"Will you encourage each other?"

"We will."

"Will you share in the burdens of the other?"

"We will."

"Will you share in each other's dreams allowing burgeoning new trails and growth to follow?"

"We will."

"Will you honor each other for all time as you honor today?"

"We will."

"Blessed be. The binding is now complete." Using the two ends of the binding cord, Rainy carefully tied the knot. She raised their hands for everyone to see. "Your vows to one another are the binding factor in this union. It matters not if you remove the cord, for it is the power within the words and promises you've chanted here today that binds your hearts together in this lifetime. Let the strength of your vows carry over and add to the power of your actions. So mote it be."

Rainy released the binding cord and placed it on the altar. Picking Jody's wedding ring up, she held it to the sky for everyone to see.

"Jared, as a sign of your love, please affix your ring to Jody's finger." She placed the wedding band in his palm.

"Jody, as Jared adjoins his ring to your hand, may you always be comforted by the purity of his love. Know now this; this ring symbolizes Jared has given himself to you and only you. May you draw strength from that during separation. May you draw peace from that when angry. May you draw comfort from that when needed."

Rainy picked Jared's wedding ring up and held it to the sky for everyone to see.

"Jody, as a sign of your love, please affix your ring to Jared's finger." She placed the golden band in the bride's palm.

"Jared, as Jody adjoins her ring to your hand, may you always be comforted with the purity of her love. Know now this; this ring symbolizes Jody has given herself to you and only you. May you draw strength from that during separation. May you draw peace from that when angry. May you draw comfort from that when needed."

Rainy allowed tears of joy for the lovers to trickle down her cheeks for all to see. The union between Jody and Jared was a strong one. Feeling blessed to be the officiate of this handfasting ritual, she couldn't have been more honored than experiencing their passion for one another first hand.

"Jared and Jody, the handfasting ceremony has concluded. You may kiss your soul mate."

Mother Earth chose that moment to embrace the couple with a gentle breeze. Applause erupted from the wedding guests.

"In love and light. Blessed be."

Chapter Three

All the guests had gone inside to toast the bride and groom, but Terry lagged behind. He concealed himself in the darkening shadows of Jared and Jody's balcony watching as Rainy performed what looked to be a ritual at the wedding altar. Spying on her was an act of outright crazy on his part and made him feel like a psycho stalker, but he couldn't stop himself. She was the most exotic woman who had ever crossed his path. Since the moment Jody had introduced them, he'd found himself inexplicably drawn to her.

Look at her, idiot. She's way out of your league.

Her dark brown mane reflected light the way stars brightened the darkened Flagstaff night. Her beauty so full and ripe, she wore little to no makeup but still managed to outshine every other woman. Her presence commanded attention. *She doesn't blend quietly into the world as I do.* He'd be willing to bet this woman escaped no one's attention.

Given the ceremony she'd just performed, it was hard to escape the fact that Rainy was substantially involved in the Wiccan religion. Terry wasn't sure if that was a plus or not. Witches had always been scary to him, but never before so divinely sensual. They were old crones who enticed children to their demise with candy. *Weren't they?* That being the case, he preferred to think of her as a layperson feeling her oats through experimentation rather than a devotee. Hell, hadn't he done some wacky things over the years while trying to discover his way in this world? Who could fault her for the same thing?

The sound of Rainy's voice floated on the breeze and nudged him out of his thoughtful deliberations. Glued to his hiding place, Terry was transfixed as her arms lifted to the sky. The ritual athame glinted in the dusky light like a beacon calling to him. She used the dagger to bury some little trinket at the base of the altar where a few short minutes ago Jody and Jared had stood to pledge their love.

Each movement flowed from one to the next and appeared choreographed like a beautiful dance. Enthralled, Terry couldn't take his eyes off Rainy as she rose and slowly turned in circles. The ceremonial knife, now carefully wiped clean on her robes, pointed away from her body and toward the ground.

Sinking further into the shadows, he continued to watch the spectacle of Rainy's ritualistic duties. The hypnotic effect persisted and strengthened. Terry's temples started throbbing to the percussive beat of her almost silent voice. His vision blurred. Images became obscured, and colors took their place. A bright purple light now encased Rainy's body. The intense glow radiated outward and arched through the athame. The luminous purple lightning sliced through the air from the tip of the ceremonial knife—creating dazzling orange flames that circled the wedding altar. Terry's mind's eye captured the brilliance of the blaze as the phantom fire steadily built and extended out to where the guests had sat just a short time ago.

"When the handfasted pair finds themselves in

need of strength, let them be drawn here to this sacred spot where the love between them was bound for all to see. Allow the vitality of their sentiment shared here to live on forever and preserve and nourish them in whatever they may need. This sacred space is now permanently protected, and the ceremonial circle is closed. With love and light. So mote it be."

A loud popping noise sounded in his head, and the magical trancelike state that had captured him so completely snapped in an instant. Blinking furiously to focus his vision, Terry jumped when he found his eyes locked with Rainy's.

Dammit! She saw me. The embarrassment of being caught eavesdropping mortified him. Without thinking, his body heaved and spun. An earsplitting, clanking, baritone racket clamored as he ran head first and tangled with the wind chimes, knocking his hat off in the process. Feeling like an even bigger idiot, Terry made a fast getaway through the back door, and into the throng of party guests. Trying to ease his humiliation, he consoled himself with the fact that it was almost dark outside. The awkward encounter could easily be chalked up to his vivid imagination running wild. *Rainy couldn't possibly have noticed me spying on her. It was too dark. I just imagined the way her accusing stare locked on mine to reprimand me for snooping.*

****

Nathan grabbed Terry's arm as he tried to rush past him. "Dude, what's wrong with you? You look like you've seen a ghost."

"Nothing's wrong with me. I'm just looking for some champagne." Terry feigned complacency and forced himself to visibly relax when a passing waiter handed him a full glass.

"Where's the stupid hat that you insisted on wearing? Don't tell me you're finally getting tired of sporting the Johnny Depp derelict look?"

Humiliation skyrocketed to annoyance. It took every ounce of energy to restrain himself from punching Nathan in the face. Terry pinched the space between his eyes to get a hold of his flaring emotions. "I took it off, okay? What the hell? Why the third degree, Nathan? Can't a man take his damn hat off if he wants to?"

Compounding his problems Terry's sharp reaction provoked a clenched jaw and an angry bulging vein to pop out on Nathan's neck. *Uh-oh.* The man's large finger landed squarely on Terry's chest leaving the hot burn of the jab as a warning to change his bad attitude. "Wait just a damn…"

"Excuse me."

Not yet willing to face the consequences, if any, to his earlier act of voyeurism, Terry winced at the sound of Rainy's sing-song voice. The gorgeous witch woman stood in front of him and Nathan. She had ditched the witch robes and wore a simple emerald green dress. Her only jewelry was an exquisite moonstone pendant. The silver figure of a woman, arms outstretched, rose from the top of the stone as if ascending to heaven.

Damn the woman was potent. All Terry could do was open his mouth. His throat closed up allowing no sound to pass his lips. "Rainy, that was a beautiful ceremony. I've never seen anything like it before." Thankfully, Nathan stepped up to the plate and would help him save face.

Her smile lifted the corners of barely glossed lips

and sliced through Terry's heart.

"Thank you, Nathan. I'm glad you liked it." She turned that dimpled smile back on Terry, and his still mutinous body left him frozen and speechless.

"I believe you dropped this." She held his hat out, but he was too mortified to accept her offering. Inching close enough for Terry to smell her seductive scent, Rainy gently swept the hair from his forehead.

"Please, allow me." Lifting the hat, she positioned it on his head. Taking great care and a bit longer than necessary to complete the task. Terry's heart swelled with her gentle treatment of his beloved hat. Her touch, while demure, left him smoldering. "Now, *that's* perfect."

Before he knew what he was doing, his hand lifted and traced the swell of her cheek. So focused on her eyes, he almost missed the surprise his touch had generated as it registered in her stance.

Nathan's hearty laughter broke the spell. "Okay. *Now* I understand why you were acting like an imbecile." The outright male pride between friends was evident when he punched Terry's arm. "Way to go, dude. Good luck with that." Leaving that thought hanging heavily in the air, Nathan winked at Rainy and made himself scarce.

Left to his own devices, the artist in Terry took over thankfully serving to banish the moron aspect of his personality—at least momentarily. "I'd like to paint you." His words were breathless as his mind conjured the canvas, the pose, and the medium he'd use to immortalize her.

"What do you think you're doing?" Jared's stern voice broke the mood. The vision immediately shattered. As if caught in a compromising position by an angry parent, Terry jumped. "You're not seriously trying to pick up the High Priestess, are you?"

Glancing back at the woman he only knew as Rainy, Terry was horrified to find the truthfulness of the title in the way her head inclined. He'd incorrectly figured—or more aptly hoped—she'd gotten ordained over the Internet or something just as trivial. He'd allowed himself to believe she probably just dabbled in the whole witchcraft scene for kicks and giggles. *High Priestess? I'm such a fucking idiot.*

Before he could answer, Jared directed his attention back to the goddess in front of him. "Please forgive him, Rainy. He doesn't get out often."

She peered at Terry waiting for him to respond, but when he didn't, Rainy broke the uncomfortable silence with humor. "Mr. Anderson said he'd like to paint me. I'm hoping he's an artist and not a masher with a bad pickup line." Jared tossed his head back and let loose a jovial laugh prompting Jody to join the group.

"Rainy, Terry's a brilliant artist! We got so caught up in our discussion last night that I didn't get a chance to show you just what he's capable of creating. Get prepared to have your socks knocked off. All of the artwork in our home is his work." Jody's arm wrapped around the goddess's waist and pulled her away—leaving Terry to stand there open mouthed. "Come with me. Let me show you his best work yet. *Solitude* is such a personal canvas that Jared won't display it out here in the main room. The portrait is back in his den."

With the women out of earshot, Jared slapped Terry on the back. "Good for you, Runt!"

Dejected by the lost opportunity, Terry uttered

through a sigh, "What do you mean?"

"You're more dense than I gave you credit for. Didn't you see the way Rainy was looking at you?"

"I don't understand. What way was she looking at me?"

Jared got a tight hold on Terry's arm and started steering him toward the den. "If my keen investigative skills are working properly, I do believe she's just as interested in you as you are in her."

Terry stopped dead in his tracks. "Huh?"

Jared's mocking sigh and exaggerated eye roll hit home. "Come with me, you idiot. Don't fuck this up. Try to grow a pair before we get to the women."

With weakened legs and knots in his stomach, he had no choice but to allow Jared to drag him into the den. As with everyone that viewed *Solitude*, a hyper-realistic portrait he'd created of Jody, Rainy stood in front of the canvas, seemingly mesmerized.

The newly wedded couple slipped from the room, leaving Terry to his own devices. He would sink or swim on his own.

"Jared has told me many times this portrait was responsible for him falling in love with Jody. By the time he met her, he was already head over heels in love. He said something within *Solitude* changed his world and opened his heart."

Rainy spun around to face him. The portrait affected her so deeply that tears pooled in her beautiful deep brown eyes. "Do you know what you've captured within this portrait?"

"I do. I'd like to hear what you think."

Holding her position across the room and even with the distance between them, Rainy's gaze penetrated deep into his core. "The pure and absolute heartache captured within *Solitude* reaches out and touches my soul. Beyond that, though, the love reaching out for Jody from past the veil to the Otherworld touches my heart. This portrait was not fashioned on the earthly plain. It couldn't have been. You were touched by all that is good and pure when you created this masterpiece. Touched by whatever you call your guiding force, the Universe, the Goddess, God, Angels. To be given such a resplendent gift reveals that you are a very blessed man, Terry."

Rainy's words left him speechless. Longing to touch her, to pull her into his arms and hang on for dear life, he managed a shaky step closer and then another.

"There you are, Rainy. Jared and Jody asked me to come and get you so they could introduce you to everyone." Nathan's unexpected interruption served to stifle Terry's forward momentum. The intrusion had him losing his newfound nerve where this beguiling witch woman was concerned.

"Certainly."

Terry's chance for spending more time with Rainy slipped away as Nathan crossed the room and offered his arm. They were almost to the door when her sweet voice glided on the air. "You've chosen the right path, Terry Anderson. You're a remarkable artist. I'm awed by your talent."

****

Jody led Rainy to the fireplace so Jared could make the introductions. "Everyone, if I could get your attention, please. I'd like to introduce you to the amazing woman that united my bride and me today." Jared placed a hand squarely on Rainy's back, gently nudging her forward. "Please say hello to Rainy Stratton, High Priestess of the Circle of the Pines Wiccan Coven."

The way things were going, Terry would be lucky to get a chance to talk to her again before the night ended. There were only a few people left milling around that hadn't converged on Rainy. Besides himself, he counted three people that weren't hounding her with questions. First there was Nathan. Then an ancient looking Native American man, who was so old he looked like a walking mummy. Next to the old codger, a young woman, probably his granddaughter, or great-granddaughter or even great-great-granddaughter for all Terry knew. Both of whom were decked out in full authentic Native American garb. He wasn't sure what tribe, but he'd seen pictures of this type of clothing before.

"Don't you dare go near her." Fingers clenched tightly into Terry's arm and added more than a little juice behind the verbal warning.

He swiped at Nathan's hand. "Hey! That hurts. What the hell are you talking about?"

"You haven't been able to take your eyes off the witchy woman all night. Don't go straying now. I'm warning you."

"Nathan, what the fuck, dude?"

"That little woman is too sweet for the likes of you. Keep your distance."

Curious, Terry glanced back at the young Indian lady. On anyone else, the traditional garments would look like a costume. Instead, Terry's keen artist's eye saw a regal Indian princess rocking the intense colors. The blouse was a brilliant shade of cobalt blue and constructed of velvet. The skirt was also velvet, but a bright shade of fire engine red. Those colors should clash when worn together, but instead, he found them beautiful. Large turquoise jewelry adorned her neck, ears, and wrists. The bits and pieces would appear gaudy on any other woman her size, but it all somehow suited her. Her hair fashioned in a knot at the back of her head, looked to be held together with twine.

If Terry had the opportunity to paint her, he'd have her on the back of a buckskin horse, sitting tall, reflecting her pride in whom and what she was. The wind of the gallop blowing strands from her tight Indian coiffure. The young Indian woman was a true natural beauty.

She continued to sit like a statue, eyes down cast, staring at her folded hands.

Terry pivoted to put Nathan in his place for jumping to conclusions. But before he could open his mouth, the dreamlike ogle on his best friend's face stopped him cold. The longing in his friend's eyes portrayed that of a man who had found something near and dear to his heart. The yearning expression spoke volumes.

"Have you gone over and talked to her yet?"

As if caught by surprise, Nathan's big body twitched. His shocked gaze zeroed in on Terry. "Hell no!"

"Since they're at the wedding, they must be friends with Jody and Jared. They've met all kinds of interesting people since moving to Flagstaff. Why don't you go and introduce yourself?"

"Jody told me the old man is a great Navajo Medicine Man. He's called Spirit Keeper and highly revered in these parts. Bright Flower is his granddaughter and under his tutelage. What do you say to the granddaughter of a man like that?"

Before Terry had a chance to nudge his friend in their direction, Nathan moaned and lumbered away.

Well, I'll be damned. The mighty have fallen. He wasn't sure why that thought brought him great pleasure, but it did.

****

The evening wound down too fast for Terry's liking. For the last hour, Rainy had the undivided attention of everyone in the room. It seemed no one wanted to leave without talking to her first. And he knew there wasn't a chance in hell of getting her alone again. Taking his mind off her had proved to be harder than he would've thought possible. Disappointment had him walking around the spacious room in circles and feeling like an abandoned pet. *Dammit! What am I doing?*

Situating himself on the back deck, Terry did what calmed him. He sketched. Having a perfect view of the craggy old Indian medicine man and his granddaughter, he allowed his imagination to take control and let his pencil have its head. The graphite moved across the page almost of its own accord.

The old man's corrugated face came to life—deep, jagged fissures from years of sun and stress were drawn in a way that represented exact proportions and dimension. Dark, sunken eyes took shape on the sketch pad as Terry filled them with wisdom and torment which were undeniably visible within their depths. In direct opposition with the shaman's age, his hair shone with vibrancy under the lights. That detail surprised

Terry because experience had taught him that salt and pepper tresses had a habit of turning dull and lifeless with time. The length was impressive as it fell in full splendor down the old man's side adding an unmistakable majestic vibe to the aged Native American. The old red cloth tied around his forehead had seen better days but appeared to match his much newer blood-red, velvet shirt.

Terry's focus shifted to the young woman who had seemingly captured Nathan's heart. Her eyes had remained hidden from him all night long, so he started with the round breadth of her face. She sported what his mother had called chubby cheeks and wore them well. On the pleasingly plump side, she was a beautiful woman. Her heritage added an age old mysticism that lent a mysterious air to her overall persona.

In the process of drawing her full pouty lips, Terry glanced up to find the young woman staring out the window. Her attention fastened to something behind him. Rather than waste time wondering what had caught her scrutiny, he focused on her eyes. Such sad eyes. He couldn't help but wonder what tragic circumstance added such deep, painful melancholy to her gaze.

Setting his pencil aside, he reviewed his handiwork. Two soft hands settled on his shoulders as someone leaned forward to appraise his work. He almost purred when Rainy's scent hit him.

"It's beautiful. You've not only drawn Spirit Keeper and Bright Flower, but you've also captured their dignity—their very heart and soul." The warmth of her hands on his shoulder and her high praise left him tingling.

"Rainy, do you know why she's so sad? What put that heartbreak in Bright Flower's eyes?"

After a long, thoughtful pause, she responded, "I can't think of a reason not to tell you. It's no longer a secret. Spirit Keeper is actively searching for her match."

Bright Flower held his attention, but Rainy's words filled him with unease. "Match?"

"Yes. Men from all over the Navajo Nation are flocking to Flagstaff to vie for the honor of betrothing Bright Flower."

Terry's body flinched under her hands. "*What? Are you talking about an arranged marriage? That's still done?*"

Rainy's hands lifted from his shoulders. The separation between them felt as though she'd backed miles away.

"Are you interested in asking for Bright Flower?"

The tone of her voice lowered and propelled his heart to beat faster. Like a blues song, the modulation of her speech had changed. Could she be jealous? Could Terry be that lucky?

Reaching out to gather Rainy's hand in his, he placed it back on his shoulder. To keep her from shifting away again, he gently stroked her fingers. Since she still stood behind him, he couldn't be sure his perception of her reaction was correct. But the impression of dissatisfaction over his possible interest in the Indian woman gave him hope.

"No. I'm not interested in Bright Flower. Would you have dinner with me tomorrow night?"

"Aren't you going back to Phoenix tomorrow?"

"Not if I can convince you to have dinner with

me."

Their combined chuckle drifted through the night air.

"I'd like that. Why don't I meet you at your cottage around seven?"

Those were the sweetest words he'd ever heard.

Chapter Four

Approaching Jared and Jody's quaint guest cottage, Rainy found there was no need to knock. Terry had left the front door wide open. Soft music played in the background, and the aroma that filled the air was a delightful blend of garlic and Italian spices. She eased her eyes shut while breathing deeply to savor the mouth watering scent.

Taking a tentative step through the front door, she called out, "Hello. Is it okay to come inside?"

Rainy couldn't help but smile as Terry entered the room with two glasses of deep red wine. He'd donned an apron copying the look of a black military flak jacket and touted in bold white letters, *'I am the chief chef, and if you don't like it, you can fuck off.'*

"Nice apron."

Spreading his arms wide he dipped in a gracious bow. "Jared made fun of the fact that I like to cook. He's not the type of man anyone tells to shut up, so I let my apron speak for me."

It pleased Rainy that laughter between them came so quickly tonight. Terry's shyness of the night before seemed to have relaxed a bit. She could get used to this new laid back side of him and appreciated his knack for making her feel comfortable even under the painful first date jitters.

Handing her a glass Terry leaned in and kissed her

cheek, being careful, Rainy noted, not to be overly aggressive. While appreciating the gentlemanly effort, she wouldn't have minded sampling his lips—especially if they tasted like the rich, tangy scent of marinara sauce currently tickling her nose.

"I'm glad you came. I've been looking forward to this time with you all day. I hope you like Italian."

"Love it. Can I help you with anything?"

"No. As soon as the oven goes…" The timer chose that moment to blare, and it was a damn good thing because the delectable aroma wafting through the air had her stomach aching to sample the food.

"Come into the kitchen with me. I've got a surprise for you." Being gallant Terry offered his arm, and she accepted.

Upon entering the kitchen, Rainy couldn't believe her eyes and did a double take. Two French doors were opened wide onto a patio covered with a trellis. Just outside the threshold an intimate little table set for two was topped with a red and white checkered tablecloth. A pair of lit candles placed in the center of the tabletop flickered in the evening air. The soft candlelight showcased a beautiful single violet rose bud. Twinkling outdoor lights left the impression of being under a star filled sky. Terry's attention to the smallest romantic detail bowled her over and magically transported her to an elegant outdoor café in Italy.

As Rainy's attention turned to the counter, she was momentarily taken aback to sue a cake, a pie, and several different types of tarts. The assorted pastries prompted her to raise both eyebrows—a dead giveaway for her astonishment at the sight of enough dessert to last a week.

Her reaction had Terry laughing. "I must have dessert. No meal should be finished off without something sweet. I didn't know what you liked, so I got a little of everything."

"Terry, did you bake all of this?"

He waved her off with a flick of his hand. "No. I bake like sh…" She could see the wheels turning in his mind as he took a moment to work through what to say without cursing. While appreciating the effort, it wasn't necessary. She wanted him as comfortable as he'd made her.

"I'm better with savory than sweet. Baking is too precise for me. All of that exact measuring is more of a science than an art." Terry visibly shuttered. "In other words, I suck at it. I prefer to cook by the seat of my pants. Do you know what I mean? A little of *this*. A little of *that*. If you ask me, you have to be creative to conquer the demands of savory cooking. I'm all over that."

"Well, I appreciate you going to a bakery then. If I ate something that tasted like *shit*, I'd probably have to think twice about eating anything else you made." Rainy offered a grin and held her glass out in hopes that he'd appreciate the humor. "To bakeries."

Laughter sparkled in Terry's eyes. "To bakeries."

****

Taking another bite of chocolate cake, Rainy closed her eyes and relished in the dark richness of the delicacy. The *'mmm'* that rattled in the back of her throat turned Terry's legs to jelly. His attention zeroed in on a crumb that rested on the side of her mouth. The way the napkin grazed her lips was so enticing that he'd created a whole fantasy around licking frosting from her body.

"Terry that was by far the best meal I've had in ages."

The sexual haze that fogged his brain every time he looked at Rainy became harder and harder to fight off. *Damn! I have to get a grip on myself.* He'd only just met her. As much as he'd like to throw the dishes from the table, bend her over and have his way with her, doing so wouldn't be right. She would never speak to him again. *It's going to be awhile before I can move from the table. Think, idiot! You don't want to scare her off. I need a subject that will occupy my mind and discourage my south of the border head.*

"Jared and Jody left for Lake Powell today. With the plans Jared made they should have quite a honeymoon."

"So *that's* the big surprise honeymoon destination? I knew there was something special planned, but Jared was so secretive I didn't have a clue as to what they were going to do. Are they renting a houseboat?"

Terry couldn't hold back the chortle which started deep in his belly. "Yep. Houseboat slash yacht complete with a crew consisting of a captain, maid service, and a personal chef. The boat—or should I say ship—even has a hot tub installed.

"So their personal time wouldn't be interrupted, he also rented another houseboat to accommodate the crew on off hours. That houseboat isn't anywhere near as luxurious. Somehow those poor hard working people are going to have to manage to get by on a measly sixty-five footer home away from home."

Rainy brightened. "Hey, maybe you and I could sign up for some of that drudgery. Those poor miserable crew members probably need a break from cruising around the lake." To complete the jest she winked at him. "What do you think?"

Their wine glasses clinked together. "I think they'd commit mutiny and just possibly slit our throats if we walked in and tried to wrangle their cushy duty away from them."

Now that supper had been completed Terry leaned in to pour Rainy more wine, hoping its gentle effects would keep her here with him a little longer.

Shifting comfortably back into his chair, Terry took a quick sip of the fruity merlot before continuing. "Jody loves to fish, and it's always been a dream of hers to go on an extended vacation to Lake Powell and see all there is to see. They left their return open-ended because Jared wants to show her the whole lake. Who knows how long that will take? My guess is we won't see hide nor hair of them for a few months."

"Wow! That sounds like a dream vacation. All kidding aside, I'm glad they have someone experienced to captain the boat, though. On any given day Lake Powell can be hazardous, to say the least, and dangerous at its worst."

Contemplating the best way to broach the next subject without betraying Nathan, Terry stared into his goblet. "Can I ask you something?"

"Sure."

"Would you tell me a little more about Bright Flower's arranged marriage?"

Terry couldn't help but notice how the atmosphere around them had suddenly turned frigid. Judging by Rainy's pursed lips he'd committed some sort of faux pas. Unsure of why her mood had turned sour so quickly, he inquired, "I'm not familiar with the customs. Is it wrong for me to ask?"

Rainy swirled the wine in her glass, but never took her eyes off him. To keep from squirming under her scrutiny, he gulped what was left in his glass. "May I ask why you are so interested?" Her voice had become clipped, and her eyes shuttered. Terry couldn't believe his luck. *Hot damn. She's jealous!*

"It's just that…" Nathan's angry mug crossed Terry's mind leaving the words to trail off.

The next few moments were tension filled. Rainy finally broke the silence. "It's just *what*?"

"Please don't think that I'm interested in Bright Flower. That couldn't be farther from the truth." Terry screwed his lips up in a grimace at the thought of betraying his best friend's feelings. "I'll be honest about why I want to know, but you can't mention any of this to Nathan."

He waited to continue until she nodded her affirmation. "I was just wondering about the custom because Bright Flower has Nathan acting like a lovesick teenager."

Rainy's astonishment at his admission was evident when her body quickly tensed. She sat up a little straighter and reached out for Terry's hand. "*Nathan* is interested in Bright Flower?"

Curious over her excitement Terry peered at her through squinted eyes. "Yes. Why?"

"Well—"she grimaced"—there are a couple of reasons. One of which I can't tell you because in doing so a confidence would be broken. But I will say that when I first laid eyes on Nathan, I knew instantly he'd make a perfect love match for…well…for some lucky woman."

Now he was the one irritated. "Really? Why is that?"

"Because Nathan is a beautiful man of course."

Terry wasted no time flicking his hand in front of Rainy's face. "Do you have vision problems?"

Swatting at him, she snickered. "No, silly. He *is* a beautiful man. His spirit comes through loud and clear. Nathan is honest with righteous morals and a great big tender heart. He'll be a good protector and an amazing lover to the woman that claims him."

Terry could only gape at her perceptive impressions of the man he'd known his whole life. Not many women had been able to see past Nathan's outer package. He was big—no, huge was a better word for it, intimidating and rather unappealing in the looks category. "How could you possibly know all of that just by meeting him the one time?"

Her eyebrow shot up, and her mouth twisted to the side in an expression that all but yelled, *'Really?'*

It was then he'd realized his stupidity had kicked in again. "Oh, yeah. Sorry. For a moment I forgot about the whole High Priestess thing. I didn't realize you had witch vision too."

Rainy's laughter at his description of her abilities was contagious and had him relaxing. Topping off their wine he stood and held his hand out to her. "Come with me. Let's sit on the porch swing. I'd love to find out more about you and how you got involved in the Wiccan religion."

Taking hold of his hand, Rainy acquiesced and allowed him to lead her to the swing. To avoid the awkward moment of having to decide what the appropriate distance between them should be, Terry risked bad manners and sat first leaving that option up to her. It pleased him that she sidled up so close their legs touched. When Rainy cuddled into his side and got comfortable, he thought he could die a happy man. Feeling bold he maneuvered his arm around her shoulders and pulled her snugly into his body. It didn't go unnoticed that she fit like a glove.

Taking a moment to get used to the intimacy, they sat silently and listened to the sounds of the forest surrounding the little guest cottage.

"I can tell you have some reservations about what I am. I like you, Terry, and I'd like to ease your mind. What do you want to know?"

"Why don't you start with whatever you're comfortable telling me?"

The fact that Terry hadn't corrected her about his comfort level, or lack thereof, hung heavily between them. He wanted to reassure her about his feelings, but she dealt with the supernatural on a daily basis. Even though he'd never had roots in any religion, Rainy's use of witchcraft did disturb him more than he cared to admit.

Her nod of understanding was almost imperceptible. "Okay. I guess it would be best to start off with my family. I'm the youngest of three kids. My sister, Carol, is sixteen years older than me. My brother, David, was eleven years older. I…"

"Wait. *Was?* Your brother *was* eleven years older?"

"Yes. David died several years back. He was a biker who lived hard and partied harder. The people in my family were all born with…h-m-m…let's just say unique gifts. I think the supernatural affected him as it did with all of us. I don't know for sure, but I believe his soul was just too sensitive which made it difficult for him to deal with the havoc that always accompanies psychic abilities. But that's a whole other story which we'll save for another time if you're still interested.

"Because there's such a huge age difference between my siblings and me, we had the unique opportunity to have several living generations at the same time. I was raised with my nieces and nephews. We were all so close in age that they felt more like brothers and sisters. It's all exceptionally confusing.

"When my grandmother was alive, we'd have a family reunion at least once a year. Now I know the reason behind that annual event, but back then I was clueless. Our folks would always push us to spend quiet alone time with her. As children, we were meant to learn from Grandma. No one ever spelled that fact out for us, and we were too busy being kids to figure it out on our own. Life moved so fast that before we knew it we were all grown up and Grandma was old.

"Back then I was too confused to discuss my abilities with anyone, even the woman meant to be my mentor. I did my best to ignore the spiritual gifts, and that was a lot harder to do than you'd think it might be. I hate to admit it, but when it came to anything supernatural or paranormal we were all a huge disappointment to Grandma. All that wisdom and knowledge was lost to us when she died.

"Grandma Stratton was a country woman with little to no education. She was the real deal—the salt of the earth. Her belief in God was unshakable. Acutely aware of her spiritual abilities, she felt privileged to have been one of the chosen, as she called it. The one lesson that beautiful soul was able to teach me before she died was that it would have been blasphemous to be given her abilities and not use those gifts to help people.

"My grandmother was a lovely person. Standing no more than four-foot, eight-inches tall, that woman was a powerhouse—fearless.

"The last year she was alive we had five generations sitting around the kitchen table." Rainy ticked each generation off with her fingers. "My grandmother, my mother, me and my sister, my niece, and my great nephew.

"As usual we sat there and listened to Grandma tell stories of her childhood and better times." Rainy rested her head in the crook of Terry's neck as she relived those family memories. "By that time in my life, I could have listened to her adventures for hours on end.

"Suddenly my great nephew, who was about eight months old at the time, reached out and pulled a mug of steaming hot coffee all over him. It was midsummer and sweltering hot, so he only wore a diaper.

"Needless to say, everyone at the table wigged out. Little Caleb was screaming from the pain of the burn. His skin was bright red and started blistering right away. As any mother would, my niece panicked and couldn't do a thing but scream and run in circles with the baby.

"At that time my grandmother's health had declined so much she was confined to a wheelchair. She couldn't get up, but her arms rose toward the baby. Somehow over the din of the commotion, I heard her voice. *'Give me that child,'* she said.

"My niece was wailing as loud as little Caleb and

didn't hear her at first. My grandmother yelled in a powerful voice that I'd never heard her use, *'Give me that boy, now!'*

"The commandment acted like a hand that came out of nowhere and slapped my niece. She handed Caleb off to Grandma immediately without thought. We all stood around in a circle and watched as Grandma placed her hands on the burn."

Rainy took a deep, nervous breath which served to peak Terry's interest even more. The reverence in her voice was a precursor to what must have been a truly magical event to witness.

"Caleb was screaming his bloody lungs out." Rainy's hands covered her ears. Her eyes slammed shut as she forcefully swallowed. "Oh, God. I can still hear his agonizing shrieks in my head."

No other words were needed to describe the horror of that moment. The trauma of the event rang through loud and clear in the way her voice wavered. Terry squeezed Rainy tighter into his side for added comfort.

"Grandma was calm as you please. Her eyes were shut, and her mouth started to move with inaudible words. Each time she worked her hands to another site of the burn, Caleb would calm a little more. After about twenty minutes the boy started laughing. His pudgy little arms were flailing around as if he were playing with some unseen force standing in front of him.

"Grandma opened her eyes and kissed the top of his head as she handed him back to my niece. The burn was gone. No more redness. No more blisters. And indeed no more pain. There was nothing but beautiful, soft baby skin and the coo of a contented child."

Rainy tilted her head, and Terry saw the

truthfulness in her misty eyes. "I know you probably don't believe any of this. Hell, I found it hard to believe, and I was there."

He responded by kissing her forehead. "I grew up with Jody, remember? Her ability to talk to spirits always amazed me. I've never known anyone that could heal before. It's fascinating. Tell me more." He hoped his interest in her family history was encouragement enough for her to continue.

"Well, needless to say, my grandma was exhausted after the healing. I wheeled her to the bedroom and helped her get into bed. It was only then that I had gathered enough courage to ask what had just happened.

"Grandma told me she talked the fire away and left it at that. No other explanation. The time for her mentoring had passed. She died shortly after that. But what I'd witnessed that day inspired me to learn more about the abilities I'd lived with my whole life. I had no idea what exactly they were or how to go about using them, so I started looking for guidance and found it within the Wiccan religion."

"Your grandmother sounds like an amazing woman. Did she have any other gifts?"

Rainy's laugh was deep. But when she placed her hand on his leg and gave his thigh a little squeeze sparks of lust shot through him.

"Grandma used to love to watch wrestling on TV. Not the Olympic sport, mind you, but the kind where men in tights jump off the ropes circling the ring and swan dive onto their opponents. At the time wrestling was televised in the wee hours of the morning. My grandma was such a devoted fan that she never missed a show. Knowing all the combatant's names, she thought of them as part of the family. Curious about her obsession, I sat with her one night." Again, she turned to look into Terry's eyes so he could see her truthfulness. "Do you know what she did?"

Her bright smile had the corners of his mouth lifting. "What did she do?"

"She prayed for her favorite wrestlers. If they were losing, she'd close her eyes and mumble. She always started out with, *'Dear Lord Almighty.'* The rest of her words slurred and I couldn't make them out. I don't know if that was a product of reverence for her prayer, or a side effect of the bottle of whiskey she kept hidden in her dresser drawer.

"Damn I miss my grandma. She was a hoot."

****

With the dishes done, Terry had run out of excuses to keep Rainy at the cottage. Tomorrow he'd go back to his life in Tempe, and she'd remain in Flagstaff.

"Walk me to my car?"

No. I want you to stay. "Okay."

"Are you going to ask me for my number?"

Terry brightened immediately. Rainy wasn't staying the night, but she wasn't saying goodbye forever either.

Taking her hand in his, they strolled outside. The late evening high country air had turned crisp. More accustomed to the warm, balmy Phoenix nights Terry's body fought not to shiver. Rainy must have sensed his discomfort because she dropped his hand and nuzzled into his side. As they walked along the path, his arm slid comfortably around her shoulders.

"When are you going back to Phoenix?"

Terry tried like hell to keep the disappointment out of his voice. Had he been asked that question a few days ago he wouldn't have been able to curb his excitement to go home. At last everything in his life had come together for him. His art had taken off, and he was finally settling down in a beautiful home that he'd waited for what felt like a lifetime to afford.

"I've got to leave tomorrow. I bought a house, and Nathan is going to help me move in over the next couple of weeks."

"That *is* exciting news! Where's your new home located?"

"Old-town Tempe. It's walking distance to Arizona State University. I'm hoping that once I get settled, you'll come down to see me."

"I'd love that."

"It's got an acre lot with a separate guest apartment at the back of the property. The outbuilding has an open floor plan. The best part about the little cottage is the walls are floor to ceiling vintage paned glass windows. All the natural light makes it perfect for my new workspace. Other than the kitchen and the bedroom in the main house the studio will be my top priority. I've got to prepare for a show next spring, and I'm starting to get nervous about having enough time to finish everything I want to include. By the way, I was serious when I asked if I could paint you."

"I'd be crazy to turn you down. I've seen your work, remember?" Her shoulder nudged his ribs. "If you'd like I'd be happy to perform a house blessing for you."

Not having any clue what a house blessing entailed, he was genuinely touched by her offer. "You'd do that for me?"

"Of course I would. I'd love to. It's an important part of moving into a new space. Especially for a home that's been inhabited before. House blessings clear out all of the previous homeowner's negative energy and make the space your own."

"Sounds great. Once I'm all moved in, I'll give you a call. I'd be happy to come to Flagstaff and pick you up."

She waved him off with her hand while making a tsk-tsk noise with her tongue. "That's not necessary. I travel to Phoenix all the time for work. I go so often that I have an apartment there. It saves on hotel bills. Besides if I can get another meal out of it like the one I had tonight I'd be a happy woman."

"It's a date then."

They'd made it to her car far too soon. He wasn't ready to let her go.

Rainy leaned on the door and peered into Terry's eyes. "I guess this is goodbye."

Before he could stop himself, he raised a hand and traced the side of her face with a gentle caress. "Not for long. I'll be back in a couple of weeks to check in on Jody and Jared's home. I'd like to see you again."

Terry had no clue how much time had passed as they stood there staring into each other's eyes. A minute? Five? Ten minutes? It felt as though time had stood still.

He moved in and kissed her forehead. Leaning into him Rainy's lips grazed the side of his mouth. Suddenly the coolness of the late summer air abandoned Terry and left him feeling warm and breathless in its place. His body betrayed him as it shivered from something altogether different than the weather. Their eyes met again when they moved together for what they'd both longed for all evening. At least he hoped Rainy had.

When their lips met, a magical current passed through their bodies and swept them away. Something akin to lightning moved between them as if they were clouds coming together in a powerful Arizona monsoon storm.

Gently cradling Rainy's face, Terry pulled away just far enough to look into her eyes. Relief flooded him when he realized the kiss had unsettled her just as much as it had rattled him. Elated to the point of wanting to whoop it up and holler he had to work to restrain himself so she wouldn't think him a fool—or possibly even worse—a horny fourteen-year-old boy stuck in the body of a sexually frustrated man.

"If you continue to gloat like that I'm going to leave here thinking some terribly unkind thoughts."

Shit. Caught again. He'd have to remember that Rainy possessed the Spidey sense.

Terry was acutely aware of the grin plastered on his face, but couldn't do a thing to stop it. *I put that look in her eyes. Me.* Pure unadulterated male pride fueled his confidence and left him preening over the fact that unkind thoughts would be the furthest thing from her mind when she left here.

His laughter was the only sound to be heard in the surrounding trees. Giddiness overtook him as he made a show of pinning her against the car door. His fingers swept through her thick silken mane.

Feeling rather smug with himself he stated, "I'm curious."

"I'm afraid to ask what sparked your curiosity."

"What was your first impression of *me*?"

Rainy's head tilted to the side as her lips pursed.

"You know, that High Priestess, witchy thing you did with Nathan where you named off the exact kind of person he is. I was wondering what your thoughts about me were when you first saw me."

She sucked that damn sexy bottom lip between her teeth, and Terry thought he'd pass out. Unable to remove his gaze from her sumptuous mouth, he watched a smile lift the corners of her lips.

"My first impression of you was that you were the most adorable man I've ever met."

It took a moment for his testosterone loaded brain to catch up with her words. Feeling a bit offended he took a giant step back. "*Adorable?* Let me get this straight. You thought Nathan was a beautiful man inside and out. You picked up on *his* superhero mentality. And I'm *adorable*?"

"You're the only man I've ever met that my abilities can't penetrate. I can't read you. In my book that makes you an enigma."

Her explanation made him feel much better. *Enigma was good.*

Rainy's broad grin let him know she could most definitely read his relieved expression.

"You're magical to me like a…like a…h-m-m…like a unicorn."

"*Unicorn?* Now you're fucking with me."

Apparently, she thought herself hysterical because the comparison between him and the ridiculous children's fantasy had her busting a gut with over the top hilarity. Rainy laughed so hard she had to bend over and support her weight on her knees. Terry's male ego took a hit and deflated again.

When she finished cackling and snorting at his expense, Rainy stood and wiped tears from her eyes. "I can see you're angry. Let me explain. Maybe *unicorn* wasn't the right choice. Let's go with international spy—man of mystery, or perhaps a sleek, sexy vampire that shifts in the night to drink from the throat of a sexy woman."

Terry rushed Rainy and caught her by surprise. Moving swiftly, he threw his arms around her and held her captive in a bear hug. "Sexy Vampire—I can live with that."

Brazenly baring her neck for him, he accepted the challenge and nibbled her tender flesh. Terry kissed and nipped the distance between her neck and earlobe. Her leg encircled his, spurring him on to a fevered pitch.

He couldn't get enough of Rainy. Playfully nipping at her chin, he moved to her bottom lip and sucked it into his mouth. Her groan sapped his strength and left his legs weak and wobbly. Given the green light, he took her mouth with a groan.

Grabbing Rainy by the knees Terry's strength surprised them both when he lifted her onto the hood of the car. Never breaking the embrace her legs wrapped around his waist and pulled him to her. Slowing and changing the pace of the kiss from needy to soft, his lips grazed the corner of her mouth and then her nose.

He pressed his forehead against hers. "Wow."

Her hands gently cradled his face. "Yeah. Wow."

Chapter Five

Following a restless night, Terry drove a little over two hours from Flagstaff in the early morning hours and finally made it to Nathan's house. Just as he pulled up to the curb, his passenger door flew open with force. A huge duffle bag was propelled over the seat and landed in the back with a thunderous thump that shook the car.

Terry couldn't help but grin as Nathan squeezed his large frame into the small vehicle. His beloved old clunker protested with a squeak under the strain of his friend's bulk. Carefully nestling a coffee cup between his legs, the big guy struggled in the tight quarters to buckle his seat belt. His girl, Rosie, might not be the prettiest thing on the road, but she always got him where he was going.

"Instead of a house, you should have spent your money on a damn car that doesn't moan and groan every time I get into it. Tell me again why I couldn't just drive myself?"

Terry waited to respond until Rosie had been thrown into first gear propelling the two men safely away from Nathan's house. Removing both hands from the steering wheel, he rubbed them together in a menacing fashion. "All the better to detain you, my dear. There will be no escaping my torture."

Nathan's lips pursed as his face reddened. "Cute,

asshole." Trying to get comfortable in the tiny bucket seat, his elbow accidentally rammed against the passenger door. "Ouch! Dammit! Seriously, aren't you the least bit embarrassed to be seen in this piece of shit?"

"Come on. Stop the bitch fest. In exchange for helping me move, I'm saving you from driving all the way across town and back. If you ask me, you got the best end of the bargain. Pfft. I go to all this trouble, and you have the nerve to insult my most cherished possession." Terry made a production of leaning forward and lovingly petting the cracked dashboard. "Don't listen to him, Rosie girl. He doesn't mean it. He's always a grumpy butt this early in the morning."

Feeling Nathan's eyes boring into him, Terry continued to console his beloved car. He had a hell of a time trying to keep a straight face.

"Grumpy butt? What are we, five-years-old again?"

Terry's attempt at containing his laughter faltered miserably as a jubilant snort escaped his lips.

Folding his beefy arms across his chest, Nathan stared at him as though he'd lost his mind. "It wasn't that funny. What the hell is…oh, wait and a minute. I forgot. You had a date with the hot witch lady last night. Since you're in such a good mood, it must have gone pretty good. Don't tell me you got lucky on the first date?"

"Dude, she's not that kind of woman, and you know it. But I did get lucky in another way. Holy shit, man, I think she's the one."

"*The one?* Have you lost your ever-loving mind? You only just met her two days ago."

"She thinks I'm an enigma." The smugness in Terry's voice rang through loud and clear. Pulling up to a stop sign, he chanced a sideway glance at his friend. It wasn't often Nathan was stunned silent. Expecting that reaction, he wished he could have had a picture of the absolute shocked expression on his friend's face.

The dumbfounded silence continued to linger longer than was socially acceptable even in jest between friends. Indignation started to rear its ugly head at Nathan's unspoken disbelief that any woman could find Terry a mystery. As if objecting to the reaction, Rosie lurched forward.

Feeling the need to back up his claim—but before he thought it through—Terry shot back, "Yep. That's right. *Me*. An enigma. An *adorable* enigma." He recognized the fatal flaw as soon as it slipped from his mouth.

It was Nathan's turn to laugh. Nathan's body shook so hard with undisguised hilarity that the cup precariously situated between his legs sloshed drops of hot liquid all over him. The prick—a man who was supposed to be his best friend—was so absorbed in laughter that he didn't even seem to feel the burn.

Before Terry would allow Nathan to rain on his parade any further, he spoke up. "You don't understand what Rainy meant. Listen to me dammit." His hand flew out and grazed Nathan's shoulder. "You know, like an international spy or a sexy vampire." His friend gasped for air between boisterous guffaws of amusement.

Nathan squelched his laughter barely long enough to talk. "What the hell were you guys smoking last night?"

"Fine. I'm not going to tell you what Rainy's first impressions of you were." Perturbed, Terry made sure to add an extra full-blown taunting inflection to his voice. That shut him up.

"Me?"

"Yep."

"Come on. From one *adorable* enigma to another. Spill."

"Rainy knows what she's talking about. I swear that woman had you pegged, dude. She said you are a beautiful man, inside and out."

"Did she now? Maybe I should ask her out. It sounds as if she may be more interested in me than you."

Before Terry knew what he was doing, his arm swung out again but this time clocked Nathan in the chest with a resounding wallop. "Don't even think about it. Besides, she said you'd be the perfect match for Bright Flower."

"*What?*"

Shit. That was stupid. "Umm. I may have mentioned to Rainy that you have a thing for Bright Flower."

"*What?*"

"Before you blow a gasket, let me explain."

"You better start talking fast, or I'm going to be forced to beat the shit out of you. By the time I'm done with you, you'll be so swollen that the EMTs will need the Jaws of Life to cut you out of this tin can."

"Rainy told me that Spirit Keeper had put the word out that he's looking for a wedding match for Bright Flower. She said that men from all around the Navajo Nation were meeting with him so he could make the perfect wedding match."

Terry felt horrible for his friend. He'd gone completely pale with the news.

"I saw the way you looked at her, Nathan. I've only seen that look between two other people. Jody and Jared look at each other like that. You need to go to Spirit Keeper and ask him to slow the process down, or you're going to lose Bright Flower before you even have a chance with her."

Terry pulled into the driveway of his new home. Seemingly lost in thought, Nathan stared out the front windshield. The only sign that he'd been paying attention was the way his jaw tightened and then relaxed as his teeth forcefully clenched together and released.

"At least give Rainy a call and talk to her." He laid his hand on Nathan's tense arm, but it was vigorously shaken off.

"We've got a lot of work ahead of us. Let's get started." Just like that, the conversation was over. The passenger door flew open. Nathan unfolded his body and spilled out of the car.

"Well, shit."

The subject of Bright Flower would most certainly come up again. Terry felt the issue far too important not to get it out in the open. For now, though, he valued his face too much to continue. Maybe after some time stewing on the problem, Nathan would be willing to talk about the predicament of arranged marriage. For now, he'd just have to put his concerns aside and let the matter drop until a little later.

Nathan's agitation showed itself as he stood ramrod straight at the front door. The man stared the barrier down as if it were the enemy.

"I've got something for you."

No response.

Terry held out the extra key he'd had made. "Here. Take it. I know my place isn't as grand as yours, but it's my home. You'll always be welcome and always have a bed waiting for you. Mi casa es su casa."

Terry was relieved to see that Nathan's firm stance had finally relaxed even if it was just a little bit. The intended gesture behind the gift of the key had his best friend looking down at his feet and exhaling to rid himself of the previous conversation's anxiety. "Okay. That means a lot to me, Terry. Thank you."

Nathan moved aside so Terry could unlock the door to his home for the first time. While standing in the doorway and peering inside, an overwhelming feeling of contentment flowed through him. He'd waited a lifetime for this moment. All the hard work he'd put into his craft had finally paid off.

"What are you waiting for? You don't want me to carry you over the threshold, do you?"

As usual, their shared humor took the edge off all the previous ill feelings between them. For the moment, at least, all was right again.

Nathan pushed past Terry. "Wow. I love it. The house is a lot bigger than it looks from the outside." Strolling over to the wall and stroking it as men often did when appreciating fine craftsmanship, he uttered, "The plaster work is incredible. Is it original to the house?"

"Yep. All the walls are original, and so is the woodwork. I think it's pretty cool. The way the plaster was applied reminds me of Adobe. You don't see walls like these anymore. They knew how to build things back in the forties."

Taking everything in, Nathan spun and went to the front window. "Man, these diamond paned windows are awesome! What wood are the frames made out of? Oak? You can tell they're vintage due to the imperfections in the glass. The small bubbles and streaks add character. Shit, man, they're stunning. I can't believe the glass has survived this long."

Terry had a difficult time tamping his pride down. "Yeah. I can't believe I got lucky enough to get my hands on this home. There's not a single house for sale in this area for over a square mile. I got a smokin' deal on it too. Do you remember when you, me, and Jody used to walk home from Tempe High School? We'd detour through this neighborhood and pick out the homes we wanted to live in when we grew up. This place was my pick every time. I know it sounds silly, but when we were kids and stood on the sidewalk in front of this house, it called to me. It was as if some force compelled me to stop and stare. I knew without a shadow of a doubt that someday I would own this home."

"Dude, that's not silly at all. That's a dream. You're a lucky man, Terry. You've worked hard, and your dreams are being realized. I'm damn proud of you."

Nathan's sentimental praise warmed Terry's heart. Smiling with pride, he offered his fist for a bump. "Come out back. You haven't seen the best part yet."

After making their way through the house, Terry opened the dining room French doors to share his little piece of paradise. To the right was an outdoor kitchen, fully equipped with a built-in barbecue.

Everything was constructed out of sandstone which continued on into the natural style swimming pool. There wasn't a single cheesy tile or any ordinary decking. Like a beach, the front of the pool slanted in a gradual decline instead of the usual steps. Lush greenery encircled a large waterfall that, when running, cascaded down and projected a tropical lagoon style feel.

"I can't wait to take a swim! It's beautiful."

"Wait till you see this!" Terry rushed to the back of the waterfall and turned it on. As the water lazily tumbled down and hit the pool, the force created swells which moved through the water to lap at the front slope. The effect was just like gentle waves rolling onto the edge of a tranquil beach.

"Damn! That's the coolest pool I've ever seen. I may have to copy the style for my place."

"You still haven't seen the best thing on this property. Come with me."

They walked down a sandstone path and found themselves in front of the second building on the property. The outbuilding looked as though it had been constructed completely out of old paned glass from about a foot off the ground to the ceiling. The blackout window treatments were closed making it all but impossible to see inside.

"This is my new studio." Terry swung the door open, but its forward progress halted as it firmly hit an unexpected barricade. Reaching inside, he flicked the light switch, but nothing happened. They squeezed through the tight opening and stood motionless as their eyes adjusted to the darkness. They encountered box after box—some piled as high as the ceiling.

"What the hell?"

"It looks like the previous owner forgot some things," Nathan stated the obvious in a deadpan tone while trying not to laugh.

"The realtor promised me all of this stuff would be gone when the people that owned the house moved out. Dammit! I don't have time for this!" Terry pulled his phone out and speed dialed his realtor. Pissed, he worked his way outside and stomped away to voice his displeasure in solitude.

Curious, Nathan made his way around some of the boxes. The only light in the room came from the front door that for now could only open partway. Navigating through the unexpected obstacle course became more difficult the farther into the building he got. Carefully bending over so he wouldn't accidentally cause a landslide of packed possessions, he squinted to make out the writing on the boxes in front of him. Some were marked with people's names—Janet, Casey, Francis, and Bill. Others, he noted, were labeled by room or occasion—bedroom, kitchen, Christmas, Easter, as well as Valentine's Day.

With each step that Nathan took deeper into the depths of the studio, the more uncomfortable he became. Blackout curtains, he realized, got their name for a reason. Their use in this space served to make the ominous shadows within the room even darker. The air smelled dank as if mold grew on every surface. The atmosphere was dense and moist as if he'd been transported deep into a dark, soggy jungle where danger lurked within every shadow. A scene from a horror flick he'd seen just the other night popped into his mind. Unsuspecting teenagers who'd had the bad luck of partying in a haunted mausoleum were unfortunate enough to have a run-in with a nasty ass demon right before their terrifying deaths. He chuckled at the thought. "I ain't no teenybopper and this ain't no crypt, so I'm probably safe."

It only took an instant for his humor to wane. The hair on the back of his neck rose just as goose bumps the size of measles started to crawl up his arms. The longer he stayed rooted in place, an overwhelming sensation of hostility began to materialize within him. It felt as though he'd entered a private sanctum without permission.

Nathan's ears prickled as a faint knocking sound could be heard coming from the direction of the side wall. While difficult to see through the inky darkness, boxes were stacked to the ceiling in that area making it impossible to tell if they covered a solid wall or more windows. He could only hope the strange sound didn't mean cartons filled with junk were shifting. If that were the case, one or both of them could be injured in an avalanche of worthless debris.

"Well, this sucks."

Carefully making his way back to the door, each step filled Nathan with an urgency to get the hell out of this building. He couldn't help but feel as though someone or something was herding him out. Picking up the pace, he carefully made his way back to the studio door. The vast sense of relief as he finally exited through the threshold had him struggling to figure out what the hell had just happened.

Terry approached Nathan, shaking his head and pinching his bottom lip between his fingers.

"What did the realtor say?"

Perplexed, he shot an unsteady glance at Nathan. "She said it was all mine. The people had abandoned everything. They didn't want any of it."

Nathan's bewildered expression spoke volumes. Without saying a word, his friend perfectly articulated how Terry felt.

"I don't understand." Nathan peered back at the studio door. "That makes no sense at all. Why pack it all up just to leave it behind?"

Terry mimicked Nathan's hands on hips as they both tried to make sense of this unexpected predicament.

"Something is wrong with this picture, Terry. No one leaves everything they've packed up behind."

"Beats the shit out of me." Terry grimaced as the palm of his hand dug into his chest. He'd had a strict plan of attack for this move, and it had all just crumbled in the blink of an eye. Never being a fan of change resulted in panic taking root.

As each minute ticked by, anxiety built within him. Terry quickly rose to his breaking point. "I planned to have the studio in working order within a couple of days. Now that's all shot to shit." He bent over trying to catch his breath. "I have to get my studio set up. That takes priority over everything else. I have to be able to work. The gallery is selling two or three of my pieces a week and asking for more paintings all the time. Plus, I have that show coming up in the spring.

"Fuck!" Not having a clue where to start, Terry's hands swiped through his too long, shaggy hair.

"Calm down, little buddy. Take a deep breath. I've got a plan. We'll pull boxes out of here one by one and go through them in the yard. Chances are they're all filled with junk so we should be able to get through them quickly. Anything you want to keep, we'll move into the house. Anything you want to chuck, we'll put in a pile. I'll rent a moving truck and take the stuff down to donate at the hippy coop over on University if it's still there. They used to give stuff away to the homeless. Remember?" Nathan's no-nonsense timbre helped ease Terry back from the brink of falling apart. "Don't worry. I'll help with this mess until the moving truck gets here. When they do, I'll work with them, and you can continue out here. Sound like a plan?"

Even as his friend took charge, Terry couldn't contain the agitation this latest obstacle cultivated. "Why the hell is nothing ever easy?"

"Dude, calm down. Just think about it for a minute. We could find Lola in here. We'd be rich."

Terry felt the muscles in his face go slack. "What?"

"Lola. You know, the long lost sister of Mona?"

Lack of sleep, driving almost two-hundred miles before seven in the morning, and a huge disappointment left Terry punchy. The ridiculous joke had him breaking out with an uncontrollable case of the snickers. "Okay. Sure. Maybe if we're super lucky, we'll find Bonah, Mona and Lola's brother. Get it?"

Always the straight man, Nathan dryly retorted, "Bonah? Really? I set you up for a good comeback, and that's the best you've got? You're breakin' my heart, Terry. Come on, Runt. We're burnin' daylight. Let's get busy."

****

With each opened box, Nathan's nerves started to ramp up. Something felt off—no, it was much more than that. The motive behind all those small family treasures being tossed aside so haphazardly seemed more along the lines of sinister than just off.

His friend's reaction wasn't helping. Terry behaved like a kid who had just hit the jackpot on Christmas morning.

Nathan held up a beautiful brightly colored afghan which had been fashioned after a stained glass window. As he inspected the handiwork, his throat began to constrict with doubt. "I don't understand what the deal is with these boxes. Look at this, Terry. This handmade blanket would be an heirloom in my family. Who in their right mind would get rid of something so special? My mom and sisters used to slave over this kind of thing for hours every night. Do you remember that? At the very least, this afghan would have taken months to make."

He bent over and rifled through the box. "There must be a dozen handmade blankets in here. How could anyone just walk away and leave it all behind?"

He might as well be talking to a wall. Terry didn't give the afghan a second glance. He was too busy ripping the next box open to see what treasure it held.

"Oh my God! Look! Look what they left for me." He held a restaurant quality stainless steel pot up in the air seemingly mesmerized by how it glinted in the sunlight. Reaching in to grab another, he yelped with delight as if just winning the lottery. "Do you have any idea how expensive these are? I can finally get rid of my old, junky pots and pans now."

Desperate to make his point, Nathan got on his knees and clamped a large hand on Terry's shoulder to get his attention. "Terry, listen to me. I think you should call and get more information on why this stuff was left behind. Something's just not right with this whole situation."

"Dude, relax. The realtor told me that I could keep anything and everything left behind by the former owners. Who knows? Maybe someone died, and the survivors didn't want the memories. Maybe they needed to downsize. There are all sorts of explanations that come to mind."

In Terry's current euphoric state, Nathan knew full well he wouldn't be able to convince his friend there might be a problem with the reclaimed booty. He decided to holster his ominous feelings for the time being. No one knew him better than Terry. Maybe he was right. *I've been known to overreact in the past.*

Nathan slipped his shoes off and hung his legs over the side of the pool. The cool water lapped at his calves and released some of the built up tension riding him. To ease his mind, he mulled over Terry's behavior the past few hours and tried to get to the bottom of his concerns. His best friend's manic demeanor since they had arrived at the house was completely out of character. The expression on Terry's face as he opened box after box unsettled Nathan. It was as if his best friend was a different person all together—someone Nathan didn't know at all. *What exactly is off?* Terry's bearing was out of kilter. His off-putting, frenzied personality was so un-Terry like. The whole situation made Nathan uneasy. Who knows? Maybe he was making a mountain out of a mole hill. He'd stay close and keep a sharp eye on his friend. For now, that was all he could do.

Since they needed a ladder and, as it turned out,

extra hands, he dialed another friend for back up.

"Jursic, it's Nathan. I've got an offer you can't refuse."

"The last time you made me an offer I couldn't refuse, we ended up hiding in the bushes to keep from getting arrested. Do you know how embarrassing it is for an FBI agent to hide out in bushes?"

"Yeah. Good times. Do you still have that pickup truck you're so proud of?"

Nathan waited to the count of five but still had no response.

"Jursic?"

"No. You can't borrow my truck. I don't care..."

"I don't want to borrow your truck. I want you to come with it and bring a ladder. I'll even buy you pizza and beer as payment. Come on. It'll be fun."

"By fun, do you mean there will be women involved?"

"Nope. Just us boys. You, me, and Terry."

"The crazy artist?"

"Yep."

"You're on. I'll be there in about thirty minutes."

"No. I need you to come to the crazy artist's new house. I'll text you the address. Don't forget the ladder and bring something to swim in."

Regrettably, Nathan put his shoes on and marched back into the studio for another box. The interior wasn't nearly as threatening once they'd opened all the heavy drapes and let some sunshine in. *I don't think I'd want to spend a night in here, though.*

The first carton he came to was labeled *Christmas.* He was almost scared to see what kind of holiday stuff people would leave behind—especially when the previous homeowners had so carelessly abandoned the other family heirlooms.

Tap. Tap. Tap.

He stopped in his tracks just a few steps away from the door. The faint knocking came from the wall still covered floor to ceiling in boxes. They all looked secure, but one or more of them had to be lopsided and ready to fall if they were shifting enough for the contents to make that sound.

Setting the carton down, Nathan paced to the wall and inspected the still standing boxes. Ever so slightly, he pushed on one stack and then the next. The whole while, he surveyed the cartons within reach to detect any movement which could explain the strange knocking sound. *Nothing. They're all stable. H-m-m.*

Nathan placed his ear to the carton closest to him and listened. *No knocking.* Maybe he was hearing things. He retraced his steps.

Time to see what Christmas trinkets Terry now owned. The knife slid easily through the packing tape. Nathan's body prickled with goose bumps and then went numb when the contents were revealed.

"What the fuck?"

"What? What did you find?"

Glancing at his friend, Nathan tried to keep the fact he was freaking out to himself. "You better come and take a look at this."

Terry leaned over the box as Nathan watched for his reaction. He recognized the initial shock on his friend's face by the incredulous stare, but then something came over Terry and had him smiling.

"I'm not sure why you're grinning. Why would anyone keep a box of broken Christmas ornaments? It's weird. *No.* It's fucking freaky."

Terry's hand disappeared into the shards of colored glass and pulled a fistful out. "Look at the colors. This has inspired me. I could make a super cool mosaic out of all this colored glass."

The dreamy expression on his friend's face unnerved Nathan almost as much as the box of broken ornaments did.

"Terry, who in their right mind stores breakable ornaments without any packing to keep them safe? Look…" He reached into the box to move the fragments around just as Terry had done moments ago. "Ouch. Son of a bitch!" Nathan jerked his hand out of the box and saw blood trickling from several cuts. *What the hell?* He bristled. *Why did I get cut and Terry didn't?* Warning bells screamed in his head. As absurd as it sounded, he couldn't shake the feeling that somehow he'd just been attacked.

Grasping his hand to inspect it, he couldn't help but notice Terry's continued interest in the contents of the box.

"What's that?"

The cuts on his hand momentarily forgotten, Nathan leaned forward to peer into the box and found a small pristine package hidden within the shards of ornaments. His stomach started to somersault as Terry reached in and pulled the pure white unblemished box out.

They removed the lid which spurred a chain reaction. Both men took a quick step back.

Terry was the first to speak. "What *is* that?"

Out of the two, Nathan was the one to man up. The pristine box held a ruined mess. If they wanted to reveal the contents, he'd have to stick his bloody hand inside. Finding something he could grasp inside the box, he yanked and released a Christmas tree topper that had once been an angel. Now it was just a burnt, barely recognizable clump of plastic and fabric.

"Well, that's kind of creepy."

All Nathan could do was stare at his best friend and wonder when he had lost his flair for the dramatic. "Creepy? *Really?* That's the biggest damn understatement I've ever heard come out of your mouth."

Nathan threw the ruined tree topper into the box, closed the lid, and picked the whole mess up. "I'm throwing all of this out right now. If you're still inspired to make something out of broken ornaments, I'll buy them for you and break them myself."

****

Jursic's big blue pickup truck pulled into the driveway just as Nathan exited the side gate to throw the eerie Christmas box into the large garbage container.

"Nice digs. Where's the beer?"

Grateful he'd have a chance to talk to Jursic about his apprehension with the studio and the bizarre boxes left behind without Terry around, Nathan crossed the yard. While approaching his friend, the moving truck picked that time to show up all but ruining his plan to share his concerns. *Maybe that's for the best. He can come to his own conclusions without my uneasiness prejudicing him.*

"You're just in time, Jursic. The heavy work is about to begin."

"I don't recall you saying anything about putting

me to work. My FBI training is telling me that the word 'fun' was used as a ploy to get me over here for the sole purpose of exploiting my spectacular brawn."

"And they say Feebs are idiots."

Jursic playfully punched Nathan in the arm. "Who says that?"

"*They* do. You know, the indefinable collective everyone's always talking about but no one can name. *They.*

"Here's the plan. Terry's out back going through boxes. While he's doing that, you and I can start putting beds together and furniture in place. That way, I'll have someplace to lay my head tonight.

"Once the basics are in place in the main house, we can help Terry finish clearing out the studio. Maybe make a couple of donation runs with that fancy pickup of yours."

"Yes, sir!" Jursic stood at attention and saluted. "Anything you say, sir, as long as I get my pizza and Dos Equis."

Chapter Six

By the way Terry's stomach rumbled, it felt as though he hadn't eaten in days. Pulling his phone out, he checked the time. *What?* Five hours had flitted by while going through the treasure the previous owners had left behind. *No wonder I'm hungry.* He'd carted too many boxes into the main house to count. But only three remained behind to be donated to charity. *Surely looting never felt this good.*

"I guess I should look at the bright side. I got a hell of a lot of good stuff out of these boxes. It wasn't such a waste of time after all."

Surveying the studio, he'd made quite a dent. Only the wall of boxes remained untouched. Curiously, many of the cartons that were left looked to be much older than those he'd already opened. There were even cobwebs connecting some of them. None of which, he noted, had been labeled either. Since it wouldn't be possible to retrieve the rest of the boxes by himself, now was as good a time as any for a break.

Before leaving, Terry took a moment to inspect the new workspace. The three glass walls thrilled him. He'd be the first to admit that the Valley of the Sun probably wasn't an ideal location to have a glass house. The air conditioning unit he'd ordered would go a long way to fixing that problem. For now, though, since none of the windows actually opened there was no way to circulate air. It was just too hot to spend an extended period of time in the building. Factoring in the heat, he may have given up on the building altogether, but as soon as he opened the blackout curtains, the natural light sealed the deal. *Thank goodness the A/C is coming this week.*

A cloud of dust particles rolled through the air as the tip of his well-worn high-top toed at the carpet. Terry made a mental note to pull the filthy floor covering up to see what lay underneath. If luck was on his side, there'd be a concrete slab that he could paint with epoxy for easy cleanup. Removing all the blackout curtains would allow the natural light to come in. Years of gunk had built up on the paned windows which meant he'd be using a lot of elbow grease to get them clean again. Moving his gaze to the ceiling and the only puny light fixture in the room, he realized installing special lighting was a priority if he wanted to work out here at night.

Leaving the door open to air the studio out, Terry made his way to the house. He'd splurge and buy some burgers for his friends. After all, they'd done the heavy lifting in the main house.

Standing amidst the boxes in his brand new ultra-modern kitchen and sipping a beer, he listened to Nathan and Jursic's raised voices coming from somewhere in the back of the house. "Nathan, you're an idiot." A loud disdainful grunt could be heard. "Just stop a minute and think. The bed doesn't go there. Look. That's a beautiful French double door which has a view of that incredible pool. Terry's going to want the bed placed where he can look out at it. If we put the bed where you want it, the only thing he's going to see is a blank fucking wall."

"Yeah? Well if we put the bed where you want it, he won't need an alarm clock. The damn sun will wake him up every morning. He's an artist. He doesn't have to get up at the butt-crack of dawn every damn day. Use your head."

Terry could imagine a very stubborn Nathan on one side of the mattress while Jursic yanked on the other side. Laughter bubbled up at the thought. *It's time to intervene before they come to blows.* He grabbed two more beers from the refrigerator and headed to the back of the house.

Just as he'd thought, there was a tug of war going on in the middle of his bedroom with the mattress. Each man strained to wrestle the heavy load away from the other. The two stubborn men were ready to rumble.

"Cerveza break."

All motion ceased. The current hostilities were forgotten, and the mattress fell to the floor where they stood. Both men hastily made their way across the room with outstretched hands.

"I've gotten as far as I can on my own out in the studio, so I'm going on a burger run. Who's hungry?" Terry handed each man a brew.

Nathan spoke up first. "I'll have my usual."

Jursic chimed in. "That sounds good to me."

Terry threw his head back and grunted. "Do you have any idea what Nathan's usual is?"

"Does it have meat, cheese, bread, potatoes and a chocolate shake?"

"Yep. Times three."

Jursic glanced at Nathan with raised eyebrows. "You eat three burgers at once?"

"I'm a growing boy. I need all the *free* nutrition Terry can get me." Nathan's thumb waved through the air in Terry's direction.

Jursic's head bobbed in the affirmative as he thought it over. "Yep. I'll have the same."

****

Nathan patiently waited until Terry left before approaching Jursic on the subject of the studio. He was more than a little interested in his friend's reaction to the unsettling vibe of the space.

"I'll clear a spot for us to eat. Why don't you get the ladder and take it out to the studio? You can use the side gate. After we eat lunch, we'll help Terry move the rest of the boxes to the backyard."

Jursic hoisted his beer in the air. "You got it."

Anxiously, Nathan paced in front of the dining room French doors leading to the backyard paradise. When his friend finally came into view stumbling with the oversized ladder, he stealthily moved out of the line of vision. He couldn't contain his snicker as Jursic carried the heavy load precariously down the stone pathway. "Yep. That's Jursic. No ordinary ladder will do. Everything's gotta be two times bigger and heavier than needed. That's the typical FBI way of doing things. Go big or go home."

As Jursic continued to lumber down the path, Nathan glanced at the outbuilding. He couldn't help but wonder why Terry would've closed the blackout curtains when there was still work to be done in there. Something inexplicable left him feeling cold and jittery. To keep his hands steady, he slipped them deep into his pockets.

Nathan leaned into the back door and watched as

Jursic finally reached the studio. Crossing his fingers, he silently prayed his friend would carry the cumbersome ladder inside rather than set it down outside. The only way to get a realistic impression would be for him to enter the one room building alone.

Nathan watched with a keen eye while Jursic opened the studio door. Suddenly, the ladder hit the ground as his hands flew up to cover his face.

"Well, that's not exactly the reaction I thought he'd have." Curious as to what had happened to garner such an unexpected response, Nathan stayed glued to the spot with a watchful eye. Jursic took a tentative step inside but went no farther. He turned his head from right to left as if appraising the interior.

Bewildered by Jursic's reaction, Nathan wondered aloud, "I wish the damn curtains were open so I could see what the problem is."

"Nathan!"

The blood-curdling scream had him quickly exiting the main house and sprinting in the direction of the studio.

"What is it? What's wrong?"

Jursic turned and gagged as if he were going to puke. It didn't take long for the smell to hit Nathan. The putrid stench of death along with an underlying hint of sulfur permeated the studio and surrounding yard. The odor was so foul, it burned his eyes—leaving a running stream of tears down his face.

"What the fuck?" Nathan yelled as he threw an arm over his mouth and nose, fighting the urge to retch.

Jursic finally slammed the front door to the studio. Instantly, the repulsive odor vanished as if it had been nothing more than a figment of their imagination.

"How in the hell has Terry been working in there all day?"

"I promise you, Jursic, the studio *did* not smell like that this morning."

"Something is rotting in there. I've been to enough crime scenes to know that smell. I know you have too, Nathan. What the hell is going on here?"

Bewildered, he stammered in search of words that wouldn't form. Mystified by this new turn of events, all he could do to answer was lamely shrug his shoulders and shake his head. The initial uneasiness he'd felt surrounding the studio had just intensified twofold.

Nathan took a tentative step toward the door. Jursic grabbed his arm and spun him around. "What the hell do you think you're doing?"

Trying to quell his growing sense of foreboding, Nathan racked his brain to come up with a plausible excuse for the putrid odor. "I've got to go in there and see what's causing that smell. It might be something in one of the remaining boxes. Maybe an animal crawled in there and died a long time ago. Maybe it didn't stink before because those boxes hadn't been disturbed." As soon as the words left his mouth, he knew how ridiculous they sounded. Recognizing his hysteria for what it was, for Terry's sake, he desperately wanted to find a reasonable explanation for his uneasiness.

Jursic's head shook in disbelief. "That's the lamest thing I've ever heard. I don't believe it for a minute, but I'm going in with you. Maybe someone in the area isn't too keen on having a new neighbor, and they're playing some sort of prank. Since the blackout curtains are drawn, and it's dark as sin in there, you go left. I'll go right. To be safe, we need to clear the interior to make sure no one is hiding."

Peering back at the discarded opened boxes on the lawn, Jursic found a little girl's baton with sparkling pink puffs on each end and a curling iron. Handing the curling iron off to Nathan, he reached for the doorknob. "You ready?"

"What the fuck am I supposed to do with this? I want your weapon."

"Tough shit. The baton's mine." Jursic looked at the curling iron and grinned. "Go for the eyes."

Doing his best to remain calm, Nathan cursed under his breath.

"One. Two. Three." Jursic threw the door open. The men moved quickly inside with the precision of a poorly outfitted SWAT team. Nathan found it telling that he would actually welcome an armed bandit over the discomfort he currently felt. At least he'd know what he was dealing with and how to respond in kind.

The air inside was thick as molasses and dead still making it difficult to breathe. The foul odor had inexplicably disappeared. Only an ominous silence greeted both men. And what was even more strange no noise from the outside world could be heard inside the room—despite the open door. Nathan felt as though he'd been sucked into a black hole where nothing but dead space hid the dark and dangerous.

"There's nothing in here. Even the smell is gone. How is that possible?" Nathan babbled, hoping beyond measure that his friend could offer up a reasonable explanation. They both took a careful step back.

"I don't understand." The shrill tenor of Jursic's voice spoke volumes. No enlightenment would be coming from him.

"Let's open all the curtains and leave the…"

Both men froze with weapons at the ready, as an unearthly raspy breathing became audible. Even in the complete blackness of the room, Nathan could tell this sound came from no living person screwing with them. Instead, it had become clear they were in the presence of something malevolent. Spinning around, he quickly opened one of the curtains to allow beams of sunlight to brighten the room. He dug his fingertips into Jursic's arm and pointed, his voice a mere whisper. "Look. There—in the corner by the remaining boxes." An emaciated black cat with its body arched and hair standing on end stood at the ready as if prepared to defend what was left of its life. The tail shot up in the air as the feline's unnaturally bright, glowing red eyes turned on the intruders. The animal's menacing growl was a warning filled with pure evil. Without moving its gaze from the men, the fiendish creature slowly made its way toward the curtained far glass wall. The cat stopped in its tracks and hissed a final warning at the intruders as it slowly vaporized into nothing.

Both men shuffled back. Nathan's mouth went bone dry, and his brain scrambled to find a plausible explanation for what they'd just seen. "Um." He sputtered before continuing. "You saw that, right?"

When no response was forthcoming, Nathan pivoted to find Jursic's mouth hanging open. He snapped his fingers in front of his friend's face to break the trance-like stupor.

Jursic's hand clamped like a vice on Nathan's arm. "In the name of all that is holy, what in the bloody hell was that thing?"

"Quick. Help me get all the curtains open." The

men ran from one window treatment to another, shoving the heavy curtains back to allow the sunlight in. They met in the middle of the last wall and turned to survey the room.

Fear of the unknown had left Nathan's legs weak and rubbery. Tightening his muscles, he locked his knees only to have them shake uncontrollably. Each man preferred to have his back to the glass wall as they crept toward the only exit in the building. Grabbing Jursic's arm, he pushed him outside. Both men stood there, baton and curling iron at the ready, silently waiting to see if anything would follow them out.

"What…I…what…a-h-h…"

"No, Jursic. I have no idea what that thing was."

Swaying slightly back and forth, Nathan was surprised Jursic stayed on his feet. Relief flooded him when the color started returning to his friend's face, and he regained enough sense to whimper. "How are you going to explain to Terry that he's sharing his studio with Satan's kitty cat?"

"Pfft. I have no idea. I'm sorry about sending you in there alone, but I needed to make sure I wasn't overreacting to this situation. I haven't had a good feeling about this studio all day. Terry hasn't exactly been himself today. I know the man better than anyone. If we try to discuss our concerns, he'll think we're punking him. Or worse, he'll believe that we're trying to rain on his parade. It's like this house has some kind of hold on him, so much so that he refuses to see reason. This move is a big deal for Terry. He won't take anything we say on the subject of a haunting seriously. And besides, since we grew up with Jody and the ghosts that always surrounded her, for the most part, we've never found them scary. But this is different. I don't know how or why yet, but whatever is happening isn't like anything we've experienced in the past. I guess we'll have to play it by ear until the right time comes up to talk to him. I have a bad feeling about this, though—an *awful* feeling."

Nathan pulled his phone out and dialed.

"Who are you calling?"

"My office. Normally I'd call Jody, our resident ghost whisperer, but she's on her honeymoon. Somehow, I don't think this can wait for her to get back. To get a better idea of what we're dealing with, I want to get the history on this place. I'm going to ask my assistant to pull all the deeds and land records she can find."

"Put it on speaker. I want to add some things to that list."

Nathan obliged. "Hi, boss…" Lynne's cheerful voice was interrupted by an ungodly static. The ear-splitting roar forced the hand which held the phone to move instinctively away from Nathan's body.

Simultaneously both men yelled into the speaker, "Lynne, are you there?"

As quickly as the ear-piercing static started, it stopped. Dead silence. Staring at the phone, neither man had a clue what to expect. "Lynne?"

"*Nooooo.*" The word, no more than a drawn out whisper, broke the eerie connection and lasted several seconds. The voice they heard clear as a bell was male and so threatening Nathan dropped the phone. The insane maniacal cackle that followed left both men quaking.

"Shit, man. That was no damn cat."

Nathan's face went slack with disbelief. "Jesus, Mary, and Joseph. What in the hell is going on here?"

****

Plopping the last bag of fast food on Rosie's passenger seat, Terry marveled at the fifty dollar lunch. *So much for going the cheap route.*

Before merging into traffic, he opened his phone and dialed Rainy. Not wanting to feel needy, he'd quashed the idea of calling her the hundred or so times he'd wanted to earlier.

Anticipation had him holding his breath as he heard the phone connect. Counting the rings, he mentally urged the woman who'd had such a huge impact on him to answer.

"Hello. This is Cheryl, Rainy's assistant. How may I help you?"

Disappointment struck him solidly in the gut. The woman of his dreams had given him the number to her work phone, not her cell phone. After a few silent moments had passed, Cheryl's voice had a ring of annoyance when she spoke again. "Hello? Can I help you with something?"

"Oh, sorry. Hello. I was looking for Rainy. Is she available?"

"Who is this, please?"

"This is Terry Anderson. I'm…" *Shit. What am I to her?* "I'm a friend of hers."

Momentarily taken aback by the woman's childlike giggle, he waited for her to speak.

"Mr. Anderson, you're all Rainy has talked about since she came in this morning."

Cheryl's unexpected reply hit him like an arrow to the heart. A warm tingle started at the top of his head and rushed through his body. Giddy, he high-fived Rosie's dashboard. Unable to contain the huge grin Rainy's assistant's words had sparked, he was certain the smile radiated through his voice. "She's been on my mind too." Feeling like a foolish teenager, he tried his best to shake the love haze. "Can I speak with her, or should I try her cell?"

"This *is* her cell phone. She had an emergency call this morning and had to rush off to the hospital to give Last Rites. This type of work takes a toll on her and the family members, so she left the phone with me to take messages."

"I'm so sorry to hear that." Disappointment laced his voice. Seconds ticked by as he wondered whether it would be insensitive to ask how long she'd be busy.

As if Cheryl had read his mind, she responded without the benefit of him asking. "To tell the truth, she's been there for several hours already. I'm not expecting her back anytime soon. Normally with Last Rites, she stays with the family until the person has departed for the Summerland. Once that's done, she will take the family home and make sure they are taken care of before she leaves them. She may not be back until tomorrow."

"Summerland?"

"Yes. The Otherworld. What you might call Heaven."

Fascinated by the terminology, his smile grew even larger. *Summerland.* The term sounded so peaceful and much less frightening than Heaven or Hell. He liked it.

Terry turned onto his street. "Would you just let her know that I'm thinking about her and I'll call to—" Pulling into his driveway, an ear-piercing static interrupted the call forcing him to jerk the phone away from his head. The noise so vile, it sounded as if an anguished cat in the throes of death had joined the conversation.

"What the hell?"

Chapter Seven

Rainy met Eric Gaines, the hospital chaplain and old friend, in the elevator. The embrace they shared strengthened their resolve for the ceremony ahead of them.

"Thank you for joining me in Iris' Last Rites. She has many family members who are practicing Christians, and I know your presence will be a comfort to them."

"It's my pleasure. Iris and I are friends and have a long history together. Many times over the years, we've participated in spirited theological debates." Eric's head hung low as he clasped his hands together. "I never won." He tried but couldn't manage to hide his grin.

Rainy's laughter bubbled over. "Don't feel bad. Iris and I have had the same discussions, and she trounced me too. Playing the devil's advocate was her favorite pastime. That old woman could talk her way out of anything, even if she didn't believe the words that came out of her mouth. The old gal's a pistol, and I love her dearly. I know you do too."

"Yes."

The mood turned somber when the elevator doors opened. Many people whom Rainy recognized as grandchildren and great-grandchildren of the dying woman she'd respected for so many years milled about in the hallway.

Taking the time to greet each person and offer condolences took a bit longer than expected, but Eric and Rainy finally found themselves entering Iris' room. They each clasped a chilled, frail hand and kissed the beautiful soul's forehead. Death was near.

Iris' eyelids fluttered, and her tired, milky eyes found Rainy's. The corners of the woman's mouth curved upward in a gentle smile as she did her best to squeeze their hands. "It's about time you two got here. I thought I was going to have to take this trip solo." The crowd around the bed erupted in nervous laughter.

Brushing the thin remnants of dull gray hair off the old woman's forehead, Rainy leaned forward. "Are you ready for me and Eric to begin?"

"Oh, yes, dear. I am more than ready."

"Blessed be, sweetheart.

"I'd like to have everyone's attention, please. Iris has asked Father Gaines and me to start the Last Rites.

"I've had the honor of knowing this sweet woman for many years now as has Father Gaines. Iris has been very specific about this ceremony and how she wants it to proceed. Many of you may not know this, but she's been planning her Last Rites for years.

"Before we begin, the bed must be moved a short distance away from the wall."

Turning her attention to Eric, Rainy nodded giving him the floor.

"Please join hands and say the Lord's Prayer with me." The Priest, the High Priestess, and the dying woman locked fingers. As Rainy proudly stated the prayer aloud, she felt the presence of her grandmother standing next to Iris' bed and gave silent thanks. The two women, unknown to each other in life but so similar in spirit, would travel the journey to the Summerland together.

"Amen."

Rainy opened her bag and donned a unique Wiccan ritual robe. Out of respect for the woman lying before her, each embroidered stitch on the eggplant colored silk had been lovingly and respectfully sewn by the coven. With Iris in mind, they had meticulously incorporated everything the woman had loved and held dear in this lifetime on the fine fabric. A rendition of mother and child held special prominence over Rainy's heart. The back portrayed a landscape of Ponderosa Pines standing majestically in the forefront of the Navajo Indian Nation's sacred San Francisco Peaks. Bright yellow sunflowers and orange Indian Paintbrush dotted the beautiful mountainside. The landscape came alive with a feeling of springtime. A pair of bald eagles soared free as a lone bull elk with his head thrown back in mid-bugle completed the landscape. And finally, stitched on her left sleeve, a likeness of her long-dead soul mate, a man she'd mourned the loss of for over three decades. The robes, a tribute to a lovely woman that she would miss with all her heart, would be gifted to Iris' family after the service.

Unfolding a note in Iris' handwriting, she cleared her voice. "Cane Henderson, please step forward.

"Cane, if you would hold your hands out, please." Placing an object in his palm, she curled his fingers over it and held him in place. "When I first met your mother, she asked me to go on a hike up the San Francisco Peaks for a special picnic.

"My thoughts at the time were, she was an octogenarian, and I'd have no trouble keeping up. Boy, was I ever wrong. Instead, Iris wore me out. She walked and walked for miles—for hours on end until finding just the right spot. Curious, I asked her what was so unique about that particular place." Rainy chuckled as she relived the story. "I mean, it all looked the same to me. She held her hand out and dropped a rock into mine. Her reply was simple. *'I was looking for something special to give you, and I finally found it.'*

"Cane Henderson, you are the man who the family looks to for guidance. As Iris Henderson's eldest son, she has requested that you stand to the North above her head and represent Earth with the stone she gave me all those years ago. Please take your place.

"Janice, please step forward."

When the woman stood in front of Rainy, she reached into her bag and brought forth the feather of a hawk. Without being asked, the grieving woman held her hands out. Rainy placed the feather across her palms and curled the woman's fingers around it. "On one of our many picnics together, Iris and I spread out on a blanket and looked to the sky. On one of those outings, a hawk circled above us. As the bird soared on a current of air, a feather fell from the heavens and was collected for this ceremony. This is that feather.

"Because your life sparkles with creativity and you share those talents with others, as Iris' eldest daughter, she has requested that you hold this gift and stand to the East representing the Air element.

"Melanie, please step forward."

The woman pushed her way forward with hands outstretched. Silent tears ran unimpeded down her face, but she never wavered. Rainy passed a match and candle to her. "Please light this white candle. You may recognize the crystal candle holder. Many a night, Iris and I would sit on her porch bathed in the soft light from this candlestick while reflecting back on the significant times in her life."

Rainy clasped Melanie's hands tightly around the crystal base. "Because you live life with passion and fire as Iris has done, your mother asks that you take the flame she used to illuminate her life and represent the Fire element. Please stand to the South.

"Father Gaines, please step forward." The surprise of being included in the pagan ceremony clearly present in his features, Eric stumbled and almost fell into Rainy. Glancing over at Iris, she wasn't surprised to see a grin on the dying woman's face. *The old troublemaker.*

After placing a wooden bowl of water in the father's hands, Rainy read from a note written with a shaky hand. *"Eric, my dear boy, I've so enjoyed our chats over the years. You've opened my mind to different ways of thinking about philosophy, religion, Heaven and Hell, and the secrets of life itself. In doing so, you've kept my spirit and mind young.*

"I know you'll forgive an old woman for including you in the middle of this pagan ceremony, as you would call it, but to me, you are the epitome of the Water element. You're the best representative I could pick for the spot. So please indulge me. I promise to put in a good word for you with the big guy upstairs when I see him." The sound of strangled snickers erupted around them.

Rainy placed her hands on Eric's. "Iris carved this bowl herself. This vessel has been marked with her blood, sweat, and tears. Over the years, you have given your own blood, sweat, and tears to others without judgment. She asks that you represent the Water element and stand to the West.

Rainy moved to the bed and took Iris' hand. "Are you ready to start your journey, sweetheart?"

It was clear that the events of a lifetime had taken a toll on Iris. The old woman who'd lived a big life had said her goodbyes and was now ready for her new journey. Squeezing Rainy's hand, Iris' lips curled up and donned the smile of an angel as she nodded her readiness.

"As you all know, Iris Henderson is not a practicing pagan nor is she a practicing Christian. She could never abide by any organized religion. Instead, Iris lived her life as a spiritual woman, one who loved others and gave of herself wholeheartedly. She has requested her Last Rites to be the best of all worlds. Let us…" Rainy stopped short and chuckled when Iris found the strength to jerk her hand.

"Before I continue, Iris, my dear friend here, would like everyone present to know that she went out of this earthly plane without pissing a single deity off." The Henderson family nodded their approval at Iris' final jest and chuckled through their tears.

"Let us begin."

Rainy held her athame over Iris' frail form. "Take Iris now to enter the Summerland.

"Mother Goddess, I ask that you protect Iris' spirit on this journey.

"I call on the Goddess of the North and ask for easy passage through the closing winter of Iris' life and into the burgeoning new spring.

"I call on the Goddess of the East and ask for a

gentle breeze to lift Iris' spirit and carry her safely to this journey's end.

"I call on the Goddess of the South to enlighten Iris' soul with the warmth of sunbeams.

"I call on the Goddess of the West to bathe Iris' spirit in love.

"We kneel before Mother Goddess and God to ask forgiveness for all of our sins. Iris is but a mere woman who has lived life to its fullest and did her best to love unconditionally those people who have touched her life.

"Iris has journeyed the Wheel of Life and is now ready to return home to the Summerland. She leaves not her family behind as she will be with them every moment of every day through their laughter and tears.

"Blessed be."

Rainy turned to face North and held her athame high. "We spring from Mother Earth to start our journey only to return in the end. Iris' time has come, and she is now ready. She asks that all remember her well and know that she is not afraid."

Pivoting East, she continued, "We flow through life on the breeze, sometimes gentle, sometimes fierce. Iris' time has come, and she is now ready to return to the Summerland. She asks that all remember her well and know that she is not afraid."

Turning South, she spoke again, "We grow and learn through trials and tribulation. The light of the fire shone brightly upon Iris and provided passion and wisdom. Iris' time has come, and she is now ready to return to the Summerland. She asks that all remember her well and know that she is not afraid."

And finally, West. "Throughout the years, Iris has cried tears of joy and tears of sadness. Life is naught without compassion and emotion. Iris' time has come, and she is now ready to return to the Summerland. She asks that all remember her well and know that she is not afraid."

Raising the athame above the heads of Iris' family members, Rainy chanted, "Iris' children, born from her blood, born from her bone, born from her flesh, think of her often and her soul shall continue to live. For wherever you shall travel, she will remain within your heart. She is not afraid of this journey. Remember her with light and love.

"So mote it be.

"We've come to the end of the Last Rites ritual. At this point, Iris asked that Father Gaines read from Psalms 23:4."

As the priest started the prayer, Rainy leaned over Iris and held her as she took her last breath.

"Amen and blessed be, sister. Safe journey."

****

Unsure what to make of Nathan and Jursic's concerned glances, Terry doled out the late afternoon lunch. "Okay. What's up? Why are you two acting as if there's a big secret that will get you into trouble when you spill it?" Terry's desire to get to the root of the problem had him leaning forward and squinting at the two men—a trait his mother had perfected in his youth when she had wanted answers.

Pretending they had no idea what he was talking about, both men shoved food into their mouths and simultaneously raised their shoulders. Maybe the gesture only worked for moms. *H-m-m. They're guilty of something.* The men ate in silence, but whatever information they withheld made the minutes ticking by anything but comfortable.

Terry passed the time, the silent treatment provided, to analyze his feelings about the two men who'd helped him throughout the day. Nathan, being involved in high-end private security—generally in the role of protecting the rich and powerful, and Jursic, being in the FBI, often worked hand-in-hand. The two men were as close to partners as it got without actually being so and had become fast friends in the process.

He wasn't a part of the bond created between them that working in dangerous and high-stress environments had generated. It stung a bit because he and Nathan had been best friends since before kindergarten. Terry liked Jursic well enough but wasn't sure he wanted him to be a part of their close-knit inner circle. After all, Jody, Nathan, and Terry had grown up together protecting each other and loving each other, more so than even blood siblings could. They'd already made room for Jared, Jody's new husband, in their little clique. Would Nathan now want to make room for Jursic? Terry wasn't sure his trust could extend to the man as it had with the others in the group. *Who knows? Maybe I'm just jealous of the bromance they seem to have going on.*

A pang of guilt jabbed Terry in the solar plexus. Trying to dislodge the knot, he dug the palm of his hand deep into the center of his gut. Here were two men breaking their backs to help him move and he was acting like a spoiled child. They didn't deserve that kind of treatment. He promised himself to do whatever was needed to keep this foul mood that had crept up on him in check.

After the uncomfortable silence had played itself

out and everyone loosened up a bit, bets were placed on how many wrappers could be shot across the room—the target, an empty paper bag. Since Nathan sucked at shooting hoops, it wasn't any great surprise that he lost with one wrapper in and two others to be collected from around the room. The real competition was between Jursic and Terry.

Impressed with the shot placement Jursic fist bumped Terry. "Shit man, where'd you learn to shoot like that?"

Terry couldn't help but notice the scowl on Nathan's face. The sneer prompted a bout of laughter. "The only sport I could ever beat Nathan at was basketball. I may be half his size, but I'm agile. I got tired of being pounded into the ground when we played football together. I always ended up at the bottom of the heap."

As if protecting his manhood, Nathan spitefully interjected, "Basketball's a sissy sport anyway. It's almost as bad as *golf* or *tennis*." The final spoken words on the subject held unmistakable derision.

Ignoring the familiar slight, Terry stood and threw the remaining garbage out. "Well, I guess it's time to get back to work out in the studio. I don't have any idea how heavy the boxes stacked against the wall are, so maybe Nathan should get on the ladder and hand the ones on top down to us. What do you think?"

The room went quiet. Terry didn't miss the shared transient expression before both men's eyes were quickly downcast.

"What?"

Jursic opened his mouth to speak, but Nathan shot a hand out and interrupted before a word could be uttered. "That sounds like a plan. Come on, Jursic, get your sorry ass up. We've got some heavy lifting to do."

"*Fine*. But I'm staying outside." To Terry, the protest sounded like a disgruntled child.

Whatever was being left unsaid made his nerves twitch. "Why? What's going on?"

As if afraid to speak up, Jursic pursed his lips. Lifting his big body off the floor with a grunt, the man made his way around Terry. "Nothing. It's nothing. Let's just get to work and get this over with."

Terry and Nathan found Jursic standing to the side of the studio door just off the path. His weight nervously shifted between his feet making his body rock. The comical image looked a great deal like a toddler trying to hold in his pee. Since Terry hadn't known Jursic all that long, he couldn't read what was behind the bizarre expression the man currently touted. Irritation at both men's peculiar antics grew when he noticed they'd shut the studio's front door and closed all the curtains.

"Why would you guys close the curtains and shut the door? I left it open so the studio would air out."

Waiting for an answer, Terry couldn't help but notice Nathan's face had lost all color. His expression had slackened leaving him looking more like a little lost puppy than a full grown man.

Nathan abruptly whipped around as he glared at Jursic for what appeared to be confirmation while answering. "We did go inside to drop the ladder off, but the curtains were closed. We thought you had shut them. To see better, we walked around the room and opened all of them before coming back to the main house." While his best friend's remarks were concise, they were filled with anxiety and didn't make any sense to Terry.

Jursic's head bobbed up and down, his mouth splayed wide open in an exaggerated, cartoonish expression.

"Wait a minute. You said the curtains were closed when you put the ladder inside?" Without giving them a chance to answer, Terry stated, "That's impossible. I left them open when I went to pick up lunch."

The more Terry thought about the situation, the clearer it became that he'd been the butt of a joke—a bad joke no less. Nathan had always been a prankster and had now recruited Jursic to do his bidding. *That* pissed him off.

Since starting the move this morning, the smallest most insignificant things had Terry's ire up. So much so that he'd felt a conscious effort had to be made to rein in his irritation. As if caught inside a dark storm cloud that influenced his mood, a bleak heaviness surrounded him. Not being a particularly angry guy, he had difficulty understanding why this was so and simply chalked it up to just being one of those days. Up until this point, he'd been able to fight off the inexplicable anger. But he couldn't—no, he *wouldn't* put up with being punked when there was so much work to be done.

Terry understood he was losing control of his temper but was powerless to stop it. The perceived teasing flared his anger at an even quicker pace. "Oh. I get it. Very fucking funny, dickheads. You're both screwing with me. Well, it won't work. Come on. I don't have time for this shit. Let's get started moving the rest of the boxes out. I want to have the studio ready to paint by tomorrow."

He grabbed the doorknob, but the damn thing didn't budge. He felt the warmth of his mounting anger shroud his face as he grimaced. Pivoting around to face the two self-appointed jokesters, he yelled, "You locked the door too? You can wipe those stunned expressions off your faces. If you don't want to help anymore, that's fine. Just say so. You don't have to prank me in the process." He whipped the studio key out of his pocket and threw the door open.

As if expecting something to jump out at them, both Jursic and Nathan took a quick step back. Terry didn't know what hurt worse. His best friend was now either tag teaming him with another person—an outsider no less, or doing his best to make him uncomfortable in his new home. Either way, Nathan's behavior cut him to the core. "Cut it out!"

Strutting into the studio, Terry opened all the curtains as Jursic and Nathan looked on from outside.

After a long exhale, Jursic declared in no uncertain terms, "I don't know what's going on with this building, but I'm not stepping foot inside by myself. Don't you even think about leaving me alone in there." He shoved Nathan while storming by to make his point.

"Everybody's in a damn snit today." Doing his best to shed his own bad mood, Nathan climbed the ladder and tapped the top box with his fist. "I think the best way to go about this is for us to remove the top three boxes in each row. Once we get those out, we'll be able to reach the rest without a ladder. Sound good?"

With grumbled approvals, Nathan shifted and tried to move the first box. Uttering a husky grunt, he had to use his weight to pry it out. "This one's heavy, Jursic. You take it."

Annoyance had Terry grinding his teeth together. "I can handle the weight. Give it to *me*." The insult he'd felt rang out loud and clear.

Nathan stopped what he was doing unable to keep his annoyed sigh from escaping. "Terry, what's up with you? That wasn't meant as a slight, and you know it. It's just that we've got muscle man here who happens to be twice your size." His head nodded toward Jursic. "He might as well pull his weight."

Jokingly Jursic nudged Terry out of the way. "Yeah, *Runt*, back it up and let the buff guy get to work."

Once the first box was removed, Nathan turned his attention back to Terry. "There's an actual solid wall behind these boxes. It's not glass like the rest are."

One carton after another was removed exposing more of the dull gray wall. "It's a good thing you'd already decided to paint before you brought any of your work in here. This wall's filthy—disgustingly filthy. It looks like it may have gotten wet at some point and oozed dirty streaks of slimy crap." As the men carried boxes out, Nathan moved the ladder to gain access to the top of the next row.

Upon removing the highest cartons of the fourth row, his excitement couldn't be suppressed. "Hey, There's a big, heavy-duty picture frame on the wall here." Only the corner was exposed, so there was no telling what kind of art lay just out of sight. "Oh my God, Terry! I think we may have found Bonah!"

Terry squealed like a little girl while clapping his hands and doing a little jig. "Didn't I tell you, Nathan? We're all going to be rich!" That produced a high-spirited chuckle from Nathan and prompted Jursic to chime in. "Bonah? What's a Bonah?"

Nathan and Terry burst out laughing at the way Jursic walked head first into the joke. Gasping for air through amused chortles, Nathan never could resist poking a little fun when the opportunity presented itself. "Terry, did you hear that? Jursic doesn't know what a Bonah is."

"Ha-ha. That's very fucking funny, douche bags. You two are morons." The pout in Jurisc's voice was unmistakable. For some reason that lifted Terry's spirits.

Nathan waved him off. The men anxiously gathered around to see what prized possession the ornate frame would reveal.

Handing the top box in the next row down, Nathan growled, "So much for being rich. It's a mirror—a big bastard too."

They worked efficiently removing the top three boxes in the remaining rows. At the far end of the wall, they found a bonus—an interior door. "I think I found a closet, or if you're lucky maybe a bathroom."

Nathan stepped off the ladder and helped take out the rest of the cartons. When the full scope of the mirror had been exposed, at five-foot wide, it turned out to be even larger than any of the men had thought. Terry gazed at the reflective surface that spanned from the ceiling all the way down to the floor. Like the windows, it had some serious age. Part of the mirror had been damaged—not broken but spotted with black flecks where no reflection showed through. The surface rippled in places and seemed to have a sparkle effect going on—a sure sign that it was an antique.

The three friends stood in front of the full-length

mirror pondering their skewed reflections. There was a definite funhouse sensation when looking into the mirror.

"If you ask me, this monstrosity is creepy as hell." Jursic tugged on the enormous gold gilded mirror frame, but it refused to budge. "Has anyone read *The Portrait of Dorian Gray*?" Chuckling at the bizarre comparison, Terry good-naturedly bumped Jursic's arm.

"I think it's a pretty kickass mirror." Stepping forward, he too gave the heavy-duty frame a yank. "It's a good thing I like it because I don't foresee this thing coming down anytime soon. I think it's bolted to the wall."

Crossing to the far end of the room, Nathan opened the now exposed interior door to find a tiny bathroom with just the bare essentials—a toilet, sink, and a miniature shower. "Well, lucky for you, you have a bathroom. Not so lucky, it's the size of a closet. I don't think this bathroom has seen the light of day for decades. If I were you, I wouldn't trust the plumbing in here.

"Uh-oh."

Terry and Jursic stilled for very different reasons and replied in unison, "Uh-oh?"

Nathan got on his hands and knees to reach for something behind the toilet. "I think an addict used to occupy your studio." After wiping the dust from a small ancient looking brown leather case, he handed it over to Terry.

After turning the case over and over in his hand, he carefully unzipped the aged container. "Wow! Check this out. It's an old shaving kit." Jursic and Nathan peered over Terry's shoulder as he pulled out a double-edged golden razor and held it up. "Look, there's a box of double edged razor blades and some green liquid called Skin Bracer. I think my grandpa used this stuff.

"How cool is this? It's like finding a time capsule."

Jursic's reaction to the kit was sketchy at best. The man anxiously swept the empty room with an intense gaze. "Am I the only one that's creeped out in here? It's so damn musty you half expect to see Boris Karloff dressed like a mummy. The air in here is thick enough to cut with a knife." He wiped the sweat from his forehead to emphasize his point. "It's like walking into a sauna."

The FBI agent's continued insistence that something was wrong, and his now ridiculous Karloff imagery, served to raise Terry's hackles again. Returning the kit to the bathroom, he ground his teeth to remind himself that the man was here helping, and he should be grateful for the assistance. "It's been closed up for God knows how long. Of course, it's going to be musty in here."

Hearing the irritation in his own voice had him taking a deep, calming breath. This dour mood was starting to sour his insides. *It's not like me to be so damn pissy. Why can't I shake this irrational anger? If I'm not careful, I'm going to come across as ungrateful.* After all that Nathan and Jursic have done, they certainly didn't deserve his caustic attitude. "You're right, though. I'm going to have to air the space out really well before I bring my canvases in here.

"Jursic, why don't you and I start going through the boxes outside? Nathan, you can use the ladder to take the curtains down. I want the light in here, so there's no reason to keep those ugly, heavy things up."

Before any objections could be launched, Jursic scurried out the door.

"Hey. You know Jursic better than I do. What's wrong with him?"

Nathan shook his head and sighed as if he'd just asked the stupidest question on earth. "He was right. Can't you feel it, man? The creepy vibe is alive and well in here. He's spooked."

"Come on. Stop it."

"No. I'm serious. Some weird shit happened when you left to get lunch." Nathan's hand waved in a dismissive motion. "We'll talk about it tonight when we're eating the pizza you promised us."

"Whatever. But I'm warning you." Terry's finger poked the air to emphasize the point. "No more joking around. It's making me mad. I'm going out to see what's in those boxes."

As Terry exited the studio, he found Jursic standing stock still and staring at the remaining cartons as if they terrified him. Taking a deep breath, he pinched the bridge of his nose. *I deserve a frickin' trophy for my self-control.* It took a Herculean effort to keep the irritation out of his voice. "These boxes aren't going to open themselves. Let's get busy."

There was no need for a knife. The dry, brittle packing tape flaked away as soon as it was touched. Upon revealing the contents, Terry's breath caught in his throat. "Holy shit!"

Jursic peeked over his shoulder. "What is it?"

"It's sketch books. The whole box is full of them."

Carefully removing the top book, he flipped it open. The pages were dingy. When touched, they crackled with age. The sketches were intense and dark. This type of subject matter wasn't to Terry's liking, but he appreciated the work that went into them. "Why on earth would an artist leave his sketchbooks behind?"

Chapter Eight

The big screen TV had been hooked up, but the satellite hadn't so Terry put some music on, and the men relaxed with pizza, hot wings, and beer on the back deck.

Nathan licked the spicy sauce off his fingers and groaned with what Terry took to be pleasure. "By the way, I got you something for the new house." The cadence of his voice was so matter-of-fact that Terry almost missed the point a gift had just been offered.

Perking up, the thought of a present had his heartbeat racing. "Yeah?"

"Yep."

The longer Terry was forced to wait while Nathan savored the next wing, the more he began to fidget. As his friend slowly devoured another spicy appetizer, he realized the anticipation was purposely being drawn out for no other reason than to torture him. After what felt like ages, finally, a broad smile crossed the guy's big mug.

"Okay. Stop squirming, Runt. I'll go get the present. It's in my bag." As Nathan passed by, he playfully nudged Terry's head with a large hand. "You're going to thank me because I went to a lot of trouble to put this together for you."

Terry rubbed his hands together in an exaggerated manner. To his way of thinking, there wasn't anything better in this world than getting a surprise present. Especially from Nathan because he always put so much thought into them.

Reappearing through the French doors, Nathan plopped a large box on his lap. Since the man had fingers the size of sausages, wrapping wasn't one of his strong suits. That being the case, he never used gift wrapping paper for decoration. Instead, layer upon layer of hot pink and black zebra striped duct tape encased the gift. The thought of someone with the hulking size of his friend picking out rolls of the funky patterned tape that was better suited for a pre-teen girl, and then standing in the checkout line with it cracked him up. He could only imagine the looks Nathan got from other customers. *And he did all of that for me.*

Layer upon layer of the heavy-duty tape made the present impenetrable to most people. But Terry had experience opening Nathan's gifts. With the help of his trusty pocket knife and after several attempts, he'd finally managed to get a side flap open.

Digging through the box and pulling the tissue paper out, he came across the gift. It took another few frustrating minutes to extract the present from the impervious wrapping. A wire connected the bulky object in his hand with something still hidden beneath the pink and black stripes.

Nathan started bouncing on the balls of his feet. Terry chuckled because his friend was one of those special people who had as much or more fun giving presents as he did receiving them. "Open the one in your hand first."

Drawing the reveal out just a little longer, Terry tested the weight of the object by lifting it several times. "It's heavy."

Nathan's big grin served to heighten the excitement. "Yep. I hope you like it. After I found out that you purchased an old house, I wanted to get something vintage to go with it. I searched to the ends of the earth to find this for you. You better fucking appreciate it." Nathan's grin turned to a warm, genuine smile. "You've mentioned in the past that you'd like to get your hands on one of these."

Terry was stunned to see a vintage 1930's pyramid art deco Bakelite telephone in perfect condition. With the braided handset cord and sparkling alpha-numeric dial, he was certain the phone had to be a prop—an amazing replica.

"I had my tech guys go over it with a fine-tooth comb. They assure me it works."

"You're kidding!"

"Nope. Check out the rest of the present."

Being careful not to tug too hard on the connecting wire, Terry set the phone down and pried the other gift from the box. Buried within the tissue paper was an old cassette answering machine. During his early childhood, his mother's landline handset had a built in feature for messages just like his cell phone. He'd never actually seen the real thing before. While the old answering machine showed some wear and tear, it had cleaned up nicely and sparkled almost as much as the rotary phone did.

"I realize the phone and answering machine are from two different eras, but I couldn't resist. After considerable hours, the geeky tech guys figured out how to connect the two so you can use them together."

Thrilled Terry jumped up with his new gadgets in

tow. "I know exactly where to put them! Come with me." He spun around and rushed inside. Arms full, he perused every piece of furniture he owned until finding the perfect table to show off his gift.

"Nathan, Jursic, grab that long bench table and put it on the other side of the kitchen against the wall by the outlet."

Once the distressed, shallow console table was in just the right place, Terry proudly displayed his gifts. He lovingly arranged them as if they carried the import of the crowned jewels. Turning his head one way and then the other, he scrutinized the positioning with a discerning eye. *Something's missing.* With a hand on his chin, he'd come to a decision. "I need one of those cool old-fashioned doilies to put under the phone." Speaking more to himself than anyone else, he continued, "Maybe I can get Jody to make one for me."

Spinning around to face his life-long friend, Terry rushed across the room and bumped shoulders. Normally he'd give the big man a real hug, but since they weren't alone a bro hug would have to suffice. "Nathan, I don't know what to say. The phone and answering machine are the best gifts I've ever received. I'll treasure them."

Nathan's giant arm landed heavily across Terry's shoulders. "I love you, man. I'm so proud of everything you've accomplished. You've never given up on your dreams of becoming an artist. Now, everything's falling into place for you. You deserve this home and so much more."

****

Even though it was September, most days the temperatures in the Phoenix area still hit the triple digit mark. The pool was a welcome relief from a long day in the heat. Temperatures, and not just the weather, had flared off and on all day. Nathan and Jursic were in the middle of the mother of all water fights. As Terry wound down with a beer, memories of what he'd considered rude remarks the two men had made throughout the day slipped into his thoughts. As their haranguing regarding his studio resurfaced, so did his puzzling anger. "*Stop it!* What's wrong with me?" Genuinely concerned by his bad attitude, he kept his voice low so it wouldn't carry to his friends.

Since the two men were currently otherwise occupied, Terry decided to look at some of the sketch pads he'd found today. Being an artist and understanding that sketches were a blueprint to an artist's vision, he couldn't fathom why anyone in their right mind would leave them behind. His curiosity was piquéd. Looking for the telltale signature, surprisingly, he couldn't find a single signed sketch or book for that matter. He was shocked to find several years of work sitting in front of him. *Who in their right mind would go to all this work and not even sign it? None of this makes any sense.*

There's an explanation here somewhere. Terry just had to look for it. Making a conscious effort to divert his attention, Terry focused on the far corner of the yard. He'd hoped that staring at the darkened studio would provide him with answers to his questions. It didn't.

Begrudgingly, he agreed something felt a little off about the building—okay, maybe even creepy at times—but he'd be damned if he lowered himself to tell his friends. All day long he'd disregarded their opinions as nothing more than insensitive jokes. His position had been made clear, and he didn't want to hear any more bullshit on the matter. So they'd finally blessedly shut their traps, even if they did still act a little skittish about the space.

Carefully turning page after yellowed page, tingles of dread pricked his skin leaving goosebumps behind. The sketches were mostly dark in nature—disturbing even to another artist. The depictions were from the deepest, darkest, recesses of the unknown artist's mind, leaving Terry to wonder just how unstable he or she had been.

A date had been scrawled on the front of each book. After arranging the sketch pads in periodic order, the time frame spanned from 1935 to 1948. The deeper into the artist's work Terry delved, the more uncomfortable he became. The troubling images generated a growing sense of apprehension. The anxiety they induced had quickly surpassed his concern over the bizarre, aberrant anger which had continued to surface deep inside him throughout the day. So much so that the feelings of instant antagonism he'd struggled with almost seemed inconsequential by comparison.

Carefully setting the last sketch pad aside he pulled his own out. He was driven by a mounting need to create something beautiful. Hopefully drawing would remove his current mindset out of the depths of hell where the other artist's depraved work had taken him. To lighten his mood, he focused on Rainy. Closing his eyes, the vision of her floated into the forefront of his mind. The memory of her raw beauty and voluptuous form rapidly filled the page. Before long, Jursic nudged him. "Whoa. Who's that?"

Curbing his first instinct to hide the sketch from prying eyes, Terry kept his voice neutral. Jursic was on the fast track to becoming a good friend, but he didn't fully trust him yet. "She's a woman I met at Jody and Jared's wedding."

"She's gorgeous. Is she single?"

Nathan slugged Jursic in the arm and chuckled. "I wouldn't be looking in *that* direction if I were you. Terry had one date and is hooked."

Jursic nodded appreciatively. "With a woman that looks like that it's understandable. Does she have any sisters?"

Irritated that Nathan still seemed to be trivializing his feelings for Rainy, Terry started to leaf through some pages in his sketchbook. "Take a look at this woman."

Holding the pad up, the drawing of Bright Flower caught Jursic's full attention. A low appreciative whistle rumbled from directly behind him. "Is this a real woman, or just some figment of your imagination?"

"Nope. Real woman. She's beautiful, isn't she?"

Moving closer, Jursic's brow scrunched as he reviewed the sketch. "Beautiful—yes. But there's more to her than that." Cupping a hand over his chin, he stroked it as if the action would provide him with a better characterization. "I'd say she's more exotic than beautiful. Is *she* married?"

"Not yet." Terry knew he was about to piss his best friend off. The angry compulsion arose again and quickly had him angling for a fight. *I'll show him.* It was almost as if a troublemaker whispered in his ear trying to goad him.

"Maybe you could introduce me?"

Before he could open his mouth, Nathan's curiosity got the best of him. When he realized Jursic was going apeshit over a likeness of Bright Flower, he shoved the man and none too gently.

Off balance, Jursic almost spilled his beer before regaining his footing. "Dammit! What did you do that for?"

Nathan couldn't tear his dreamy gaze from the beautiful Indian woman's likeness.

"Come on, man. What's the story?"

Seeing his friend's genuine heartache released his building anger in a heartbeat. Terry remained silent and hoped Jursic would have more luck getting Nathan to open up about his feelings. He knew the only way the big guy would have a shot at the Indian woman was to recognize what he was feeling so he could act on it. With an arranged marriage looming, he'd have to suck it up and evaluate his emotions quickly.

"There's something about…" Nathan's mouth pinched the words off. On a deep sigh, he drew a long swig of beer.

Jursic and Terry exchanged telling glances as the silence continued.

Apparently unwilling to speak about Bright Flower any longer, Nathan's jaw clenched with resignation. "I'm going for another swim. You two assholes coming?"

"You go ahead. I'm going to make a call." Terry held his phone out as if to confirm the task.

As an afterthought, the good guy in him—who, he had to admit, had been absent most of the day, leaned forward. "Hey, Jursic, we've got plenty of beer, the fridge is stocked with junk food, and I've got a spare bed. Why don't you stay here tonight? You won't have to make the drive across town."

"Thanks, little buddy." Jursic rotated his head and locked his gaze on the now dark studio. "But unlike you two slackers, I have to work tomorrow. So, if it's okay, I'll take a rain check."

"Sure. Anytime."

Since Terry hadn't heard from Rainy, he figured he'd probably be leaving a message but didn't care. Punching her contact information on the phone, he noticed the other men had become quiet. When he glanced up, they were staring at his cell phone—their expressions quizzical. As it rang, his free arm shot out with a shrug to silently ask what their problem was now.

"Hello. You've reached…" Screeching static halted any possible communication. The explosive racket, so unexpected, propelled the phone out of Terry's tight grasp and almost landed it in the pool.

"What the hell?" The disturbing shrillness of a cat being tortured could still be heard from several feet away without the use of the speaker. It was the same tortured screeches he'd heard earlier when his conversation with Cheryl had been interrupted. Terry rushed over to end the call. Dumbfounded he stared at the now silent cell phone.

A strong wet hand grasped his shoulder making him jump. "That's one of the problems Jursic and I had earlier. The studio creeped me out so bad that I wanted to get some background on the people who've lived here. Anytime we tried to make the call, it was as if someone or something stopped us."

Moving back to his chair, Terry ran a hand through his hair to calm himself. "*Someone* or *something*? Come on. Listen to yourself. Don't you think you're being just a little overly dramatic? *So what* there's static? I used the phone earlier when I talked to the realtor, remember? I didn't have any problem then."

An idea suddenly popped into his mind. "Hey, maybe it's sunspots?"

Nathan looked at him like he was a sad little boy grasping at straws. Terry hated that superior expression. "The problem we've had with the phones is not the only incident, Terry."

As if a puppet, his body felt guided by someone else's hand. He jumped to his feet and stood—his firm stance a clear warning of trouble to come. Unable to hold his fury in check, his hand shot out to stop any further discussion. "I'm going for a walk." He refused to give Nathan a chance to impede his exit.

Chapter Nine

Walking at a leisurely pace, Terry decided to wait and call Rainy until he was a fair distance away from the house. Wanting to explore the neighborhood, he crossed the road and headed north up Ash. Each long stride under the mature trees transported him farther from his dream home. Curiously, he noted, his frame of mind started to calm. Built up stress he'd been carrying around all day like extra pounds, melted away with each step. Terry knew he'd have to explore the reason behind those feelings sooner or later, but right now he was enjoying the solitude too much to reflect any further on them.

The evening was beautiful but hot. Even with the sun bedded down for the night, the temperature still hovered at right around ninety-five degrees. Since he'd lived in the desert all his life, the heat didn't bother him in the least. In fact, he'd choose hot weather over cold any day of the week.

Unable to hold off on calling Rainy any longer, he hit the send button. The remaining negativity surrounding him dissipated at the sound of her voice on the message. "Hello. You've reached Rainy Stratton. I'm sorry I can't take your call at the moment. At the sound of the tone, please leave a message, and I'll call you back as soon as possible."

Beep.

"Hi. I knew you were probably still busy, but I couldn't stop thinking about you. Apparently, I don't have great cell phone reception at my house." As if she could see him, he lifted his shoulders. "Maybe sunspots. I know it's only been one day, but this move has been a bear. Oh, Jeez. I'm sorry. I'm complaining about a stupid move, and you've had to deal with the death of someone today. I hope you're doing okay. If you need anything—anything at all, please let me help you.

"I thought that if you're not busy this weekend, I'd come up and stay at Jody and Jared's guesthouse again. I might be convinced to make a little supper and open a bottle of wine if you'd like to join me. Well, anyway, I just couldn't get you off my mind and thought I'd call. Since I'm having phone issues, make sure to leave a message if I don't answer. Bye."

Just as the call was disconnected, Terry looked up to find himself standing at the edge of his property line. A sensation of someone or something reaching into his chest and clamping icy fingers around his heart stilted his breathing. His legs started to feel like rubber and wobbled. *How the hell did I get back here? I was walking in the other direction.*

After taking a moment to get a hold of himself and shake off the unreasonable fear, Terry strolled through the front door to find Nathan leaning on the kitchen counter chugging a beer. Loud country music was blaring from the back of the house.

"Where's Jursic?"

"He's tired." Nathan clicked his tongue and grinned. "He didn't want to get chlorine on his pretty new truck seats, so he's taking a shower. He'll be done…" The old-school answering machine came to life as Terry strolled by it.

"You have thirty-six new messages."

"Oh my God! You got it to work already?" Focusing his attention on the machine, Terry started pushing buttons. "What do I have to do to get the messages?" When no response was forthcoming, he turned back to Nathan. Terry had no idea what to make of his slack-jawed expression.

"*What?* Come over here and show me how to work this thing." When Nathan didn't move, Terry crouched down to read the well-worn faint lettering above each button. Pleased with himself, he found the message retrieval button and pushed it without thinking twice.

The machine came to life and spoke with a broken computerized voice. "First missed message."

Giddy with his new toy, Terry beamed at Nathan. "Did you hear that old-fashioned computerized voice? That's the coolest…"

"No one cares." The ghoulish sounding voice, nothing more than a whisper, put a halt to Terry's excitement in an instant.

Beep.

"Second missed message."

Shrieks, nightmarish screams of the damned, could be heard in the background before the message concluded. Terry felt every muscle in his face sag. Glass broke behind him. He spun around to glare at Nathan who stood at attention with a busted beer bottle at his feet.

Beep.

"Third missed message."

The sound of a cat surely being tortured rang

through loud and clear making Terry's body seize from the strangled cries.

Beep.

"Fourth missed message."

A deep growl from something that could only be classified as a grizzly supernatural creature pierced the air. Terry's blood pressure spiked and left him reeling.

Trying to shut the horrifying sounds out, Terry covered his ears and rushed over to Nathan. "How could you? Why would you do this to me? Make it stop!"

Nathan forcefully grabbed Terry's arm and squeezed while pushing him over to the answering machine. Bending down, he lifted the plug off the floor. He had to scream over the piercing noise coming from the possessed gift. "Look dammit! The answering machine isn't plugged in! It *can't* be working."

Trying to release himself from Nathan's hold, Terry yanked at the viselike grip that held him firmly by the upper arm. "You're doing this on purpose. Make it stop now. It's not funny, Nathan!"

Beep.

"Fifth new message."

With one quick move, Nathan grasped Terry in a tight embrace and screamed at the top of his lungs. "Call the witch lady. Call her right…"

Before he could finish his statement, the antique phone came to life and started ringing even as the messages continued to play. In one sweep of the arms, Nathan scooped up the gifts he'd been so proud of and ran out of the front door. Horrified, Terry watched as he chucked them out onto the lawn. Only then were the menacing messages silenced.

The joke had gone too far and sent him over the edge of reason. When Nathan entered the room, Terry sucker punched him. One swift movement and Nathan had him pinned to the floor.

Tears burned the back of Terry's eyes at Nathan's betrayal. "How could you do that to me? You know what this house means to me."

Nathan shivered, took a deep breath, and closed his eyes. When they finally opened Terry saw raw fear.

"What the fuck has gotten into you? Use your brain. Look, Terry, I'm good, but even I can't make something work without electricity if it needs to be plugged in. Think about it a minute. You're the one that sat the phone and answering machine on the table. Did you plug them in? Besides that, you don't even have a landline yet. It's not possible for the phone to connect if there's no landline installed."

Not wanting to hear any excuses, Terry struggled beneath him. "Dammit, get off me." They sat on the floor glaring at each other.

Jursic sauntered into the room. "Since mom and dad are fighting, I'm going to leave now." Chuckling at his own joke, he started for the door. "Thanks for the food and beer. If you need any more help, just give me a call. I don't have anything planned in the evenings this week, so I'm free if you need me and my exquisite brawn."

Nathan shoved at Terry's arm and nodded at Jursic's back so he'd acknowledge the hard work the man had put in today.

"Thanks for your help." Terry's voice sounded forced and insincere, even to his own ears, and earned him an elbow to the ribs from Nathan. The unspoken *'don't be a douche bag'* evident in the gesture.

"Jursic, I'm sorry I was such a dick today. I guess it was all the stress. I really appreciate everything you did and your offer to keep helping out. It means a lot to me."

Nathan stood and made his way to the front door. "Hold up. I'll walk you out."

Shutting the door behind them, both men moved toward Jursic's truck. "I need you to do me a favor. Call my office and talk to Lynne. She gets in around six, so call her early. Have them drop a company vehicle off here and whatever information she can find on this place. I want the past owner's names, contact info, all of it. Include any research you can think of that might help too. I need it by late morning. Have them leave the documents in the car when they drop it off. It's important."

Jursic nodded acknowledgment as he stared at Nathan's gifts scattered in the grass at the edge of the property. "What's up with that?"

"Don't ask."

"All righty, then."

There wasn't a chance in hell that Nathan was going to take his gifts back into the house. After collecting the phone and answering machine from the front lawn, he sat them in a darkened corner of the front porch. Not sure which Terry he'd find when he opened the front door, Nathan leaned heavily on the frame and stared at his friend. "I—"

Terry's hand shot out. "Nope. No more tonight. We both probably got overheated today working out in the studio without any air conditioning. It's late, and we need some sleep. We'll talk about it in the morning when our tempers aren't so close to the surface."

Retreating down the hall, Terry stepped into the bathroom that only moments ago Jursic had occupied. Shutting the door, he leaned heavily against it. "What the hell is going on?"

Since the master bath was still in shambles, Terry would clean up in here. He'd feel like a new man once some of this moving day filth covering him was gone. Turning the shower on to warm the water, he leaned against the sink and rubbed his tired eyes.

A loud banging on the door made him jump. "Hey, are you almost done in there? I'd like to take a shower too."

Steam from the hot spray overran the small washroom making visibility almost nil. Terry had no clue how long he'd been watching the shower run. It felt as though he'd fallen asleep on his feet. His mind was drawing a complete blank.

"Oh…a-h-h…sorry. I'll be out in just a little bit."

A strange sound caught Terry's attention while bending over to untie his Chucks. The hair on the back of his neck stood at attention. Prickles of unease swept through his body. As panic started to set in, his breathing became forced. His fight or flight instinct kicked in, and everything inside him told him to run—to get the hell out before it was too late. Instead, going against every instinct, he stood and slowly turned. As he gazed into the mirror, pressure built deep inside his eyes as they bulged from outright shock.

Someone was painstakingly scrawling a message in the condensation on the mirror. Each stroke of the unseen finger vibrated and jumped creating an awful squeaking noise.

No one cares.

After the immediate shock wore off, Terry vigorously wiped the mirror down with his towel. "Okay. I give up." He whispered to himself. "First thing in the morning I'll give Rainy a call. She'll know what's going on here—better yet, she'll know how to get rid of whatever it is."

Instead of the long, hot shower he'd been looking forward to, he was stuck with a quick, cold dousing.

Terry bumped into Nathan in the hallway and wasn't able to look him in the eyes to apologize. "I'm sorry, I took so long. You might want to wait awhile for the hot water." Without saying another word, he sequestered himself in his room for the night. By the time his head hit the pillow, he'd talked himself into believing the handwritten message was just a daydream. Yeah. *A nightmarish daydream.* With the abundance of negative talk today about bad vibes and creepy feelings, who could blame his mind for wandering as it had?

****

The touch of Rainy's lips forced a wanton groan that resonated from deep within Terry's belly. As she leaned over and looked down, her silken hair splayed out around his face cocooning him. Her naked body straddled him, and he couldn't resist running his hands up her thighs and grasping that luscious bottom.

His firm hold pushed her body up so he'd have access to her bountiful breasts. He could die a happy man with his face cradled between her womanly curves. Terry's mouth hungrily sought out an erect nipple. She teased him by gently pulling away and then lowering her body. Rainy continued to move the taut nub of her breast in and out of his reach until he caught the peak between his teeth and growled, unwilling to let her withdraw another time. Suckling her, he drew as much of her large breast into his mouth as possible.

"Terry, oh God, Terry!" Hearing her utter his name in passion was like a prayer being answered.

Rainy's muscles tensed, as her hips started to undulate. The movement stirred his erection to an all new need as her warm womanly sheath cradled him. Crying Terry's name out again and again, her need for him became frantic. Roughly pulling her breast from his mouth, she clasped his erection tightly and held him in place as she took him into her body. Everything else ceased to be. The sensation of being one with this mysterious woman had him seeing stars. Never in his life had he felt this need, this drive to love someone and make her as delirious as she made him.

With her head tilted back and her breasts thrust forward, she was a vision and his for the taking. He reached out and pinched her glistening nipples. Closer than he to the point of release, her hands tangled in her hair just as a mewling sound left those tantalizing lips. Terry drove into her at a frantic pace.

"I love you, Terry." Rainy's words floated on the air with a passionate whisper.

Just as her body crested the precipice and clamped down on his, an ominous black shadow slithered out of the darkness. Before he could utter a sound, the inky blackness was upon Rainy—grasping and tearing at her flesh. The entity smashed into her with stunning force, propelling her away from him. Terry's arms flew out trying to hold on without success. She hit the floor with force, creating a loud whomp sound as vital air whooshed out of her lungs.

Something larger than a man and blacker than the surrounding shadows picked Rainy up and threw her against the wall. Screams—both his and hers gushed forth at the sound of breaking bones. Terry jerked from side to side but was powerless to break the invisible bonds which held him firmly spread-eagle on the bed.

"Watch what happens to the witch if you tell her about me."

The attack felt as if it had lasted for hours. Unable to move or even speak, Terry could only watch, horrified, as the beast tore his woman from limb to limb. Finally, the hold on his body broke, enabling him to move. Scurrying across the floor, he reached Rainy's broken, bloody corpse and hung on for dear life as grief overtook him. Gashes from claws and chunks of missing muscle and skin where the beast had attacked with its razor sharp teeth oozed. Cradling her in his arms, he listened to her chest for any sign of life. Nothing. No sound. No heartbeat. No gurgling. Only silence. Blood ran from her nose and ears. Dead eyes stared up at him, blaming him. Terry had been forced to watch while Rainy had been thrown around and mangled as if she weighed no more than a ragdoll.

Kissing her fore head, the pain of his grief escaped as he cried out in anguish. "I didn't know, Rainy. I didn't know. I'm so sorry, baby. All of this is my fault."

The black mass slithered toward Terry and leaned in. A demonic face appeared from the mist. Rainy's blood dripped from its fangs. Where muscle and skin should have covered the beast's face, there was only ragged and torn sinew. The monster that stared back at him was inhuman. The demon's eyes, filled with such hatred, reminded him of red-hot molten lava. When the grotesque creature opened its mouth to speak, the fetid scent of death permeated Terry's senses making him ill.

"Remember this feeling, Terrryy." His name slithered like a snake out of demon's mouth. "I know what she is. I'm stronger than the witch. If you speak of me to her, she'll die."

Terry awoke fighting the tangled, damp sheets. Struggling to catch a breath, he forced himself to sit up. His chest heaved with exertion. Cold sweat dripped down his hair and ran into his eyes. All the while the smell of rotting flesh and sulfur engulfed him.

"Remember this." The disembodied voice was more like a rumbling growl than actual speech. Quickly reaching for the bedside lamp, Terry's fingers found the switch and turned it on. Scouring every inch of the room and finding nothing, it was clear that whatever had threatened him and Rainy had taken its leave.

Terry threw his shaking body back against the pillows. Something stiff and unforgiving was beneath his shoulders. Panicked, he jumped off the bed and stared at an old sketch book. Shock and dread rattled through every fiber of his being. The depiction in front of him was new. A large black figure held onto one of Rainy's feet and dragged her badly mangled corpse through the studio door.

Unable to control the terror any longer, he wailed, "I won't tell her! I won't! Don't hurt her."

The only response was dead still air.

Chapter Ten

The majority of Wiccans were nurturers by nature, and Rainy was no different. She took great pride in officiating over Last Rights, but it always proved to be a difficult task and demanded much of her energy. Most people thought she was nuts, but taking care of the dying and their family members provided her with a tremendous sense of accomplishment. Even those folks who had a different set of spiritual beliefs had sought out her services as a dying and grief counselor.

Her path—this life's work she'd chosen—while both physically and mentally grueling, touched people in their hour of need in a positive way. Beyond that, her profession as a High Priestess put her squarely in the public's line of sight to help them through a multitude of tough times and make a difference in their lives. What more could she possibly ask out of life? She'd been put on this earth to serve others and did her best to provide that service with grace and dignity.

Since the downtown public parking lot was located a few blocks from her shop, each morning, rain, snow, or shine, Rainy greeted the new day with a leisurely walk. The five-minute jaunt was her *me* time of the day. Those few early morning moments were always used to ground herself and prepare for the challenges of the day ahead.

Although always enjoying the stroll from her car to

Natural Sense, her business in downtown Flagstaff, her tired, aching bones left her feeling a little flat this morning. With a pronounced roll of the shoulders, Rainy did her best to relax the strained muscles in her neck. The Last Rights she'd performed yesterday continued with the family deep into the night and had taken a toll. By the time their needs had subsided, the hour had grown late. She'd gratefully accepted the offered bed to lay her weary head down before making the drive back to the city.

Passing by the quirky stores near her business encouraged the first smile of the day. She never got tired of viewing the eccentric window dressings. The little storefronts were a window shopper's dream. That alone made it impossible to get tired of her daily constitutionals through the streets of old town Flagstaff.

Many people, tourists mainly, jokingly referred to the little shops in the historic district as the hippy trade. On the surface, Rainy supposed, the reason for that tagline was clear. The displays in the windows sported handmade jewelry that was a cross between Native American and what she liked to call Gothic Gypsy. The funky at heart could easily find clothing designed for their unconventional style—the majority of which were lovingly created by hand from homespun natural materials. And of course, who could pass up the handmade candles that at times could be smelled from miles away? There were also breweries, bakeries, and eateries that catered to every type of palate. A vegan who eats like a bird or someone with a heftier appetite who prefers to partake in Arizona big meat favorites could savor whatever their hearts desired. Rainy was particularly fond of the succulent steaks that were the size of platters. If she were feeling particularly naughty, perhaps she'd order the gooey cheese stuffed hamburgers that were big enough for two and oozed yummy goodness all over her hands. "We have it all," she proudly declared to herself as delight in the small town filled her with joy.

The downtown Flagstaff tourist district was located on the old Route 66 and in Northern Arizona University's back yard. The place was loaded with Wild West history. The long-established Hotel Monte Vista's iconic signage was in plain view from Rainy's storefront. The old beauty was built in 1927 and still operated today. In its heyday, the grande dame of downtown Flagstaff had seen the likes of long gone celebrities such as John Wayne, Bob Hope, and Freddy Mercury, just to name a few. The once lavish lodging sported many ghost stories of its own prompting those who stayed overnight to stop by her mystical shop and share their ghostly encounters. Between tourists and college students, the local shops got all the commerce they could handle every business day of the year.

Momentarily lost in her surroundings, she'd traveled on foot faster than normal. Finding herself just up the street from Natural Sense, the time had come to start the first of her morning rituals—a prayer to kick start the day.

Mother Goddess, thank you for this beautiful day.

Thank you for giving me the strength and desire to help those in need.

Thank you for being with the family last night and offering comfort only you can.

Thank you for providing me with the right words to soothe the sting of the loss of a loved one. And, above all else, thank you for opening up the Summerland for another beautiful soul.

I ask that you guide anyone needing help or comfort today into my path and lead me to the appropriate way of ministering to their needs. Help me have the courage to open myself up to their troubles, whatever they may be, and offer the proper assistance to relieve their suffering.

Blessed Be.

The bell above the front door tinkled upon Rainy's entry. As usual, surveying the store provided a sense of whimsy and prompted a giggle. Since the blessed day of Cheryl's arrival, her beloved business had soared to new heights. It turned out that Rainy's apprentice slash assistant was an astute marketing genius. Sure, Natural Sense did well enough before the woman had become an integral part of the coven. But with her assistance, the daily tourist foot traffic had grown substantially.

Cheryl's ideas had run the gamut from the fantastic to the fantastical. Playing up what she called the metaphysical angle with gemstones, crystals, athames, as well as figurines of dragons, cats, and fairies. There wasn't a single mystical creature left out of the mix.

Before Cheryl's arrival, Rainy had always done well enough selling her candles, lotions, potions, and herbs for healing and other benefits. The public seminars she'd sponsored in the shop's bookstore had been a huge success and continued to guide those seeking spiritual clarity. She'd taught everything from the importance of white light protection and the art of meditation to the basics of the Tarot.

Her clientele consisted of a mixture of spiritual beliefs—those of the Jewish faith, Christians, Wiccans,

Buddhists, just to name a few. Their choice of religion mattered not to her. She welcomed everyone and tried her best to slant her teachings to the beliefs of her clients and teach tolerance ultimately helping people grow as better human beings. Throughout her adult life, Rainy had tried to live up to her grandmother's legacy which was love and tolerance of all, not separation. In turn, everyone, no matter their spiritual beliefs, felt comfortable with Rainy. She did not judge. Therefore she was not judged.

With Cheryl's astute marketing acumen focused on Natural Sense, people came into the store in droves which generated huge sales numbers. Even more significantly, the young woman's presence provided Rainy with the opportunity to do more specialized work to help those in need.

Over the years, she had worked her ass off to dispel one of the seedier sides of the profession. Without a doubt, she still had people asking her to perform spells ranging from bad to worse—anything spanning from gray magic, such as love spells and financial spells, up to and including black magic incantations which would be even more harmful.

When those people approached her, for the most part, they didn't realize just how dangerous their request was. Now rather than turning people away with a curt 'no,' Rainy had time to teach folks about karma and the devastating effects on everyone concerned if she were to fulfill such a request. Bending a third party's will for your own satisfaction negates their free will. As the spell seeker, they would gain a personal advantage by placing someone else at a disadvantage. Doing so would have a harmful effect on everyone involved including herself for implementing such a request.

Something else the general public didn't realize about casting spells was that it was damn near impossible to reverse the effects of an incantation once completed. Rainy had some meager successes with spell reversal in the past but was only batting right around a fifty percent success rate.

It wasn't as if you could practice this skill. Every incantation was different. Every caster of spells was different. There were just too many variables which made it necessary to fly by the seat of your pants and hope for the best when trying to reverse someone else's dirty work. Rainy had been a firsthand witness to how the negativity of *any* enchantment affected people. Never would she lower herself or her moral compass to entertain performing spells for customers. Doing so was just too costly to everyone involved.

Over time Natural Sense's high-profit margin, which Cheryl was instrumental in producing, had been so large that Rainy no longer charged for spiritual readings. In her field, it was standard practice to get paid an hourly fee for such things. Some were reasonable. Some were exorbitant. She would never fault another person for doing so. For Rainy, though, it had always gone against the grain to charge folks who needed and sought out spiritual counsel. When people requested advice from someone with her gifts, she was well aware that many times the action was a last ditch effort for them. With her assistant's aid, she was now in a position to gift that particular service free of charge. If a client insisted on paying, Rainy would suggest they pay it forward with an act of kindness to someone in need.

Cheryl appeared from the back office. The ever-present cheerful smile she sported along with her willingness to help any customer who entered their humble little business was front and center. Her assistant's beaming expression never faltered, but Rainy caught a spark of concern in the young woman's eyes. Knowing she would be worried about her well-being, Rainy flashed a brilliant smile. "Good morning."

"You come over here right this minute and sit down." Sounding more like a mother hen than the beautiful young woman she was, Cheryl patted the back of the overstuffed chair to make her point. "I've just brewed some of your favorite tea." On that note, her assistant disappeared back through the office door from which she'd come.

Rainy raised her head in gratitude. "Thank you, Goddess, for the gift of Cheryl."

They weren't expecting a rush on the store until around ten. Once the stampede hit, they wouldn't slow down again until closing the doors at eight that evening. The first flush of the morning would be the only opportunity for mentor and protégée to catch up and recap the prior day's events.

Cheryl strode out from the office and handed Rainy a steaming cup of tea and her phone. "Before I forget, your new gentleman friend called yesterday."

Rainy instantly perked up. She couldn't help the crooked smile that bloomed on her face. "Yeah?"

"I must say, he seems quite smitten with you. I enjoyed talking to him. By the way, he left you a message last night, but I didn't listen to it. I figured it was probably too personal."

Suddenly aware that her heartbeat was fluttering, Rainy allowed the warmth of her desire to fill her body. Being careful not to give the full extent of her emotions away, she cleared her throat. "I know it sounds crazy because I just met him, but I've had a difficult time getting him off my mind." She could only hope her timid smile hid the memory of the erotic dreams she'd had last night that had just popped into her mind.

"Well, I don't care how long you've known each other. That man's hooked. I heard it every time his voice softened when he said your name."

Ms. Hopeless Romantic's candid words wheedled a girlish snicker from Rainy. "Stop it. We've only had one date."

"Whatever." Cheryl's lips puckered to the side of her face as if she had all the answers to love at her disposal. "I *know* what I heard in his voice. I also know you. I've never seen you so excited about a man before. It's about time you found *muirn beatha dan*."

Hearing the Gaelic words which meant *'my one true love'* roll off Cheryl's tongue affected Rainy profoundly. *How many times have I prayed to find my soul mate? Too many to count.* Rainy didn't know yet if Terry was that man, but he was certainly different than all the rest who had journeyed in and out of her life.

Muirn beatha dan. As the beautiful phrase meandered through her mind, she took a sip of tea. Unfortunately, her mouth had frozen into a grin which made the simple act of drinking difficult. Doing so resulted in the warm liquid dribbling down her chin. Embarrassment swept a warm tingling sensation across the back of her neck as she quickly dabbed with a tissue.

The feelings she was experiencing for Terry were new to Rainy. It was far too soon to be discussing them with anyone just yet. Apparently, her unspoken thoughts on the matter were understood because Cheryl thankfully changed the subject.

"How are the Henderson's?"

Rainy chanced another sip of tea and sighed with pleasure. *A-h-h. Just right.*

"They're doing well. Thank you for asking. Iris Henderson was a beautiful person. Her entire family came from all over the country to spend the final hours with her. Blessed be for the love and tenderness of folks like Iris. I wish more people would take the time to love and cherish the way that woman did in her lifetime."

"Yes. Blessed be."

"Her sons and daugh—" Rainy abruptly bent forward, falling off the chair and landing on all fours. Her prized possession—Grandma Stratton's fine china teacup—flew through the air sending the tepid liquid in all directions. The swift impact to her midsection was so painful that it felt as though she'd been kicked in the gut. Air whooshed from her lungs. She endured punch after brutal punch—the blows coming out of nowhere. The violent force of each unseen strike left her with an unforgiving stabbing pain and feeling as if several ribs had snapped in two. Struggling to catch her breath, Rainy recognized this supernatural event for what it was. Prayers tumbled from her mouth but had no immediate effect on the psychic pain.

Panicked Cheryl knelt beside her and cried out, "What's wrong? Rainy, what is it?"

Searing, agonizing pain radiated throughout her body. Ribs, arms, legs—not a single extremity was spared from the trauma. Only her head and face were free from the explosive attack by the unseen perpetrator. In the blink of an eye the reason behind the pain formed in her mind. Unfortunately, Rainy had suffered through similar abusive psychic events through many of her female clients. Her spine stiffened, and the heat of rage filled her as she began to comprehend the nature behind this brutal attack.

The only way out of this psychic assault was to muddle through it the best she could. Rainy slammed her eyes shut and tried desperately to catch her breath. *Someone's in deep trouble.* Snapshots of images started to appear and roll like a disjointed movie through her mind's eye. Doing everything within means to work through the excruciating pain, she turned her focus on the people in the visions.

A flash of an unknown man shot across the back of her eyelids. He dangled a thick rope with large knots and stood threateningly above a cowering woman. Another burst of light provided a glimpse of the stark fear clearly visible on the cowering woman's face—her pallor a sickly ashen. As if she were an animal caught in a trap, her lips trembled with fear but no sound emerged. To protect herself, the injured woman had wedged her body into a corner of the room to become as small of a target as possible. As the scene played out, it became apparent she'd been too severely injured to fight back or even to mount a getaway. The helpless woman's fear was palpable and momentarily urged Rainy's sensitive psyche to free herself from this vision.

Turning all attention toward the attacker, Rainy felt the man's unwavering rage. His blood pounded murderous intent throughout his body. The lethal emotion elevated to a point in which it became as tangible as the floor she now found herself kneeling on. It only took an instant to realize that if events continued to unfold as they were, the maniac was one horrific beating away from killing the defenseless woman. The time had come to intervene.

The fierceness in which Rainy stated her plea could only compare to that of a lioness about to do battle for her cub's life. Digging deep and distancing herself from the fear, she put every ounce of energy she could muster into the entreaty. "Mother Goddess, I beg of you, let the bastard hear my words." Without thought to her own personal safety, Rainy forced her spirit into the murky blackness of the murderous man's mind to battle for the woman's well-being.

"Stop! I can see you! You'll be caught if you kill her. Back away." Feeling the enraged man's strength of will as he mentally fought her words off, she knew an extreme change of tactics would be needed to get through to him. To spare this woman's life, Rainy was up for the challenge. "If you touch her again, you sorry son of a bitch, I'll track you to the ends of the earth and haunt you till your dying day. You'll never have a moment's peace. I swear it! Back away from her!"

The fearful shudder which ran through his body rocked Rainy as if it were her own. Time seemed to stand still as her vision went black. The bastard had somehow found a way to kick her out of his mind. The stark terror-filled image of the severely beaten woman and the wail of a small child, somewhere in the distance burned into her mind.

Slowly Rainy's spirit came back into her corporeal

body. The knowledge Mother Goddess had just imparted spoke directly to the critical events soon to follow. The guiding forces were giving Rainy notice that these two people would soon be in her presence, and she needed to prepare for the worst. Unable to shake the pure madness of the evil man she couldn't help but momentarily give into the terror and tremble.

Trying to keep the wobble out of her voice, she clutched Cheryl's hand for strength. "We're going to need some help at the shop today. A dreadfully dangerous man is going to come in with a woman. I'll need you to distract him so I can speak with her. Call Sarah and Camille. We'll need them to come in and work with the customers, so you and I can do what must be done to help this poor woman."

Rainy allowed Cheryl to lift her up from the floor and hoist her back onto the chair. Her ice cold hands shook uncontrollably. Doing what she could to calm herself, she ran her fingers through her mass of disheveled hair. The phantom pain in her ribs still lingered but would thankfully subside in a short period of time, unlike the woman who had suffered the injuries.

"I've got to call Detective Branch and let her know there's an emergency coming in today."

Chapter Eleven

Sleep didn't come again until the bright morning sunlight entered Terry's room. Only with the perceived safety that came from sunbeams filtering through the French doors would he relax enough to turn the light off and shut his eyes again.

Feeling a little better after a few dreamless hours of shut eye, Terry sat back with a critical eye and reviewed the events of the following evening. If anyone could help it would be Nathan, but he didn't dare talk openly in the house. Whatever was here had made it crystal clear that he...it...*the entity* was acutely aware of everything going on.

Hating the thought of looking at the horrific sketch again, he knew it would be impossible to ask for help from Nathan without it. Only then would his friend know what was at stake. Everyone's safety was at risk. From this point forward, Terry would have to ensure that he took all precautions. Carefully folding the old sheet of sketch paper, he slipped it in his back pocket as nonchalantly as possible all the while nervously looking over his shoulder.

Nathan's demeanor up until the time they pulled out of the driveway was unreadable. Terry knew his friend was holding something back and also knew he, himself, was at fault for that. The way he'd jumped on everyone yesterday at the drop of a coin still confounded him. But the idea of someone else controlling his emotions had started to take root. *Was that even possible?* There'd been no logical explanation for his riotous feelings. Driving through downtown Tempe served to push the bad attitude away for the moment at least.

"This was an excellent idea you had."

Nathan shot a suspicious glance in his direction and then focused back on traffic. "What idea?"

After the way I behaved yesterday, who could blame his skepticism. "Going out to breakfast. How did you get the car?"

"The office dropped it off for me."

Nathan's curt clipped answers reinforced the notion that Terry had some apologies to make. Picking up a file folder, which was thrown haphazardly on the bench seat, he started nervously leafing through the papers without actually reading them. Nathan grabbed it out of his hand and slapped the paperwork back down on the seat.

"Don't tell me you have to work on your vacation?"

"Nope." The word hung in the air until Nathan decided to elaborate. "You and I are going to go through the documents in that file. I didn't want to mention it at the house. I can't explain it, but it feels as though I'm being watched there. That's just one of the many things we need to discuss."

Terry exhaled a heavy sigh. "I know you're not going to believe me, but I understand what you're saying. I'm sorry about the way I acted yesterday. I don't have a clue as to what my problem was. I knew I was behaving badly, but I just couldn't stop myself."

"I know, Terry. You *weren't* yourself. That among other things worries me." Pulling into the waffle restaurant parking lot Nathan found an empty spot and cut the engine off. When his best friend shot an icy, piercing glance toward him, the pit of Terry's stomach lurched. They were on the same page now. Nathan just didn't know it yet.

"Let's talk about this when we get inside. I feel like I could eat a horse. You know how irritable I get when I'm hungry. I may just kick your ass into tomorrow if I don't get some food soon."

Terry grabbed Nathan's arm to stop him from exiting the vehicle. "Before we go in I have something to show you. I don't want to take a chance that anyone in the restaurant will see it."

Rubbing the back of his neck, Terry tried to simmer down. Nathan had taught him that the only way out of a problem was to trudge through it. He had a hell of a problem on his hands and wouldn't be able to fight his way to the other side without his best friend beside him. "Something happened to me last night when I was in the bathroom."

Nathan's hand slammed down on the steering wheel. "I knew it! Why didn't you…"

Trying to calm his friend, Terry reached out to Nathan. "Stop. I didn't tell you because I wasn't sure what had happened. I only knew that *something* had happened. Before I finally got into the shower, I'd stated aloud that I was going to call Rainy and have her get rid of whatever is there at the house."

"Finally you're making some sense."

"Not so fast." Pulling the offensive sketch from his pocket, he reluctantly handed it to Nathan. "I had a dream."

Terry tried to be strong, but the force of the image he was about to reveal was so disturbing his nerves got the better of him. The panicky tic in his hand had the folded paper shaking as he handed it off to his friend.

Nathan took a long, deep breath and braced himself before unfolding the sketch. As if it burned his fingers, he quickly tossed the drawing back to Terry. "What the hell, man? Why would you draw something like that?"

Unable to continue eye contact Terry glared at the grisly image. His revulsion over the grim picture resulted in a fierce shake of the head.

Pressure built deep in his chest. It was beginning to sink in just how much the fear for himself, for Rainy, and for Nathan weighed him down. His voice dropped an octave. "Nathan, I *didn't* draw that. Whatever is in my home left it for me as a warning. He…it told me that Rainy would be killed if I said anything about him. The shadow man said he knew what she was and he…*it* is stronger than her."

Concern creased Nathan's face. *"He? It? Shadow man?* You *saw* it? You *spoke* to it?" Lowering his voice to a whisper, he stated as calmly as possible, "I *knew* that place was haunted. It was the only explanation that made any sense. I figured a dead homeowner didn't want you in his space." Offering support Nathan grabbed Terry's shoulder and squeezed. "Are you telling me that you actually saw something? That you believe this is more dangerous than some old harmless ghost trying to scare the shit out of us or just get us to leave?"

"I have no idea what's there, but I *do* know it's bad. Somehow we've got to come up with a plan to figure out how to get rid of it without letting Rainy know." He cringed when his gaze fell on the crumpled paper. "We can't risk her. I *won't* risk her."

"I hear you on that." Nathan agreed.

"Maybe we can find some clue in the documents you have." Terry crumpled the sketch into a tiny ball and threw it under the seat. "Let's go inside and start reading."

****

"May I help you, gentlemen?"

Nathan, the ever-present gentleman, dug deep and offered up a warm smile for the cute waitress. Terry wished he was capable of turning off his anxiety at the drop of a coin like his friend.

"I'll have the T-Bone medium, with eggs sunny side up, an order of your biscuits and gravy, two sides of bacon, and keep the coffee coming, please."

Terry waited until the waitress finished scrawling Nathan's order down. "I'll have two eggs soft scrambled, with hash browns, bacon and a biscuit, please. Why don't you just leave the pot of coffee?"

With their orders placed, Nathan pulled his phone out and searched through his contacts. Terry's stomach rolled over. "You're not calling Rainy, are you?"

The stark panic in his voice sparked a twitch in Nathan's features. "No." But he didn't offer any more of an explanation.

Putting the phone to his ear, Nathan became aware of Terry's unease. "It's going to be okay, Runt. I'm not calling Rainy. I don't even know her num..." His finger shot up in the air to silently halt the conversation.

"David, hello. It's me, Nathan Gordon. How are you doing?"

Terry hated listening to one-sided telephone conversations. Eavesdropping made him feel helpless, so he remained motionless as Nathan nodded his head.

"That's great. I have a big favor to ask. I know we haven't seen each other for—gosh, what's it been— over a year already? I should never have let time slip by like that. But…"

Nod.

"Yeah. You're absolutely right, man. Umm—I was wondering if you have any free time today or tomorrow? A friend of mine and I have a problem. With your background, I think you might be the only person that can help."

Feeling more out of the loop than ever, Terry bit his lip and watched Nathan's head bob and weave while his attention remained focused on listening to whoever the hell Dave was. He scoured his memory but couldn't make any connection between Nathan and anyone named Dave. His leg started bouncing, so he slapped his knee to stop the nervous twitch. *Damn leg has a mind of its own.*

"I've got a big favor to ask. I wouldn't normally be calling out of the blue like this, but it's become apparent this situation is out of control. It's critical that we get your insight and specialized help on the matter. A good friend of mine just purchased a home in the Tempe area, and some strange things have been happening. I was…"

Nod.

"That's right. I was hoping that maybe you could come by and do a house blessing. It would make us both feel a lot better."

The tension in Terry's muscles was pronounced

and lifted his shoulders an inch higher as Nathan's head continued to bob.

"Well, let's put it this way. You know me. I don't like jumping to conclusions. But we both believe that Terry has an uninvited guest.

"Yep."

Nod.

Nathan was starting to look like a damn bobblehead. Terry wanted to scream his aggravation at the top of his lungs. *'What's he saying? It's gotta be good, right? Otherwise why all the damn nodding?'* Doing his best to keep quiet, he bit his lip so hard he thought he tasted blood and eased off.

"That's right. The invisible kind. Do you want me to tell you what's been happening?"

Nod.

Unable to keep the frustration at bay any longer, Terry pushed his fists into his eyes. *Please, Dave, whoever you are. We need your help.*

"Okay. That's great! We'll see you bright and early tomorrow morning." Nathan's exhale of relief was audible.

"Thanks so much, Dave. I'll text you the address. Right. Bye."

Before Nathan could press end, Terry jumped in. "Who's Dave? Can he bless the house? As in banishing whatever that thing is?"

The waitress picked that time to start piling plates in front Nathan. Terry was frantic for answers. The young woman cast a sideway glance at him when he loudly harrumphed his disgust at the untimely interruption.

"Please, excuse my friend. He's a little anxious this

morning. Thank you. I'm famished." *Again with the damn smile.*

The waitress, Jenny, or so her nameplate stated, giggled flirtatiously and left.

"Dammit! Tell me! Can Dave help us?"

"Yes, he can." Terry didn't miss the confident ring in Nathan's voice. "Dave is the Phoenix Police Department's Chaplain," he stated as a chunk of steak made its way through the self-satisfied grin. "He recommended that we keep the mood and emotions light at your house. No angry outbursts. No mention of anything amiss. We don't want the shadow man to know someone's coming to toss him out on his ear. Sound good?"

Feeling like the weight of the world had just been lifted from his shoulders, Terry was finally able to relax. "Sounds *great* to me."

"Okay. Let's eat before everything gets cold, and then we'll take a look at the file."

Finishing off the last bite, Nathan gulped the remaining drops of his coffee. "I still want to go through the information on your house that Lynne found because we may have something here that will help Dave. I know you have a lot of people coming to work on the house this week. What are the plans exactly?"

"Well, I thought today that you and I could sand all of the crud off the one solid wall and ceiling in the studio and paint. I also want to schedule an electrician to put different lighting in, and I need to call a plumber. I have the air conditioning guy coming over Thursday to install a small unit. After we've finished all the dirty work, I want to pull that nasty carpet up and see if I can epoxy the floor. Oh! I almost forgot. I need to schedule a phone guy to come out and hook my landline up too." Terry's fist appreciatively bumped Nathan's arm.

"That's already taken care of. The phone people will be at your house on Wednesday."

Nathan's thoughtfulness never ceased to amaze Terry. "Thanks, man. I really do love your gift. H-m-m, let me rephrase that. I *will* love it after the exorcism. I plan on keeping it in the closet until the spook is gone." The men shared a lighthearted chuckle.

"Let's see what we have here." Nathan plopped the file folder down heavily on the table and opened it. There was a three-inch stack of paper.

"When did you ask for all of that?"

"I talked to Jursic before he left last night and asked him to call work this morning."

Scratching his head, Terry couldn't believe the vast number of documents that had been gathered in such a short amount of time. "How in the world is it possible they found all this information?"

Nathan scoffed. "Did you forget that Jared is my partner? Between his P.I. side of the business and my security team, we have access to just about every database in operation. Some legal. Some not so legal.

"Here's what I'm thinking. Since you're not responsible for that sketch, then whatever's in the house drew it as you said. Let's call him what you did, Shadow Man for now. You found…" Nathan's jaw dropped as he perused the first page.

"What? What did you find?"

Scratching his head, Nathan turned disbelieving eyes to him. "Your house was built in 1946. Do you have any idea how many owners there have been since then?"

Not sure if he wanted to hear the answer Terry shook his head.

"Fifty-four."

"What? No. That must be wrong."

Nathan held a paper up that summarized facts about his home. Unwilling to reach across the table and grasp the page he squinted to read it instead. Dizziness hit him making his eyes feel as though they were rolling back in his head.

Nathan clutched Terry's hand to get his undivided attention. "Your house is a little over seventy years old but has had fifty-four different owners. That's…" His facial features scrunched together as he did the math. "That averages out to roughly a year and a half per owner. That's a *huge* red flag."

Before Terry could say a word, Nathan was punching numbers into his phone.

"Who are you calling now?"

"Look at the names of the owner's you purchased the house from." Glancing at the paper Terry couldn't make a connection.

"I don't know those people. Should I?"

"Janet and Casey Fastbinder. You don't recognize those names?"

Clueless, all Terry could do was lamely shrug his shoulders.

"Those two names were on some of the boxes you went through yesterday. They couldn't have had possession of the house any longer than two weeks. Yet they left everything they had behind. I want to know why. Don't you?"

Two weeks? Terry reviewed the list again. *Oh, my*

God. He's right. Two weeks.

Bracing himself, Terry watched as Nathan waited for someone to answer the phone.

"Hello. My name is Nathan Gordon. You don't know me, but a friend of mine purchased the home you sold on Ash in Tempe, Arizona. I was…"

Nathan's pursed lips had Terry leaning forward. "What?"

"She hung up on me. Apparently, we're not going to get anywhere talking to them."

Terry recognized Nathan's thought process. Anytime his friend had a problem, his face would turn stern with a scowl. It would stay that way until the issue could be resolved in his mind—or at the very least until he came up with pertinent questions that needed answers.

"Our best lead is that disturbing drawing. Do you think you can connect that with the sketch books you found?"

Terry bit his thumbnail as he thought about the question. Coming to a conclusion he nodded. "Yeah. I can see that. Every artist has their own style. The work I looked at in those sketch books was disturbing as hell, but not nearly as gruesome as the present left on my bed. But I think there *are* striking resemblances with style and technique. Yeah. I'd say it would be a safe assumption that the same person could have sketched both."

"Okay. Good. We've got a starting point. Were you able to determine the time frame for those sketches?"

"1935 through 1948."

"The house was built in 1946, so my best guess is if Shadow Man lived there, it would have been somewhere between 1946 and 1948." Nathan shuffled through the paperwork and found information for the original owner of the home.

"Jack and June Forman were the first homeowners. They purchased the house in 1946 and stayed there through 1950. *Dammit.* They're both dead now." He furiously continued the search through the documents. "I can't find any police reports or newspaper clippings for those years."

Pushing part of the stack toward Terry, Nathan mumbled, "Look for any deaths, anything pertaining to an artist, or anything that seems out of the norm. The summary sheet Lynne gave me shows a high number of police reports over the years. See if you can figure out what that's about."

Feeling a little better because he was finally doing something—anything—to get answers, Terry dug in.

They'd finished eating an hour ago but remained seated at the table. The breakfast crowd had long since vanished as had the lunch crowd.

Frustrated, Terry rubbed his eyes. "I…" His phone suddenly came alive and blared Witchy Woman. "It's Rainy. I've got to take this.

"Good morning."

"Good morning to you too. I got your message. I hope I didn't catch you at a bad time to talk."

"Perfect timing. Nathan and I were just taking a break. It's so good to hear your voice."

"That's sweet. Thank you. I've been looking forward to talking to you as well."

"Are you free this weekend? I was thinking about coming up to check on Jody and Jared's house. I'd love to have you over and cook for you again."

"That sounds great, but something has come up. It looks like I'm going to be in Phoenix this weekend. I was wondering if you'd like to come to my apartment in the Valley and let me repay you for the wonderful dinner you fed me the other night?"

Terry's heart jumped. "I'd love that!"

"If you're ready for the house blessing, I can also come by and do that for you."

"No! I...no. Um. I'm not ready. I don't want you to see the place until everything is taken care of." Nathan kicked him under the table. "I mean, you know, put away."

"Okay. Whenever you're ready to have it done, just let me know. I'll text you my address in the Valley. How about you come by around six on Saturday night?"

"I'll be there."

"Great. I won't keep you."

"Okay. Rainy, it was so good to hear your voice. Goodbye."

Her giggle melted him. "Goodbye."

Terry hit end and smiled at his phone.

"Mauh. Mauh. Mauh."

Terry snickered at Nathan's production of blowing kisses. "Pfft. You're just jealous."

Chapter Twelve

Rainy had listened to Terry's message from the night before a couple of times. It was silly to keep it, she knew, but who cared? She'd learned quickly that the sound of his voice momentarily settled jittery nerves. And there was plenty to be jumpy about today.

Several hours had passed since the morning's horrific premonition. Standing behind the counter and rearranging trinkets, Rainy's field of vision abruptly went dark. A brilliant flash in her mind's eye, much like the bright strobe of a camera, revealed the couple she'd been expecting. Hastily pulling her phone out, she dialed Detective Branch.

"I'm five minutes away. Are they there?"

"They're close. The man and woman should be walking through the door anytime now. I didn't glimpse the child in my vision, but it feels like the boy is with them too."

Without another word the phone disconnected.

The bell above the door clattered leaving Rainy to harness blinding fear. The usually soothing tone signaling arriving customers suddenly sent her nerves all ajar. It wasn't necessary to look at the people who had just entered. Instinctively she knew they were the couple she was expecting. Her fingers gripped the new burner phone in her pocket. In preparation for this meeting, she'd activated the disposable cell only moments after the early morning episode.

Moving to Cheryl's side, she whispered, "It's show time. We're going to do this just as we discussed. Nothing more. Nothing less. I don't want you going all cowgirl on me. Not only is it too dangerous, but we must stick to the script to make sure everything goes as planned. Play to his ego. Smile and touch his arm as if you're coming on to him. He'll…"

"Do you want the nonchalant make-him-think-it's-his-idea mode or bitch in heat?"

Not following Cheryl's train of thought, Rainy could only stare. "What?"

"Do you want him to think he's making the moves, or do you want me to wipe the floor with him?"

Rainy couldn't help but grin. "Oh honey, make him bleed. I need him to move away from his wife and child, so I can approach her and talk freely. Do whatever you have to do to keep him occupied but don't under any circumstance leave with him. Don't forget to set up a time and place to meet him tonight."

Cheryl's high-spirited spunk momentarily lost focus as she cringed.

"I know it's difficult, but you're not actually going to meet him. Remember why we're doing this. I just need to get that bastard out of the house so we can get the wife and child to safety. It has to be tonight. After what I witnessed there's no time left. If this doesn't work, he'll kill them both before we get another chance to act."

Rainy was fascinated watching Cheryl transform herself into a beguiling Siren. Her apprentice added a slight pout to her mouth, licked her lips, and with an added sparkle in her eyes, she moved out to do her part."

Damn. That girl is good.

The savage brute's attention quickly shifted to the sultry enchantress throwing some heavy-duty moves his way.

"Praise the Goddess! I knew there was a good reason to come to work today. I could feel it in my bones. Someone special was going to walk through that door and change my life. And here you are!"

Nudging him none too gently away from his wife, Cheryl talked to the man as if he were the answer to any woman's prayer. She even brazenly caressed his powerful arm as she batted her eyelashes at him. The narcissistic bastard didn't know what hit him.

Having no regard for his wife at all, the glint in the abuser's eyes revealed nothing but a feral attraction to Cheryl—fitting behavior for the dirty dog he was. The fact his wife and son were present didn't bother him in the least and that pissed Rainy off even more.

With his attention drawn in another direction, the bully's wife noticeably relaxed. Seemingly grateful to be free of the jerk's scrutiny, she moved in the other direction deeper into the store. The abused woman was obviously used to hiding injuries because her limp was slight. But the pain was evident in each step she took if anyone bothered to pay attention.

Where on earth was her family? Friends? But Rainy knew the answer to that question. He'd probably separated them and built a wall between them years ago. Abusers didn't abide by any outside interference.

Gingerly pushing the stroller which held a beautiful sleeping child, the woman reached out to touch a crystal tchotchke. The pain such a slight gesture caused was visible as it quaked through her body. She quickly retracted her arm with a flinch. The morning beating had taken a high toll on her ribs.

Closely observing, Rainy sent tendrils of psychic power toward the woman who had managed to live through an unforgivable nightmare. Without surprise, she noted that the lady had completely emotionally withdrawn. No matter how potent her psychic ability was, the woman's disposition had been buried so deep it wouldn't be possible to penetrate and get a good read on her.

Allowing her vision to blur, Rainy tried a different technique. This practice made viewing auras a little easier. In the past, she'd seen the electromagnetic field around battered women pulled in close to their bodies but never to this extent. The woman's life force, which for an ordinary person held vibrant colors, was completely devoid of any hue. Black spots encircled what was left of her translucent aura as if all light and life's vigor had been sucked dry and stored away into the inky blotches.

Knowing it would be difficult for the woman to trust a complete stranger, Rainy extended her own aura to include mother and child. She focused her energy on love and light and compassion. In doing so, she hoped to convey that positive energy to the woman who so desperately needed it. Being careful not to make any sudden movements, Rainy approached her. "Excuse me."

Not wanting any attention drawn to herself, the battered lady recoiled and tried to turn away. Rainy held her hand out and insisted she listened. "You don't know me, but I'm here to help you. I don't want to scare you, so I'm not going to ask for your name. I know what he's doing to you. I saw a vision of what happened this morning."

Ignoring the woman's sharp intake of breath, Rainy continued before she could retreat. "I'm not going to sugarcoat this. You need to leave tonight, or he *will* kill you. I was only able to stop him this morning because we were somehow connected. I scared the shit out of him. Next time there may not be a connection for me to help.

"Here's a card. In case your husband finds it, it says Summit Pediatric Clinic. The name is Dr. Jessica Branch. She's not a doctor. Jessica is the best cop I know, and her life's work is with domestic abuse victims. I know you're terrified of being caught but take a glance at the woman standing behind me."

Before doing so, the battered woman carefully looked around for her husband. When satisfied he was nowhere in sight she moved slightly to her left and glanced several feet behind Rainy. No mirror was needed to know that Jessica had somehow made her presence known.

"That is Detective Jessica Branch. She has a dedicated line for the number on this card and will answer any time of the night or day. She'll come to you when you call her. If need be, Detective Branch will protect you and your son with her life. She'll get you both out to safety. You're not alone. We've used this same system for over five years now and helped many, many domestic abuse victims. There's *never* been a flaw in this arrangement. You must get out tonight." Rainy knew she had to spell it all out for the woman, or her words may not be heeded. "If you don't, you *and* your child will die at his hand before this week is out."

The broken woman secreted a petrified glance back to her husband who had reappeared but was still busy with Cheryl. Depleted of all self-esteem, the woman wouldn't look into Rainy's eyes. "He said he'd kill us if I ever left him. I can't leave. I can't risk it. I've got Marcus to worry about."

"Look at me."

After several moments the woman raised her eyes to peer meekly into Rainy's. In an instant, she faltered and dropped the gaze.

"I want you to understand the truth behind what I'm telling you. I've been in your husband's mind. He's not going to let either of you live. He's already prowling for a new victim. Just look at him!" Rainy nodded her head in his direction.

She let the woman momentarily examine the man who'd promised to love her forever. The same man that had so brutally beaten her this morning leaned in close to smell Cheryl's hair. It was a move meant to be seductive but instead was utterly skivvy. Then the prick whispered something in her ear turning Cheryl's complexion a bright shade of crimson.

"While we still have time, let me help you another way." Rainy braced herself to feel the woman's pain.

It was a serious matter taking on someone else's pain, but Rainy knew she must. Their only means of privacy was a small bookcase between them and the husband. She gently laid her hands on the woman's cracked ribs. Both women flinched. To ease the lady's emotional discomfiture, Rainy called on *her* spiritual belief system. As she'd heard her grandmother do all those years back, she started to whisper. "Dear God

Almighty." Even with her eyes closed, the healing words weren't merely spoken but felt also. Therapeutic heat transferred from her hands and penetrated the woman's body easing the soreness and mending ribs. The bruises would remain, but at least the sting of pain would be lessened. She continued to move her hands from wound to wound.

****

Cheryl had gone above and beyond granting Rainy another fifteen minutes to work her healing magic. She'd taken on as much of the woman's pain as she dared. Only when certain there had been success with the healing did she step back. Between old injuries and new, Rainy had a difficult time catching her breath.

"I call on Mary the virgin mother, and Jesus son of God, to hear my prayer. Satan, I rebuke you in the name of Jesus Christ. Mother Goddess, I beseech you. I ask that the divine white light of protection encircle this woman and her son." The air around the women and child came to life, crackling and spinning with warmth on the heels of the powerful protection. Wind chimes hanging from a nearby shelf started to twirl and dance in the heavenly breeze. "Keep them safe. Allow nothing harmful to penetrate this defensive shell."

The protection held firm. While the atmosphere around the women was currently vibrant and alive with God's and Mother Earth's loving light, the protective barrier wouldn't last for much more than a day.

"Detective Branch and I have formulated a plan for your husband to be out of the house tonight. Don't do anything until he leaves. Call Jessica as soon as it's clear he's gone and pack one bag only with whatever you and your son need. You must be quick."

"You don't understand." The woman's voice shook with terror. "My husband's rich. I have no money of my own. He'll find us. He won't stop looking until he does. We'll never be free of him."

Rainy slid the burner phone from her pocket and hid it beneath the diapers at the bottom of the baby's bag. "I have friends, Jody and Jared Bastion. They own the leading security firm in the country and live right here in Flagstaff. They are aware of my work with abused women and children and have offered their services pro bono for anyone in need. With their help your husband will never find you."

The woman grabbed Rainy's arm and looked deeply into her eyes for the first time since they'd met. The healing power provided a glimmer of hope now visible in her gaze. "I trust you. My name is Amy. My son is Marcus. If he leaves tonight I'll call on the phone you've given me. I promise."

Hearing Cheryl wrap up the discussion with the vile man signaled the close of Rainy's conversation with Amy. Unable to safely say anything else and still suffering from the pain she'd taken on, Rainy inched her way to the back office.

"For you, sweetheart, it's on the house. I hope you decide to come out and play tonight. I'd love to get to know you a little better."

"You can be sure of it, little darlin'. I've got some special plans for you."

Amy was jumpy but who wouldn't be in her position? The moment the door closed behind them Jessica entered Rainy's office.

"Her name is Amy. Her son is Marcus. I didn't get a last name."

Cheryl ran through the office door waving something in the air. "Here's his card. It has a name and phone number on it. Marcus Grosic the fourth—as in IV. He never missed the opportunity to let me know that he comes from a long line of money. What a pretentious bastard."

Rainy tried to rub the exhaustion from her eyes. "She'll call tonight. I'm sure of it. She can sense the change in him. I just hope she lives until then."

"I saw what you did for her. No matter what happens you've helped her." Jessica moved in for a hug. "I'm going to follow them for a while and make sure things go as planned."

Chapter Thirteen

Terry dug tightly clenched fists deep into his lower back and stretched, trying to release the kinks that came from holding a heavy-duty sander flush to the wall. *Thank God there's only one wall and a ceiling to clean before the painting begins.* Even with the rented electric power tools, the sticky goop that covered the room's two solid surfaces proved to be a real bitch to get off. In many places, he'd had to strip the paint all the way to the drywall as if the wall itself had bled the sludge. At least the gunk wasn't on the glass.

Revulsion over the slimy, sticky substance sent tremors of disgust throughout his body. He had no clue what the gunk was and didn't want to delve too deeply into what it could be. However, Nathan had aptly dubbed the foul sludge ghoul snot.

Thanks to the three exterior walls of antique paned glass, the temperature inside the studio had become overwhelming as work progressed into the late afternoon. The windows were no match for the desert heat and offered no insulation whatsoever. Terry felt as though he were spending an afternoon in a convection oven and would soon be cooked to well done. *That will teach me to wait so late in the day to start any hard labor before the air conditioning gets installed.*

To stay as cool as possible, both he and Nathan were shirtless. With the rate of the sweat that poured out of him, it didn't take long before every stitch of the loose fitting board shorts clung to his body. They had become so waterlogged that he struggled to keep them on his hips. With each slight movement, the saturated material grew heavier and slid farther down his legs making the work even more miserable.

Stepping outside, Terry yanked at the face mask to get a breath of fresh air. Jerking at the rag hanging from his back pocket, he swiped at the caked on crud covering his goggles. Instead of cleaning the clear plastic eye protection, the sweat and dust smeared making it impossible to see anything.

Removing the protective eyewear, Terry glanced back into the studio to find Nathan standing on a ladder. The *w-r-r-r* of the power tool roared steadily as the sticky slime was painstakingly scraped from the ceiling. Nathan's muscles bulged and even shook from the strain of holding the sander above his head. *He's going to be sore tomorrow.* Tiny paint particles swam through the air as if a blizzard had settled in the small space. The fine white dust was drawn to his friend's waterlogged body and stuck like glue. Laughter caught in Terry's throat as he yelled, "Dude, you look like a snowman."

With a pronounced jerk, Nathan swatted at his ear as if Terry's words were a pesky fly that had just dive bombed him. More than a little perturbed by his friend's quick dismissal at the attempted humor, he snapped, "Well, if you're going to be an asshole about it, you can get your own damn beer."

As he turned to walk away, Nathan yelped. Terry spun around just in time to see the big guy lose his grip on the sander which had been held precariously above his head. The power tool came down hard grazing the side of Nathan's face. Instead of clutching what had to be a budding lump the size of a goose egg, Nathan's arms flailed around his face. Panic induced a hysterical shriek while his hands swatted through the air as if he were under assault from a swarm of angry bees.

Because there wasn't a single insect in sight, it took a moment for Terry's mind to catch up and understand the danger his friend was in.

All at once, his brain clicked that Nathan was teetering high up on a ladder and about to fall. Terry's body propelled forward. Before he got through the threshold, something at the far end of the room caught his attention. He froze. The mass wasn't solid but carried enough density to disturb the flow of particles floating through the air. Whatever that thing was, it moved stealthily and with purpose. The shimmering mass parted the paint dust as if it were the Red Sea and moved in a straight shot right at Nathan's back. Blinking to clear his vision, he strained to get a better look. *Shadow Man. It had to be him.*

In a matter of seconds, pulse racing fear turned Terry's mouth into the Dust Bowl. "Stop!" His tongue was so dry that the word came out sounding more like a squeak. Thankfully, the noise that did emerge was loud enough to divert the phantom's attention.

As if surprised it had been discovered, the entity paused. The hair on Terry's arms stood at attention. Now that movement had ceased, paint dust settled on the creature creating an outline of sorts. The thing across the room lowered itself in what Terry perceived as a defensive crouch and growled. The temperature inside the studio had to be well over one hundred degrees, but raging fear induced an ice cold chill that ran the length of his spine leaving a tingling sensation in its wake.

The air surrounding him became molten hot as if a furnace had been switched on. Any second now, Terry expected flames from the depths of hell to shoot from the floor and scorch him. Sparing a quick glance at Nathan, Terry was relieved to find his friend climbing down to safety.

The slow, hulking gait in which Nathan descended was a huge red flag that the man had no clue of the immediate danger. "Hurry, dammit!" Panic dried the words in his throat. No way was his friend going to hear them over the sound of the power tool that was now buzzing around the floor.

Peering back at the Shadow Man, all thought seemed to slow and dull. It was as though the creature had reached inside his head and flipped the off switch, lulling his brain to sleep. His mind had somehow become lumbered—almost to the point of being stagnant—leaving him bewildered and unsure how to proceed.

Shadow Man was manipulating his mind, but Terry couldn't do a thing to stop the intrusion. Clamping his eyes shut was the only action he could think of to possibly reverse the effect. He realized his mistake immediately when the demon took advantage. Terry's gut twisted in agony when the Shadow Man slithered up beside him. *"I've tired of your friend. He must go."* The words hissed into his consciousness on the breath of decaying flesh. The vile stench roused Terry from the dreamlike state, and he forced his eyes to open.

Before he could get his bearings, Shadow Man

rushed toward an unsuspecting Nathan, who'd only made it halfway down the ladder. He'd never get to his friend before he was knocked off. Legs unsteady, Terry willed them to move for Nathan's sake.

As feared, the entity's gelatinous mass slithered so quickly across the room that it hit Nathan before Terry could reach him. His best friend lost his footing and tumbled from the ladder. The unseen assailant had charged right through Nathan's large body. Closing in just in the nick of time, Terry threw his arms out to break the big man's fall. His own size and weight were no match for Nathan's. Instead of catching him, he ended up sprawled in a heap on the floor with Nathan on top just like the old football days when they were kids. Only this time, Nathan was unmoving and silent. Dead weight.

Unsure if another attack was coming or not, Terry squirmed from beneath Nathan and jumped on top to protect him while he was defenseless. The electric sander was dangerously close to Nathan's now still legs. Reaching out, Terry grabbed hold of the cord and yanked just in the nick of time. Another moment and the power tool could have sliced through skin and bone.

Agonizing moans started to rip through the air and scared Terry more than the entity ever could have. Staying on top, he wiggled his way around until he could reach Nathan's face. Just as expected, the heavy sander's handle had left a nasty goose egg where it had drilled his friend's forehead. *Thank God none of the working parts had touched his skin.* Yanking at the mask and goggles, Terry saw the extent of pain in his friend's expression. Tears trickled from the corners of tightly clenched eyes leaving tracks through the paint dust on Nathan's cheeks.

Believing another attack was imminent and with Shadow Man nowhere to be seen, a frenzied mania took over all rational thought. Hoping that adrenaline would kick in and give him some much needed superhuman strength, Terry jumped to his feet and grabbed Nathan's arms but couldn't budge his friend's massive body.

"Come on. Help me. We have to get out of here."

Nathan's answering groan resonated all the way through Terry's core. Still holding his friend's arms, he pivoted around to get a better hold and tried to drag him out to safety. *No luck.* He didn't have the strength to move him a lousy inch. Bending down, Terry screamed into Nathan's face. "Get up! Now!"

Nathan's body jerked as if he'd been hit. His head shook trying to clear the cobwebs.

"Don't just stand there looking down at me. Help me up, dammit." The sound of Nathan's weak voice was music to Terry's ears. Once standing, Terry wrapped an arm around his friend's waist and shuffled him through the studio's exit.

They stumbled from the building and once free, toppled onto the grass. Terry watched Nathan's abdomen rise and fall as he caught his breath.

"Are you all right? Talk to me, Nathan."

"What the hell happened in there? Why did you smack me? I feel like I've been hit by a bus. And where did all those flies come from?"

"I didn't hit you!"

"I *saw* you run up behind me and take a swing at me. Why would you do that?" The accusatory tone of Nathan's voice struck home.

"I swear, it wasn't me. Shadow Man is playing

with both of us. There weren't any flies, either. That must have been another head game."

"I couldn't get them to leave me alone. All of a sudden, there were thousands of them swarming me."

"I'm telling you there were *no* flies. It was a trick. Shadow Man—well, at least I think it was Shadow Man—ran right through you. I couldn't get to you in time. I'm sorry."

Nathan winced and tried to reach behind his back. "Fuck, man, I feel like I've been torn to pieces." Finally, finding the strength to sit up, the exploration of his back had left Nathan's hand covered in blood. Terry blanched and swallowed deep to keep from making the situation any worse by puking all over his friend.

"What the hell? You've got blood all over you!"

Sliding behind Nathan, the first thing Terry saw was his friend's back streaked with fresh blood. He came close to fainting when the cause became evident. "Stay here. I'm getting the hose to clean you up and take a better look."

Kneeling behind Nathan, Terry directed the flow from the hose down Nathan's shoulders. The cool water cascaded over taut muscles and caused goose bumps to rise on Nathan's overheated flesh. Terry cleaned the remaining blood and paint dust from his friend. The initial assessment of the injury was confirmed.

"I don't know how to tell you this, but you've been bitten. The bite punctured your skin in several places. The wounds look pretty deep."

The door to the studio, mere feet away, slammed shut. Both Nathan and Terry jumped to their feet primed for another attack, but one never came.

The rigid set of Nathan's shoulders reflected his

resolve. "I'm calling it. We're done in the studio for the day. Give me that hose. I'm going to finish washing off, and then I'm taking a much-needed plunge into the pool to cool down."

Terry could feel his sanity slipping away. "Are you crazy? That thing just attacked you, and now you want to go for a fucking swim as if nothing happened?"

Nathan was on him in a second. Huge hands cupped Terry's face so fast he didn't have time to escape the grasp. "Get a hold of yourself. Remember what we discussed earlier? We're going to forget any of this happened and act like everything is business as usual. For the time being, we are done working in the studio. After a nice relaxing swim, we're going to treat ourselves to some expensive steaks, which *you're* going to grill in that fancy ass outdoor kitchen. Got it?" Nathan squeezed Terry's face so he'd think before replying.

Terry closed his eyes and took a few deep breaths. "It doesn't want you here. That monster told me so. You're not safe. If anything were to happen…"

To comfort Terry, Nathan wrapped his massive arms around him all but smothering him. "Shut up. Business as usual. We can handle this until tomorrow morning. We're not going to let that thing chase us off." Terry's ear was nestled against his best friend's chest and listened to the slam of his heartbeat. Nathan was scared to death but wasn't going to back down.

Pulling away, he forced a smile in case that thing was watching them. "You're right. Everything's fine."

Nathan bent to pick up the hose when Terry jerked him back. "If you end up with rabies, I'll fork out the money for the treatment." His grin was no longer forced. "I love you, man."

Nathan's lips curved up. "Now there's the Terry I know and love. Douche bag."

****

"Damn! There's nothing like watching the Dbacks on a big screen. It's almost as good as being at Chase Field." Nathan sipped his beer and threw some popcorn in his mouth.

"Not that I don't enjoy your company, Nathan, but it sure would be nice to have a couple of women sitting next to us. Do you think Rainy likes baseball?"

At the mention of Rainy's name, Nathan stiffened and shot Terry an incredulous look. Realizing his mistake, Terry waited for Shadow Man's wrath. He didn't have to wait long.

Both men froze when an unexplained clicking noise sounded from the back door. They watched as the handles slowly pushed down. The French doors gently swung open. Terry jumped to his feet when the kitchen sink's faucet turned on by itself. Like a snake, the sprayer lifted out of the sink and came alive slithering and shimmying through the air. Water squirted everywhere.

Looking to Nathan for insight on how to handle this newest twist, Terry's heart stilled when the big guy's eyes bulged with unbridled fear. His knuckles were white from grasping the armrests.

A trail of water materialized from the kitchen floor into the living room. The men watched as puddles formed and appeared all the way down the hall. The shower came on in the bathroom. The toilet flushed. Looking as though he'd finally had enough, Nathan jumped to his feet.

The moment when Nathan's fear turned to anger was evident in the way his jaw flexed. The man's body all but vibrated with rage. With teeth bared, Nathan's menacing grimace commanded in no uncertain terms that Shadow Man was not welcome. Any mortal man would be running for his life if confronted with such a heat filled glare. When he did finally talk, a seething ferocity punctuated each word. "I'll turn off the water in the kitchen. You shut the faucets off in the bathroom. Grab some towels while you're there. We'll have this mess cleaned up in no time at all."

Not expecting those words and not sure he'd heard his friend right, Terry stood and stared with his mouth sagging open. Nathan's eyebrows rose denying any challenge. "Now."

Not daring to cross his friend when he was this pissed, Terry moved to the bathroom and did as told. Once the water trail on the floor had been taken care of, they sat back down in front of the TV.

A loud bang sounded on the coat closet door. The antique phone nestled within started to ring. Both men glared at the closet.

The cracking sound of Nathan slapping his legs ricocheted through Terry's head and made him cringe. Nathan stood, his face contorted into an apologetic look. "Okay. That's it. I'm done dealing with this shit tonight. We're going to my house." Pivoting, he spoke to every corner of the room. "But we'll be back tomorrow and start work first thing in the morning. You may have won this battle, Shadow Man, but you won't win the war. If I were you, I'd think about making a hasty retreat while you still can."

Nathan turned and defiantly stared at Terry.

Knowing that look, he raised his hands to remind his friend that he wasn't the enemy.

"Hey, you'll get no argument from me."

Chapter Fourteen

They'd just settled into Nathan's sedan for the drive across town when Terry's phone started to play Witchy Woman. Finally having something to smile about, Terry fumbled in his pocket for the cell. "Rainy, I was hoping I'd get to talk to you tonight."

"It's good to hear your voice too." Alerted to Rainy's nervous tension through the slight quiver in her voice, Terry sat up a little straighter.

"Is everything all right? You sound a little stressed."

"I'm waiting for some people to show up. There's a slight problem here, and it looks like I'll be coming to Phoenix sooner than the weekend. I could use a little down time. I was hoping to coax you away from the responsibilities of being a new homeowner long enough to join me for supper one evening. I know Nathan is staying with you. I'd love to have him come and join us too."

The news he'd be seeing Rainy sooner rather than later sent little bolts of electricity through Terry and amped up his depleted energy in a matter of seconds. The spurt of power had his butt bouncing in place. Unabashedly, he fist pumped the air.

Not wanting to seem too eager, he took a few deep breaths to control the giddiness which would surely be heard in his voice if he couldn't contain himself.

Nathan's easy laughter broke through all his antics. Terry shot his friend a goofy grin. "I'd love to come over and see your place. What day are you going to be down?"

"There are some legal issues which must be taken care of first. But once that's done, Cheryl and I will be transporting a woman and her child to Phoenix. I'm hoping we can get everything resolved tomorrow, but it will probably be late Wednesday or early Thursday before I can leave."

"Wait. Legal issues? What does that mean?"

"My coven runs a safe house for abused women and children. We're getting a woman and her baby out of an abusive household tonight. They should be here any time now. While I'm in Phoenix, I'd like to discuss some security issues with Nathan if he's got any spare time."

His excitement at hearing from Rainy had suddenly turned to panic. *My girl is in trouble.* Unable to catch his breath, Terry heard the whoosh of blood rushing between his ears but not much else. He knocked his temple with the heel of his hand a few times to hear better. "Wait. What?"

"Well, I…"

Not waiting to hear her out, Terry turned to Nathan. "We need to get to Flagstaff right now. Rainy needs me."

"No! Terry, listen to me. I'm fine. I'm safe. And, by the way, that's the sweetest thing I've heard in months."

"But I want to help you."

Nathan punched Terry's arm and sent him head first into the passenger door's window. "Get a grip,

Terry. Put Rainy on speaker, so I can hear what she's saying."

Before Terry could get a word out, Rainy stated through a giggle, "Go ahead and turn the speaker on, so I can calm both of your worries at the same time."

Reluctant to share even a moment of his precious time with Rainy, Terry sighed and punched the button. "Okay. You're on speaker. Talk to us. But if you can't convince me you're safe, I'm coming to get you myself."

"Everything is going to be fine. I promise you. I work with the Flagstaff police and help domestic violence victims remove themselves from the threat. We help them with the courts, get a new start, and do everything in our power to keep them safe from their abusers.

"We've done this for a long time now. Please trust me when I tell you that I am safe and will be surrounded by Flagstaff PD as long as there's any danger.

"I didn't call to worry you. I had a little free time and just wanted to hear your voice. Now, if Nathan is satisfied that I'm safe, please take me off the speaker phone, so I can tell you how much I miss you privately."

Before he could punch the button, Nathan spoke up. "If you need us, don't hesitate to call. We'll come running. When you're here, I'd be happy to discuss safety measures with you."

"Thank you, Nathan. That means a lot to me."

"You're off speaker now. Can I just say that you never cease to amaze me? I have a superhero do-gooder for a best friend. And now I find out that I've got a kick ass girlfriend too."

After a lengthy pause, Rainy purred, "Do you think of me as your girlfriend?"

Realizing the mistake his loose lips had just made, words—any words—suddenly escaped him. There were thousands of expressions rushing across his brain to cover his stupidity, but nothing came out. He didn't want to scare Rainy off, but the big *'g'* word had just felt so right it had slipped right off his damn tongue. *Shit! Say something moron.*

"Terry? Are you there?"

"Yeah. I'm sorry. I don't mean to rush things between us, but I feel such a strong pull to you. I can't stop thinking about you. Every time I close my eyes, I see your face." His head hit the side window again from another blow to his arm. Nathan whispered, "Dude, get a grip. You're not a teenager. If you keep gushing like this, you're going to scare her off. Before you know what hit you, she'll be running in the other direction. And who the hell could blame her?"

Oh Jeez. "I didn't mean that in a stalker way. It's just…"

"But you did mean it, didn't you? After all, I'd feel terrible if I were the only one in whatever this relationship is that felt such a strong pull. I'm going to share a little secret with you. I want to kiss you again, Terry. I want to hold you in my arms and feel the calm you bring. And then I want to kiss you again."

Did I just hear that right? Terry's hand slid up to his heart. His body suddenly felt so light that he imagined himself floating away on the desert heat waves. Turning momentarily stupid, a heavenly sensation of pure joy suddenly overwhelmed him. *She feels the same way I do!*

"Runt! If you keep breathing that heavy into the phone, she's going to think you're jacking off."

Apparently, Nathan spoke louder than Terry had thought because Rainy's laughter carried him out of the love haze and straight into mortification. "Don't listen to anything Nathan says." Desperately wishing he could be alone with his phone, Terry made a feeble swipe in his friend's direction to shut him up.

"Rainy." After what she'd just confessed, he wasn't going to waste time and hold back anymore. *I'm going to be honest and tell her like it is.* "You take my breath away. Maybe you could come to Phoenix tomorrow?"

"I don't think that's possible, but it's nice to know you want me. I'll come to you as soon as I can."

"I do want you. Oh, God, I do."

"Then we'll have to do something about that." After a slight pause, her voice became strained. "I've got to go now, Terry. They're here. Call me when you can. Goodbye."

"I will. Please be safe and call me if you need me. Goodbye."

****

Detective Branch opened the apartment door and rushed Amy and Marcus inside. Relief flooded Rainy when she saw everyone was okay. The most dangerous time for a woman was the moment she left the abuser. Dashing across the room, she ushered the frightened woman and sleeping child to the couch.

"Everything's all right now. You and little Marcus are safe."

Anxiety and nerves had Amy breaking down in

sobs. "Thank you for helping us."

Rainy embraced the woman and held her while she cried. "Come with me. We've got a crib set up in your bedroom for Marcus. Let's put him down so you can decompress and start to relax while we talk."

Before she could be guided into the bedroom, Amy stopped. The years she'd been subjected to submission reflected in her body's stance. The woman's shoulders were slumped forward, and her head tilted downward looking at the floor instead of into Rainy's eyes. Tears trickled down her face dripping from her chin onto Marcus' blanket.

"There's something I have to say to you before we go any farther." Her shaky words were barely above a whisper. Amy bit her upper lip so hard Rainy thought she'd draw blood.

"Of course. You're free to say or do whatever you please now, Amy."

After a few deep breaths to gain the courage to speak her mind, Amy raised her head, and her gaze captured Rainy's. "You don't understand. Both of you got Marcus and me out of that hell alive. Before this morning, I could never afford to hope that would happen. I sincerely believed the only way out of my husband's reach would come by being placed in a body bag."

The despair and defeat in Amy's voice was heartbreaking. Rainy straightened her spine and spoke with resolve. "You're stronger than you know. Until you can call on that strength by yourself, you have both Jessica's and my support. We'll keep you out of harm's way until that time. From this point moving forward, the only people around you will care about *your* needs and the needs of your son. In those times that fear has you in its grasp, we're here for you. Now, why don't you put Marcus down, and I'll make us some tea."

Rainy, Jessica, and Amy had just settled in when a light knock sounded at the door. Amy whimpered and made a break for escape to the bedroom.

"It's okay! It's Cheryl bringing supplies for you and Marcus." Amy stopped at the bedroom doorway but wouldn't move until she was certain who was on the other side of the door.

Jessica unholstered her gun and crept toward the front door. "Yes?"

"Jessica, it's me. Cheryl. Let me in." After a collective sigh of relief, the front door opened admitting Rainy's assistant who had an armload of groceries.

Still standing in the bedroom threshold, Amy stood her ground. Cheryl dropped the food on the kitchen counter and practically danced across the room to engulf the young mother in a tender embrace. "Are you doing okay?"

Creases formed on Amy's forehead. Backing out of Cheryl's arms, she stepped protectively in front of the bedroom door where her sleeping child lay. "You're the one that went to meet my husband." It was a flat statement rather than a question.

"No. I'm the woman that gave him an excuse to leave the house so we could get you out. You can trust me."

Jessica stepped forward. "We can all confirm that, Amy. Cheryl is going into hiding with you. We have a feeling that when your husband realizes it was her that led him away so you could gain your freedom, he'll come looking for her."

Amy's face went slack and lost all color. She reached for Cheryl and clung to her. "Oh my God. You have no idea what kind of enemy you've made. If he thinks you betrayed him, he'll never stop looking for you. Why would you do that? Why would you put yourself in danger like that?"

"Because you needed help. Let's face it. Your husband is a pig. You and that boy in there deserve better."

Rainy watched the exchange and was saddened by the surprised shock that crossed Amy's face. It was clear that the monster she'd been living with had stolen her self-worth.

Slowly moving so she wouldn't startle the woman, Rainy reached out to touch Amy's arm. "You and little Marcus are out of harm's way now. Come and sit down. We're going to discuss the plans for the next couple of days and how we're going to get you to safety. If we do our job right, you'll never have to be afraid of him again. We…" Rainy's arm swiped through the air to include everyone, "along with the help of many others always get our women to safety."

Chapter Fifteen

Since the Shadow Man's reach only seemed to extend out to the property line, Nathan parked the car in front of a neighbor's house to wait for Dave. Both men were in agreement that the best way to approach the house, and the demon within, would be a sneak attack. Hopefully, in doing so, they'd have a slight advantage. Neither man was fooled. They both expected all hell to break loose once Dave stepped on the property. If the mere mention of Rainy's name sent the ghoul's ire into overdrive, then inviting a holy man over to kick some demon ass would most definitely be construed as an attack. So they used these last final moments to gather whatever confidence they could.

Terry couldn't keep from fidgeting. Up until this point, biting his nails had only resulted in drawing blood. Worse yet, the bad habit did nothing to stop the images of the nasty creature from saturating his every thought. Struggling to control the terror which persistently throbbed through him, he'd tried everything he could think of to gain the upper hand over his fears. In the end, no action he'd taken had come close to soothing the frayed nerves.

Flipping the car's stereo to a classic rock station, Terry lost himself in the frantic beat of a drum solo. He loved playing air drums and pictured himself on a stage in front of thousands of fans behind an impressive set of

Pearls. His arms flew through the air, expertly pantomiming the strike of each imaginary drum to shred the radio's tune.

Finally able to lose himself in some emotion other than panic, Terry was abruptly pulled out of his make-believe drum solo when Nathan's fist connected with his bicep. The radio blinked out leaving dead silence within the car. "Ouch! What did you do that for?"

"Get a grip, Runt. Your nervous energy is making me more anxious than whatever that thing is in your house. I've got your back. You've got mine. Dave will get rid of whatever it is. Just keep your cool. Between the three of us, that piece of shit won't know what hit him. Now breathe."

To the count of three, Terry inhaled through his nostrils and exhaled out of his mouth. Feeling a little better his head bobbed confirmation. "You're right."

"Of course I am."

Continuing the slow, deep breathing Terry focused his attention on the tree lined street that had been a big draw for him to this neighborhood. Living on this road and in this house had been a childhood dream. Surprisingly enough, throughout the years this place hadn't changed an iota. There was something so appealing and peaceful about a street cocooned in mature trees. Even though this area was in the heart of the Phoenix Metropolitan area, and less than a mile from the high-energy Arizona State University campus, this little piece of paradise he'd worked so hard to attain had a small town feel. Closing his eyes again, Terry allowed the resolve of taking back what was his wash over him. *No way in hell am I walking away from my dream home.*

The preacher man should be arriving anytime now. Painfully aware that he'd been squeezing his knuckles, Terry stretched each finger and focused on the movement to relieve some of the remaining tension.

Glancing over at his friend, Terry noted that as usual Nathan was the picture of confidence. The only tell the guy had that he wasn't serene was the way his thumb nervously tapped the steering wheel. Trying to ward off any negative feelings, Terry did his best to keep the shrillness from his voice. "I need you to tell me one more time that this is going to work."

Without an ounce of hesitancy, Nathan smiled. "Yep. Everything's going to be just fine."

Terry wasn't afraid to admit this ghost bully—who had enjoyed running him out of his home the previous night—scared the shit out of him. Since the meeting with the preacher had been set up, he'd had almost twenty-four hours to think about what would happen and everything that could go wrong once the man stepped foot on the property. Up until this point, he'd been scared to share his concerns aloud—afraid that he might somehow jinx the whole spirit cleansing ritual. The time had arrived to discuss his apprehension.

He took a brief moment and cleared his throat, hoping he'd be able to voice his concerns in an intelligent fashion rather than sounding like a raving lunatic. "What if Shadow Man hides from the preacher? What if Dave thinks we're full of shit and does a half ass job because he believes we're nuts?"

Nathan slanted a glance at Terry and chuckled in a way that said, *You're such an idiot*. "Why are you calling Dave a preacher? He's a chaplain."

Without a moment's hesitation, a surly harrumph

escaped his lips. "You're kidding, right? Think about it, man. When you hear the word *chaplain*, who comes to mind? I'll tell you who. Father Mulcahy from M.A.S.H. That dude's the meekest of the meek. But when you hear the word *preacher*, who do you think about?" When no answer was forthcoming, Terry issued a disgusted grunt. He couldn't believe how thick headed his best friend was being. "Jeez, Nathan, the answer is obvious. You think of Clint Eastwood from Pale Rider. Who do *you* think is better equipped to deal with Shadow Man? H-m-m?"

After a moment of stunned silence, Nathan closed his mouth and rolled his eyes. Opening the car door, he leaned back toward Terry and spoke through gritted teeth. "Dave's here. If you are disrespectful, I swear I will pummel you. You need to be on your best behavior. Don't even think about embarrassing me with stupid ass things like that coming out of your mouth. The man is here as a special favor to me. I'd appreciate you giving him the respect he deserves."

Before exiting the vehicle, Nathan took a deep breath himself and then offered Terry his most reassuring grin. "Look. Don't worry about that thing hiding. I've gone over this in my mind a hundred times. Shadow Man doesn't want to hide. Whatever that thing is, it wants everyone to know it's there. Hell, if you ask me, I think the bastard wants the attention. Stop worrying. You're retaking your house. In an hour, you're going to be wondering why Shadow Man was ever a problem at all."

Nathan climbed out of the vehicle. "Come on. Pull yourself together. You're going to like Dave."

The confidence with which Nathan spoke left Terry

feeling much better as he also got out of the car. That is until Preacher Dave stepped out of the sedan. The man wasn't anything like Terry had imagined at all. After seeing the guy's appearance, it would have been a serious understatement to say that he had some reservations. Instead of a crusty old Clint Eastwood type—someone that could easily kick some demon ass—Dave turned out to be a young, slightly built man that carried his demon fighting tools in a worn out backpack. Gone were the images of the renowned black satchel that Terry remembered seeing in the Exorcist. Hell, this guy made Father Mulcahy look like a badass. The preacher boy even had freckles on his face for God's sake. As his hopes for a successful duel with the Shadow Man were dashed, Terry's knees started to buckle as though the earth had dropped from beneath his feet. To keep upright, he leaned heavily on the side of the car.

Once the introductions were made, he stood idly by as Nathan described the events Shadow Man had heaped upon them over the last few days. As his best friend spoke of the trials they'd been subjected to, the preacher boy kept glancing at Terry. He couldn't help but wonder if they were serving this young holy man up for breakfast.

Deep in thought, Terry almost fell over when Nathan unexpectedly nudged him with an elbow. Rubbing his arm, he sheepishly admitted, "Sorry. I was lost in thought. Um, are you sure you're going to be able to handle this thing? You're not really what I was expecting."

Preacher Dave held his small hand out and offered a gentle smile. "Thank you for your concern, Terry. I assure you, all will be well." As he clasped the younger man's hand, an unexpected peaceful feeling blanketed him. Tingling started in his fingers and moved in waves throughout his body doing wonders to compose his fears. Gone were the quaking tremors he'd suffered through the night before. Out of nowhere, he now experienced an overwhelming sense of peace and contentment.

"May I call you Terry?"

"Of Course."

Preacher boy nodded and smiled reassuringly. "Terry, I don't know what's in your house. For reasons I'm sure you can understand, I'm not taking everything Nathan tells me as gospel. I need to make up my own mind about what's there if anything.

"Please, don't worry. I see how upset the both of you are, and that tells me that something is not right. If you have any remnants of a dead soul around, I promise that I will do everything in my power to cleanse them from your home." As if he'd just been dismissed, Dave pivoted to face Nathan.

Terry didn't want to upset the preacher boy but felt he had to be honest with the man. Otherwise, it would be like sending an innocent lamb off to slaughter. Pursing his lips, he interrupted. "Um. Excuse me, Dave. If I can just interject that *'remnants of a dead soul'* is a term that doesn't come close to what we're dealing with here. Whatever Shadow Man is, I doubt it's ever lived a day in the human world. And if that thing *was* ever human, he must have done something terrible in life to end up the way he is now. Please don't go in there underestimating this thing's power. If Shadow Man can bring down a man the size of Nathan, I have no doubt it

188

could break you in two."

He could see in the preacher boy's eyes that the words of warning had hit home. Dave nodded and placed a hand on his shoulder for reassurance. "Thank you. You're right. I respect everything you've just said, and I'll be careful."

He didn't know why, but Terry believed him. Something about Dave oozed tranquility and a gentleness of spirit. The peaceful vibe surrounding the kid sparked a hint of excitement that they might just have a chance at getting rid of the problem. They were about to pit good versus evil. His momma had always said that good would prevail over evil any day of the week.

Opening the backpack, Dave donned a black robe and gathered the needed tools for fighting Shadow Man. He filled three bottles with what Terry perceived to be holy water. Preacher boy opened an incense burner and added several different colored cones. As they were being lit and stoked to burn hot, Terry couldn't help but wonder not only why incense, but why so many different kinds were used together? As a matter of fact, he was full of questions but didn't want to interrupt whatever process the preacher boy was implementing. In the end, none of that mattered as long as they beat the crap out of some demon ass. Several minutes passed as Terry watched Dave lower his head and pray. Speaking Latin wasn't in his repertoire. He'd be more comfortable if he knew what was being said. But again, he didn't feel it would be in his best interest to butt in.

Dave held the incense burner in front of Nathan and finally started a prayer that Terry could understand.

Saint Michael, the Archangel, was being called on to defend them all in battle. He liked the sound of that. Terry couldn't help but picture Saint Michael resembling Clint Eastwood. *Now we're talking.* Preacher boy stated the prayer over and over as he doused every inch of Nathan with the incense and then holy water. After repeating the ritual on Terry, Dave handed both men a vial of holy water and a prayer card.

"I don't know what's going to happen in there, but if you feel as though you are being attacked, state the Lord's prayer aloud and spray holy water around you. Doing so should be enough to protect you. If you still feel as though you are under attack, clasp the hand or arm of your friend and continue to pray. The show of unity will let whatever we're dealing with know that we come as a combined force. If we are successful in calling the entity out, do not, under any circumstance, engage the spirit. Leave that to me. Don't give in, and don't show fear. Get angry. Fight for God's love to shine through the evil."

Taken aback by the preacher boy's transformation, it was like a miracle had occurred right in front of Terry's eyes. No longer was he looking at a young man. They were in the presence of a warrior. His artist's mind momentarily wandered, and visions of how he'd paint the person standing in front of him flitted across his mind's eye. Images of a backpack hiding a mighty sword came to mind leaving a smile on his face.

Quickly moving across the front lawn, Terry pictured the three of them as a badass assault team. They swooped through the front door with a precision that left little doubt as to why they were there. When nothing happened, he glanced over at his friend. By

Nathan's vibe, it was evident the man was just as shocked by the anticlimactic entry as he was. While having no clue what to expect, absolutely nothing happening had certainly never been on their radar. Somehow, the quiet made this whole experience all the more frightening.

Moving stealthily from room to room, they sent incense smoke into every crevice and corner of the house. Holy water doused every inch. Holy oil anointed each doorway and window. By the time they'd reached the kitchen, Terry had started to relax. Was it possible that Shadow Man had run for the hills when he saw preacher boy coming? While that scenario didn't seem probable, it was certainly a possibility.

With the main house cleansed, they walked through the back French doors anointing and praying over every square inch of the outdoor kitchen. Terry's breath caught in his throat when the preacher boy suddenly pivoted and stood frozen in place while glaring at the studio.

Everyone's attention turned to the back of the yard. A deep rumbling thud sounded off as if someone played a bass drum over some wickedly loud speakers. A pulsating wave could be felt in the air as if the studio had a heart and they were feeling the percussive beat. Each fragile window pane started to rattle but held in place.

Visions of the neighborhood children Terry had seen at play raced through his mind. *Oh my God! What if they heard this racket and came to see what all the fuss was about?* He'd just have to cross that bridge when and if curiosity got the best of the kids. If the need arose, they'd somehow find a way to protect anyone that showed up.

Inside the studio, paint particles from the previous day's work started to float on the air obscuring any possible visibility within the glass walls.

With each second that passed, the vibration grew stronger. Terrifying thump after thump rattled the vintage studio windows. The glass rumbled and shimmied as if alive. Knowing the fight was just beginning, each man stood stoically and waited to see what would happen next.

They didn't have long to wait. Terry's skin started to crawl as each strike of the pulse brought with it a sensation of ice cold fingers pushing against flesh. The impression created an invisible, but all too real, barrier between them and the targeted studio. There was no question that Shadow Man had set restrictions on progressing into the yard. The men were not welcome to go any farther.

Testing the boundaries, Terry leaned forward. Unseen fingernails poked and prodded his chest insisting that he retreat. His entire lifetime, he'd always heard there would come a time when fight or flight would be his only available options. His rational mind was alert enough to understand that this moment was that time. Unfortunately, no one had ever mentioned a third—obviously less popular option—freezing in place. It wasn't heroics that held him still. It was terror beyond anything he'd ever experienced before. He just didn't have enough control over his mind or body to run like hell. So he stood there glued in place and tried not to panic.

Doing his best to figure out the next move, he focused on preacher boy and his stance. After the initial shock had worn off, Terry sensed a change in the man. As if a breeze had just broken the stagnant air, the preacher boy's robes billowed and it seemingly filled him with a fierce determination that Terry hadn't seen before. Dave stood a little straighter. Fear had gripped this young man and shown itself through his pursed and puckered lips. Terry recognized the moment an inner resolve seized the preacher boy. He could've sworn Dave had grown a foot taller right before his eyes. The young man's newly gained power served to release the invisible hands which had previously stalled their forward momentum. While unable to explain the transformation, it appeared to Terry that they were in the presence of a previously unknown superhero getting ready to kick some serious demon butt. *Hell yes!*

Without removing his gaze from the studio, preacher boy spoke to both Nathan and Terry. "Because of the dust particles floating around, we're going to need face masks and eye protection. Do you have those available?" His voice had taken on an otherworldly and oddly deeper timbre.

Nathan ran into the house and quickly returned to pass out goggles and paint masks. After donning the protective gear, Dave spoke with a fire in his voice. "Join arms and continue to pray, no matter what happens. Do not separate and do not back down. Do not run from this thing or you'll never be rid of it."

Once again the Archangel Michael's name crossed the preacher's lips, as he started to move slowly and with definite purpose toward the studio. With each step closer to the outbuilding, rivulets of sweat appeared and began to streak down the preacher boy's face.

By the time the three of them stood in front of the

studio entrance, Dave's clothing looked soaked through. Reaching out toward the doorknob, the man suddenly gagged and turned away. Jerking the mask from his face, he wretched what was left of his breakfast. Overcome, he fell to his knees but somehow had kept his demon arsenal—a cross, incense burner, Bible, and holy water—clutched in his hands. As instructed, Terry and Nathan continued to clasp each other's arms as they bent down to check on the preacher boy.

"Don't let go of each other," the man-boy urged through gasps.

Pulling himself up from the ground, preacher boy's shoulders flexed back as he forced a deep breath into his lungs. With a fierce resolve, Dave started to recite the Lord's Prayer through clenched teeth. It was the first time in Terry's life that he'd ever seen God used as a weapon. It was a powerful moment. "Please start reciting the Lord's Prayer. No matter what happens, do not stop and *do not* engage the demon."

Doing his best not to faint, a shiver of stark raving panic ran through Terry's body. Not only did preacher boy just say the dreaded *'d'* word, but he'd recited it with such venom his statement solidified just how much trouble they were facing. The danger they'd been in all along had just become real.

This time Dave took care as he reached for the doorknob. Just as he was about to touch it, his hand drew back. Raising a stiff arm above his head, it swung down in an arc spraying holy water in its wake. Terry's knees buckled when the holy water hit the door. The droplets sizzled and boiled away as if they had landed on a scalding hot stove-top. *Oh shit.*

Horrified, they watched through the vintage glass as the paint dust parted. A black mist whirled around the inside of the door. First, it took the shape of an animal. Not your everyday, run of the mill animal. If Terry were a betting man, he believed what he'd just seen was a devil dog or demon hound ready to pounce on anyone willing to cross the threshold. As soon as the misty specter fully formed, the inky black vapor became fluid again. Twisting and swirling, pieces of the phantom separated into a multitude of different entities. Terry almost laughed as he thought of a bubble machine until each of the black orbs turned into contorted, terrorized faces. Screams of agony simultaneously rang out creating a horrific opera.

Preacher boy stood strong in the face of pure evil and recited scripture meant to cast the demon out of the studio. Instead of the mist dissipating, each agonized face gathered into a single unit which formed into the demon Terry had met in his dreams. It stood on the other side of the glass, leering at preacher boy, sludge dripping from its fangs.

"In the name of Jesus Christ, I command you give me your name." Dave's voice had such an otherworldly quality to it that for a moment, Terry didn't believe he had actually spoken the words.

Shadow Man threw his head back and cackled. "Is that the best you've got?" In an instant, the thing lunged for the door and screeched, "Go away. You cannot enter here. This place is my sanctuary." The demon moved silently out of view, hiding within the swirling paint dust.

Preacher boy threw the door open. The stench of death met us. Standing his ground outside of the doorway, Dave didn't question but demanded, "I command you in the name of God to give me your name, demon. You have no sanctuary here. You can no longer hide. Tell me your name."

Yanking at Nathan's arm, Terry pulled his friend's big frame down to his level. "Why is he talking to it? Who cares what its name is?"

"Concentrate, Runt. I have a feeling this is important." Continuing to pray aloud, both Terry and Nathan watched with growing concern as Dave seemed unable to enter the studio. Even though the door was open, there was an invisible barrier keeping the holy man at bay. At that moment, young Dave refused to be denied entry. Backing up, he made the sign of the Trinity, threw his shoulder out and ran as fast as he could to gain access through the unseen blockade. For a moment, time seemed to stop. The holy man was suspended in air as if he was being held off the ground by an invisible shield. When the force field lost its power and the preacher gained entry, Terry was sure it was the man's untainted devotion that finally broke the barrier.

Showing more courage than Terry had ever seen, preacher boy moved quickly within the studio. Holy water flew into all corners of the room. Incense parted the paint dust like it was a knife running through soft butter. The air inside was stagnant and heavy enough to crush the breath from their lungs. Gasping for air, Terry and Nathan continued to wield the Lord's Prayer as if it were a sword. The words slashed through the thickness parting the air as if the spoken word had the power to seek out and destroy the demon.

"In the name of all that is holy, I demand you leave

this place and crawl back into the pit of hell. You are not welcome here and must leave this minute."

Unsure whether the noise was just in his head or if he actually heard it, a high pitched scream wailed through Terry's brain. Wincing, he did his best to cover his ears and still hold onto his friend. The only thing keeping him sane was Nathan, so Terry locked onto his friend's arm with the force of a hungry shark.

"Spray your holy water on every window. Keep saying the prayer. The demon is getting weak." Dave's orders rang through but sounded muffled as if he were a football field away instead of in such close quarters.

Preacher boy shuffled to the mirror and doused it with holy water and then incense. A gale force wind hotter than a blow torch picked up and tried to blow the men free of the building.

Terry's attention turned to the mirror, now under assault by the preacher. Images appeared of a man sitting on the floor doing terrible things to a cat in the name of the dark one. Then the same man appeared in front of an easel, erratically drawing as if possessed. Suddenly, the man faced the mirror and shed his skin as if it were a Halloween costume instead of flesh and blood. The monster Terry had become so familiar with over the last few days revealed itself.

The demon charged the mirror but couldn't pass through. The dark one clawed and screamed as it tried to find any means of escape. Terry and Nathan quickly scooted across the room and along with preacher boy, shot sprays of holy water onto the mirror front. The temperature in the studio started to fall as the wind decreased. Dave anointed the mirror with holy oil, and everything came to a stop. The silence was deafening.

Not daring to move, they stood there waiting for something to happen. The only remaining reflections were those of the three living men.

Terry bit down on his lip until he drew blood. Finally, the feeling was starting to come back into his body. Swiping his arm over his mouth, he did his best to swallow. Terror had dried up his spit. Using the blood to moisten his mouth, he finally choked out, "Is it over? Is that thing gone?"

Preacher boy continued to stare. Before saying a word, he collapsed on the floor. Nathan and Terry picked him up and carried him outside.

It took ten minutes before the man could speak. "Well, that was scary."

Nervous laughter bubbled up from Terry's chest. That wasn't exactly what he was hoping to hear. "Is that thing gone? Is it safe now?"

Dave looked through the studio glass walls and sighed. "It's gone for now. It'll take some time before we know if it's gone for good."

"I don't understand. What does that mean?"

"To be sure a demon leaves, you must weaken it enough to give you its name. Even though I felt that thing grow weaker, it never gave its name. Whatever that thing was, it was strong. Never in my life have I faced anything so evil. The room feels as though the demon left, but who knows? If we just weakened it, that's going to be one pissed off entity when it returns. I'm afraid that only time will tell."

"How long will we have to wait to know for sure?"

"There's no way to know. I'm going to leave my incense with you and some holy water and oil. Every day, I want you to walk through your house and studio and do a spiritual cleansing using these items. State the Lord's prayer in every room and then declare that this is your home and nothing negative is allowed to stay. If something happens, call me. I'll come running. That's the best we can do for now."

Chapter Sixteen

Just to be on the safe side, both Nathan and Terry decided it would be wise—for a while at least—to enter the studio in pairs. Terry waved the incense and stated the Lord's Prayer as Nathan followed behind with the holy water. Once done, they stood in the middle of the room to survey their handiwork. Standing back to back, each man opened themselves up to the vibe of the space. Following Preacher Dave's advice, they'd been vigilant and conducted this now daily ritual for the last three mornings. So far, so good. Each rise of the sun brought a deeper calm to their surroundings.

The previous few days had been blissfully quiet. There'd been no unexplained mood swings. No fugue states where chunks of time went missing. No baffling puddles of water. No doors opening and closing on their own. And not even an inkling of a bad dream.

Even though the landline had been hooked up, the phone still currently resided in the closet, but it too had remained silent. After the scare the antique had given both of them, neither man was interested in hearing that ring for a while, even if it proved to be an actual live caller on the other end. Truth be told, Terry had no idea how long it would take him to get comfortable with that sound. *Will the ring tone always remind me of the boogie man?* He hoped not. He would just have to trust in the fact that time healed all. Once Terry's comfort level rose a bit more, all that had to be done for the phone to be activated was to plug it into the phone jack.

While Terry maintained a positive attitude and focused on his troubles being far behind him, Nathan and Dave remained cautiously optimistic. Preacher boy had called each day to get an update. Since the demon had been banished, the previous difficulties with their phones had ceased.

Nathan, being the worry wart he was, still insisted on having an escape plan in the event Shadow Man decided to make another appearance. While the thought rankled Terry, deep down he understood the concern and gave in to Nathan's safety requests. So the men made sure they carried their wallets and car keys with them at all times. They each had a duffle bag with a change of clothes in their vehicle in case a fast getaway was needed. In the end, Terry was a little more relaxed knowing they didn't have to stop for anything if a run for the cars proved necessary.

Even with all the setbacks, the studio's remodeling schedule had miraculously remained intact. The electrician had come and gone completing the new lighting. The space was now expertly illuminated and would allow Terry to work in his studio around the clock once the floor had been sealed and finished with epoxy. The plumber had taken care of the small bathroom, and Terry had painted the tiny restroom a bright white to match the rest of the walls. The miniature one-person shower had been scrubbed three times. He'd even taken the time to pick up some glass paint and created a mural on the small glass door to give the room more character. Those tasks combined with the new commode and pedestal sink left the small washroom gleaming and sparkling. No more gloom or any sign of an ominous presence remained. Anyone entering would think it just an insignificant bathroom. But the space had been successfully reclaimed by the living. Leaving Terry with a sense of much-needed peace where previously he had none.

Besides having the air conditioning installed and taking care of the floor, all that was left to do was to cart in his work tools and supplies and arrange them in the best possible position. He could barely contain his excitement because the light at the end of the tunnel had finally crept close enough to see. While Terry had been careful never to voice his concerns aloud, he readily admitted to himself that there was a time he didn't know if it would ever be safe to move in.

"What's on tap for today?"

Terry pulled his phone out and checked the calendar. "The air conditioning guys are due here any time now." Clicking his tongue, he kicked the floor with his sneaker. "I thought that once they finished, we could finally rip this nasty carpet up and see what kind of shape the floor is in. Hopefully, the foundation is level, and we won't need to rent a concrete sander. Maybe we can start the sealing process this afternoon. From what I gathered with my research, doing the floor shouldn't be difficult, but it will need to be done in stages and will end up being pretty time-consuming. Since Rainy's coming into town today, I'd like to quit a little early, so we're not late for dinner. We're supposed to be at her place by six."

"That sounds like a plan. Speaking of Rainy, I think I'm going to bow out tonight. I'm not anxious to be a third wheel."

Terry shot a quick glance at Nathan and looked away. Nervous energy had him shifting his weight from foot to foot. "She wants you to come with me. You can't beg out now. It would be rude."

Nathan remained quiet until Terry peered at him again. The bastard touted that all knowing smile only a best friend brandishes when he knows the truth of the matter. He would never consider going with the flow and missing the opportunity to have a little fun at Terry's expense. "You're scared to be alone with her."

Shit. It's like he's a mind reader. "No, I'm not! I just don't want to disappoint her. She's expecting both of us. You *have* to come with me. You can leave after supper."

"Don't bullshit me. You're scared."

Feeling foolish, Terry's chin dropped to his chest. All pretense aside, maybe Nathan had some good advice to offer. He'd never steered him wrong in the past. "What if she sees me again and decides she's made a terrible mistake? What if I can't keep the conversation going and she realizes that I'm nothing more than a boring jerk that she has nothing in common with?" Trying to relieve the pain these thoughts caused, Terry massaged the space above his heart with the palm of his hand.

"I can't stop thinking about her. She's become so important to me. I've built this whole relationship up in my mind. What if Rainy decides she doesn't like me?" Raising pleading eyes to Nathan, he begged, "You *have* to come and keep the conversation going if it lags. You *have* to stop me if I say something stupid or act like a damn fool. Maybe, if the opportunity arises, you could come up with a conversation or story that makes me look good."

"Is that so? And what exactly would you like me to say to make you look good?" Nathan playfully lunged forward and shoved Terry's shoulder. "Wait! I've got it. I can tell her about the time you saved those baby birds."

Terry perked up. "Yeah. That's a good story. You can tell her how I picked up the nest and braved the angry mother bird to put it safely back in the tree. Women love stories like that."

"Should I leave out the part where you climbed the tree and knocked the nest down in the first place?"

"Jeez, Nathan, way to focus on the negative. Come on. Let's go and wait in the house for the air conditioning people to get here. We'll come up with some good stories while we're waiting."

****

Blessedly cold air blasted through the newly cut air conditioning vents. This was a huge moment and another small victory. Any further hard labor in the studio would be done in relative comfort. *Yep. Things are definitely looking up.*

Terry strolled through the room with a deep sense of accomplishment. They'd been through a lot this week, but the results were undeniable. The all important workspace should be ready to set up by the weekend. Barely able to keep the skip out of his step, giddiness from the opportunity to create his art in this space took hold. It was as if the small outbuilding were planned and built so many years ago with him in mind. With the diamond shaped antique paned glass windows, the building itself was a work of fine art. In his mind's eye, he could visualize the artisans honing their craft to create this masterpiece. To honor those master craftsmen, Terry would create beautiful pieces of art here to keep the spirit of their work alive.

"You're going to have one hell of an electric bill in the summer months. Other than that, this space is perfect for you. I've always imagined you working your magic in a place like this. I can't wait to see the first canvas you create here."

Terry couldn't help but beam at his ever supportive friend. Taking in his surroundings, he rushed across the room while sweeping his arms in a large arc. "I'm going to put my easel here. And right here, my supply table." Rushing to the only solid wall, he stopped and lovingly brushed the stark white surface. "On either side of the mirror, there's enough space to hang my newly completed canvases to make sure they're perfect before I ship them off to the art dealer.

"Come on. Let's get this carpet out of here and see what kind of floor we have to work with."

Each man pried at the carpet's edge until they had a good hold to start ripping the musty covering up. Once loose, they rolled the carpet to carry it outside. Nathan picked his end up with no problem, but Terry couldn't budge his side. Grunting, he put his back into it but still had no luck lifting the heavy floor covering.

Sweat dripped from Nathan's brow as he complained, "Dammit. Just push your end if you can't pick it up. I can't hold this weight much longer." Terry's shoes dug into the now exposed carpet pad as he threw all his weight into shoving the heavy roll outside.

With the chore completed, both men collapsed. Terry, shaky from the exertion, sprawled on the ground and moaned. "I'm using muscles I didn't know I had."

Nathan erupted into laughter. "Runt, I hate to break it to you, but the reason you didn't know you had those muscles is because you *don't* have them. You've really got to get to the gym with me. You're a pathetic male specimen."

Unaffected by Nathan's harsh criticism and still unable to move, Terry decided lying limp was the best course of action and slammed his eyes shut. "I think I'm going to take a nap right here."

He was forced to move a few inches when the toe of Nathan's shoe gently kicked at his hip. "Come on. Get up. That carpet pad isn't going to unstick itself. If we have any luck at all, maybe the glue disintegrated over time, and the pad will come up as easy as the carpet did."

Terry grimaced up at his friend. Still splayed out on the lawn, he stuttered, "Luck? Really? With everything that's happened, the only luck we've had so far is bad." He allowed a slow growing grin to cross his lips. "I have an idea. I'll stay here and think positive thoughts while you go in and pry the pad off the floor."

Nathan moved so quickly Terry didn't have time to protest. In an instant, his limp body had been picked up and set on his feet. "I'm going to let go, so you better lock your knees if you don't want to fall."

Terry wasn't sure if his shaky legs could hold him up or not but was pleasantly surprised when he didn't slide back down to the ground when Nathan stepped away.

"Come on, Runt. Stop messing around. Let's get this done so we can go to the store and get what we need to start sealing the floor."

Even with the air conditioning blowing at full blast, the exertion required to remove the stubborn glue and pad from the floor left both men covered in sweat. Every muscle in Terry's body burned from the hard work. Being an artist, the majority of his time was spent seated on a stool in front of a canvas. Never before had so much physicality been demanded from his artist frame. He cursed himself for it now. *Maybe I should take Nathan up on his gym offer.*

The kinks in his muscles had kinks. Consoling himself that each scraping motion meant he was one step closer to the end of the physical labor, Terry concentrated on the annoying grinding sound of each pass over the concrete. By doing so, he hoped to momentarily forget about the effect the constant motion was having on his aching body. Diving back in, he'd just started to see some forward progress when Nathan cursed under his breath.

"What?"

"I don't think it's going to be as easy to seal the concrete as we originally thought. We're probably going to have to paint it first. It looks like someone spilled something on the floor. The pad is ground in and stuck to whatever this gunk is. Come over here and help me get this section up so we can see how bad it is."

Dragging himself to the center of the room, Terry grunted as he bore down on the floor scraper to help uncover the damaged surface. Once they were confident they had exposed the entire area, both men turned to see how bad it was.

It took a moment for the image which had been scrawled on the floor to settle into Terry's brain. But once his mind locked on the symbol and identified it, a paralyzing fear swept through his body. Rendered speechless his jaw went slack. A distressed whimper passed through his lips. They'd just stumbled into the demon's web and unwittingly uncovered a clear path for re-entry into Terry's home.

The foundation beneath their feet started to vibrate. As if the old concrete sub floor had become liquid, the ground pitched and shook—leaving the men off balance. Terry's startled mind couldn't seem to move past the terror and keep up. Trying like hell to make sense of what he was experiencing, the motion reminded him of videos he'd seen of earthquakes as the ground rolled like waves. *This is impossible.*

Movement to his left jarred him back to reality. Nathan's big body slammed to the ground. He came to rest within a circle directly on top of a pentagram which, at some point in time, had been permanently affixed to the studio floor with blood red paint. At least Terry hoped it was paint. Completely out of character for Nathan, his best friend emitted a frightened squeal. The sound so aberrant, Terry would have thought it a joke except for the fact the man was wildly flailing and doing his best to scurry on hands and knees to any place beyond the symbol.

Trying to stay on his feet, Terry grabbed his friend and tugged with all his weight. All movement in the studio's foundation instantly ceased. While the ground beneath his feet had become still, his body continued to lurch to and fro as he wrestled with the abrupt lack of motion. It took a formidable effort to stay upright.

The only noise to be heard was each man's staggered breathing.

Time stood still as he waited for whatever would

come next. As the realization hit home that they were experiencing the calm before the storm, tremors born from terror poked and pinched every nerve ending in his body. Trying to get an idea of where the next brutal attack would come from, Terry tuned into his senses. The air was thick and oppressive. Breathing became difficult. Dire hopelessness washed over him. All he could do was wait, and that pissed him off. Always being on the defensive was tiring and by God, he'd do something about it.

As if Shadow Man could sense a change in Terry's demeanor, a fluid movement within the mirror became apparent and shifted both men's focus. Their reflections disappeared. Darkness manifested and festered behind the glass surface—*no*—darkness was too simple a term for what lay within the mirror. It was suffocating and despairing, a place where all light died, and only evil resided. Wisps of a mist started to form and circle spiraling deep within the mirror's depths as if it had purpose. Suddenly, the veil between hell and earth was just a breadth away.

Enthralled, Terry couldn't look away. *The demon. Oh shit!* Something within his mind came alive and snapped him out of the stupor. With speed he didn't realize he possessed, Terry grabbed Nathan's arm and lifted him to his feet.

The wall on either side of the mirror came alive. No longer a solid mass, it rippled as if constructed with a thin fabric instead of drywall. Disembodied fists pushed against the barrier trying to break free. The wall, now pliable, revealed knuckles as they swiped and scraped downward trying to break through. A deep rumbling pulsated as if the building were readying itself to attack. The threatening reverberation emulated the loud clackety-clack of a freight train at full speed. Each vibration grew stronger and more intense. *Surely the neighbors will hear the commotion and come to our rescue.*

Before the men could make their escape, the mirror flashed and crackled. It bowed and stretched outward. Knowing they should run for their lives but mesmerized by what they were seeing, all the men could do was gape in horror. Having their full attention, Shadow Man ran from the depths of the mirror toward them at breakneck speed. At the last moment, Terry and Nathan scrambled for the door. Before they could exit, the mirror exploded into thousands of pieces spraying shards of glass into the tiny room.

Terry pushed Nathan through the door and slammed it behind them. The tactic was useless at keeping Shadow Man at bay. The demon caught Terry by the neck and lifted him off the ground. Fear surged through his body while he felt his eyes bulged out from the constricting hold. Kicking furiously, he punched out with his fists. The feverish attempt to escape the grasp of the entity was useless. Stars appeared in his field of vision, and he knew the demon would kill him. Somewhere in the back of his head, Preacher Dave's voice could be heard wielding a prayer to the Archangel Michael. With his body too weak to fight any longer, Terry focused his mind and spirit on each word of the powerful entreaty. To his dismay, the prayer had no immediate effect.

From a distance, Nathan's voice could be faintly heard screaming obscenities at the beast that held his life in its hands. No longer feeling the pain or panic,

Terry let go and allowed his mind to wander and float on the breeze as a dying leaf might drift on a current of air. The weightlessness sucked him in. Something internal made him aware that nothing could harm him in this state. A state that encouraged him to linger and explore this new experience for as long as possible.

The gentle breeze that carried him off grew with furious intensity until it was a full blown gale. The force tugged at his legs and yanked him out of the peace. A sharp stabbing pain in his knee snapped him out of the dreamlike state. Nathan had a hold of his legs, firmly yanking him back to the ground. His friend had effectively released him from the Shadow Man's grasp, and his subsequent escape into what Terry now realized was death.

The entity turned on Nathan. Terry's mind barely registered the brutal attack. Suffering multiple hits like that would surely have killed a smaller man. Nathan flew backward and landed in a heap near the pool.

Dazed and clutching his throat, it took several tries before Terry could get to his feet. His knee, dislocated from Nathan's attempt to free him, screamed with pain. Still seeing stars and having difficulty breathing, he was no match for the demon. Instead of rushing Shadow Man, Terry taunted the entity with every foul name that came to mind. It worked.

The demon turned his attention back to Terry and menacingly slithered to his side. As if playing with a fly, the bastard increased the fear level by circling him—once, twice, three times. Attempting to shrink away, the entity dug sharp claws into Terry's arm and held him in place.

"Get out. I will kill you if you come back." With

those parting words, Shadow Man disappeared back into his lair.

The demon's fierce attack came to an abrupt halt.

The good guys would live to see another day.

Terry wobbled to his friend and helped him up. Ready to get the hell out without any further disturbance, they both staggered for the side gate instead of going through the main house. There was no telling what would happen if they entered the home, so they bypassed it. Without a glance back, they helped each other to their vehicles. Tires squealed, and rubber was laid as they made their escape to the nearest emergency room.

Not wanting to involve the police, Terry wracked his brain for a believable whopper to explain their numerous injuries. Tired and scared, his brain couldn't focus. Somehow, they'd just have to wing it.

Chapter Seventeen

Butterflies had swooped and swarmed in Rainy's belly all day. Time seemed to meander by at a snail's pace. It felt more like an eternity instead of a scant few days since she'd last been in Terry's embrace. The opportunity for them to spend some quality time together had finally arrived. Tonight's date was too important to leave anything up to chance. Every detail had been second guessed. It was nerve-racking. Since the moment he'd agreed to come to her place in Phoenix for dinner, she'd fussed over every element of the evening—what to wear, what to serve, how to make her second, less used residence homier. Knowing full well that Terry had the keen eye of an artist motivated her to move trinkets from one shelf to another and back again.

With Terry's obvious reservations about Rainy's religion, the first impression of her personal space became more important than ever. The only way they'd get past that particular roadblock was to make him as comfortable as possible in her surroundings. Only then would he relax enough to understand that she was no different than any other clergy out there. She didn't have ghosts lurking in her closets or Fae Brownies mopping the floors.

Coming from a Christian background herself helped in recognizing the stereotypical fears Terry may have about anything Pagan. That being the case, every decision grew in importance. The pressure was overwhelming. It was never Rainy's intention to convert Terry, but she did want him at ease. So much so that she currently sat in front of three scented candles and stared at the giant pillars. The hope that perhaps the wax possessed an ability to shed some light on which fragrance would best serve to relax and soothe Terry's apprehensions hadn't materialized.

Slapping her hands on her legs, Rainy scolded herself, "This is ridiculous! I have to get a hold of myself." Grabbing one of the large three-wick candles, she situated it on the dining room hutch atop one of her grandmother's handmade doilies. Doing so would provide a soft, serene glow while they ate. Striking a match, she took a moment while igniting each wick to envision her own unique inner light brightly shining. "There. Everyone loves vanilla. The scent is warm and inviting. Now stop over thinking everything so damn much." *If only.*

Turning her attention to the kitchen, Rainy sighed. Fretting over the discouraging inability to compete with Terry's cooking skills, the last few hours had been fraught with devising what she hoped would be the perfect menu. Determined to knock his socks off, she'd buckled down and came up with a plan. Her special enchiladas made with sinfully scrumptious handmade tortillas were ready and waiting to pop into the oven. Only somewhat comforted by the fact that everybody raved about her Mexican food, Rainy had concocted a strategy for guaranteed success. To ensure her efforts at cooking dinner were a hit, she'd start the evening off with some deliciously sweet and sour margaritas. Not above plying Terry and Nathan with alcohol to distort their palates, the high tequila content was deceptive. If nothing else, the powerful drink would deaden taste buds.

The closer the time got to six, the more Rainy fidgeted. Over the last week, there wasn't an hour that went by in which her mind hadn't wandered to Terry. Their last kiss had left her in a perpetual state of longing and served to keep her awake many a night. When sleep did come, she'd dreamt of being in his arms sated and safe. If he only knew how foreign those feelings and urges were for her. Rainy was mystified over the speed with which Terry had burrowed his way so deeply into her consciousness. She could think of little else. If her lifestyle had taught her anything, it was to accept life's gifts as they were offered.

Delightful tingles rippled through Rainy when a light rap sounded on the door. Feeling like a school girl again, she couldn't help but bob up and down on her toes. Taking an extra moment to calm herself, she said a little prayer. "Mother Goddess, please help me keep my composure. I know that Terry's path has converged with mine for a reason. I vow to remain open to all possibilities. Blessed be."

Reaching for the doorknob, Rainy did her best to subdue the huge grin. The smirk was fixed on her face when she thought of the man standing on the other side of the door. Trying for an expression of somewhere between *you-haven't-been-on-my-mind-at-all* and *take-me-to-bed-right-this-minute*, she scolded herself. "Oh, to hell with it."

All pretenses fell once the door opened. Terry looked sheepish and stood with the aid of crutches.

Angry red marks smudged his beautiful neck. Rendered speechless, Rainy turned her attention to Nathan. Terry's friend brandished a lopsided grin, and he wore a pair of sunglasses that did nothing to hide his bruised and swollen face.

Competing forces of emotion took over. Anger that someone had hurt her man fought with her nurturing side. The resulting indecision left Rainy confused. As if rooted on the spot, all she could manage to do was stand there like a complete idiot. Not having a clue what to say, she finally gathered herself enough to usher the men inside and guide them to the couch.

Sitting beside Terry, Rainy clutched his hand. Waiting for an explanation, she looked from Terry to Nathan and back to Terry again. The uncomfortable silence went on for minutes. They looked like two little boys who were caught red-handed stealing cookies. When no details were forthcoming, she willed her voice to be calm.

"Who did this to you?" Considering her fury—which had manifested at a blistering pace—over someone beating two gentle souls, Rainy was proud to have maintained an even pitch. Inside, she was boiling mad and wanted to do a little ass kicking herself.

Encouraging an explanation, Rainy locked eyes with Terry first. *Nothing.* The man offered no answer. Her gaze turned to Nathan. Neither man was willing to speak. She waited for Nathan's aura to envelope her and provide answers without the benefit of words. But the man had built a wall around himself, completely closing his emotions down. *Why? What are they trying to hide?*

"I suppose there's a simple reason the two of you

aren't telling me what happened. Since no one is speaking, then please, at least tell me you're all right."

Terry tightened his hold on her hand and kissed her cheek. "We're okay. It was just a little fight." Frustrated that the man was psychically unreadable, Rainy casually leaned back and called upon her other more mundane senses to provide answers. There was something off in the tone of his voice. For the first time in her life, she wished she could probe someone without their knowledge. Even if that were an option, it wouldn't be possible with Terry. And with Nathan's wall being so strong, she'd just have to wait for one of them to slip up and spill the beans.

Trying to draw a little peace of mind from Terry's touch, she squeezed his hand. "First things first. If you'd let me, I'd like to help with the pain." Rainy waited for both men to acknowledge their agreement before beginning the healing process.

For better access to his wounds, she situated herself on the coffee table across from Terry. "I will expect some answers once the healing is complete."

Without waiting for a reply, Rainy laid her hands on Terry's brace covered knee. In an instant, a negative image resembling an x-ray of the injured limb popped into her mind. Feeling heat build in her core, she envisioned the potent energy moving steadily through her body. Once the healing force ramped up, it traveled through her hands directly into his knee. The energy, which materialized in her mind as a luminous white light, pooled in that area, circling and penetrating through bone and tissue rejuvenating everything in its path. Feeling the searing pain in her own body, she had no doubt the healing was working. *That's something at least.* Envisioning the caustic pain moving down her leg and out the bottom of her foot, Rainy sent it deep into the earth where it could harm no one else. When the healing treatment on his knee concluded, she focused her attention on his throat.

Keeping her touch light, Rainy internally fought the irrepressible urge to lash out at whoever was responsible for hurting this sweet man. Immediately recognizing that the damage to Terry's throat was far more critical than his leg, a healing spell gently crossed her lips. "Healing desire sent into this night, deliver the blessings to one so bright. Set free into this night the restorative white light, and cocoon my love in your blessed delight. Mother Goddess, I trust in your aid. With love and light. So mote it be."

Feeling the power of the chant running through her veins, she transferred his pain into herself. Rainy felt the exact spot each fingertip had dug into Terry's throat and the force behind the grip. Stars appeared in her field of vision. Images of Terry's death at the hands of someone she couldn't identify brought her back to the here and now. Her throat burned, and the muscles felt badly bruised. Her eyes fluttered open. Terry's broad smile was the first thing she saw.

Still clinging to his hand, she brushed his palm against her cheek.

"Am I your love?"

Feeling the heat of embarrassment bloom on her face, she tried to remember what she'd chanted in the spell. "What?"

Kissing the top of her head, he whispered, "When you were chanting, you called me *your love.* Am I?"

Since every situation was different, especially with

healing, the years had taught her to listen to a higher power for casting healing spells instead of using standard phrases. For the life of her, she couldn't remember what she'd said. *Well, this is embarrassing.*

"U-m-m, I need to work on Nathan now." To show just how serious she was, Rainy placed her hand over Terry's heart. "When I'm finished, you *will* give me answers." Leaving no option for anything but agreement, Rainy slid behind the couch and removed the sunglasses that did nothing to hide Nathan's deep, puffy contusions.

Upon first viewing Nathan's injuries, they appeared far more impressive than Terry's. But Rainy felt no hint of impending doom as she touched his face. Submitting to the trance like state needed for healing, she found that Nathan's wounds involved tissue and only took a fraction of the time to heal that Terry's injuries had taken. When the pain subsided, Nathan audibly sighed.

Leaning his head back, Nathan offered Rainy a warm smile. She felt a deep sense of pleasure because the remaining bruises were much lighter in color. *Yes. These wounds were not nearly as dangerous as Terry's.*

Gathering her wits, she was bound and determined to get to the bottom of what happened. She placed a light kiss on top of Nathan's head. "I'm glad you're feeling better."

Her attention switched to Terry who'd moved across the room without his crutches and stood in front of the fireplace mantle. His gaze locked on a pentagram affixed to the wall that the coven had made when she became their High Priestess. It was one of her prized possessions. As if entranced, he stood in place

219

motionless. Still partially in an altered state from participating in the healing work, Rainey recognized small changes in the atmosphere surrounding Terry. An alteration in his aura was her first indication that there was a problem. The energy surrounding him turned a dark shade of red and tightened close to his physical form. The aura shimmered and started to ripple as his body began to tremble. *With what? Anger? No, it's fear.* She didn't have to be psychic to see that his response to her precious gift was a negative one.

Knowing beyond a shadow of a doubt that this moment was important to their future relationship, Rainy spoke quietly. "Terry, is something wrong?"

Before she could react, he reached up and tore the pentagram from the wall. Small polished stones broke away from the pentacle and flew through the air. He snapped the twigs which had been carefully collected and tooled into the symbol of her religion. Precious stones representing each element were severed from the wood and thrown across the room.

As if he'd struck her, Rainy fell to her knees and clutched her stomach. Terry's rage was tangible as it connected from across the room and took hold, suffocating her in its cruel embrace. Weakened from the healing, she didn't have the strength needed to conceal her anguish. Tears fell unimpeded, and she struggled to catch her breath. Bewildered by the malicious actions of someone she cared so deeply for, Rainy began to gather the precious stones within her reach. Glancing up at Terry's hateful expression made her want to shrivel up and disappear.

"*Why?* I don't understand. Why would you do this?"

"*Why?* If I weren't so pissed, *that* would be funny."

To keep him from causing any further damage, Nathan converged on Terry. One arm clutched his body in a tight grip, and the other clamped over his mouth.

Grunting and snorting through the struggle like a caged animal, Terry kicked out trying to free himself. Nathan screamed and pulled his hand away. "Ouch! You fucking bit me!"

"It was you, wasn't it? I didn't have any problems until I met you. My life was finally going in the direction that I wanted. I was happy. And you stepped in and took it all away. *Why?* Why did you send that monster to me?" Rainy felt the full force of the venomous attack. Each hateful word connected with her body and broke her heart.

Continuing to fight Nathan's tight hold, Terry redirected the poison. "Let me go dammit. I can't stay here another minute."

"I will *not* let you go, you stupid shit." Nathan lifted Terry so his legs were no longer on the ground and forcefully shook him. "You're not going anywhere. I'm putting you on that couch. If I have to, I'll sit on you. You're going to listen to what Rainy has to say. And if I'm right, which I always am, you're going to have to find a way to apologize. That is, of course, if she doesn't kick your sorry ass out right this minute."

True to his word, Nathan carried Terry to the couch. His body crumpled as it hit the sofa. An angry growl vibrated deep within his chest. She didn't know if the frightening sound was directed at her or Nathan. Her attention turned back to the remnants of the destroyed pentagram.

"Rainy?" Nathan's voice was little more than a

whisper and full of torment. "I'm so very sorry. There's something that I need to tell you. It will help you understand why this idiot flew off the handle. Please, come sit down and let me talk to you."

Feeling stripped bare, Rainy stood on shaky legs. She and her religion had been attacked before, but never from someone who'd stolen her heart. Sitting on the chair facing the men, she wiped her eyes and tried to stifle the pangs of grief. Unable to look either man in the eye, she sat silently with her head bowed.

Nathan wrestled with Terry and finally gave him an ultimatum. "Don't you dare move. I'm going to try to fix this. If one muscle on your body so much as twitches, I'm going to lay you out flat."

Pulling a wrinkled and aged piece of paper from his back pocket, one that looked to have been previously crumpled and discarded, Nathan reluctantly handed it to Rainy. As soon as her eyes landed on the paper, a jolt of dread erupted within her. Lifting her gaze, she locked eyes with Nathan.

"I didn't want to show you this, but something told me to bring it tonight. I think you need to see this so you understand why this imbecile reacted the way he did." Being the good man he was, Nathan set the paper down on the table in front of Rainy. He was giving her the option to either kick their butts out or get to the root of the problem.

Terry had suddenly become quiet. The only thing she heard was his heavy breathing, but the unmistakable heat of his stare bored into her. Tentatively, Rainy reached out and touched the paper with her fingertips. A burning sensation ran through her veins, and she quickly retracted her arm shaking her hand in the process. Both men remained silent.

Panic set in as dread crashed through Rainy's senses. Closing her eyes, she requested protection for all in the room. A flaming pentagram burned brightly in her mind's eye. Only then did she find enough courage to grasp the paper and unfold it.

The image shocked her. Her gaze burned into Terry looking for any sign that he had been the one to pen this atrocity. *No. This evil is not in him.* Someone or something wanted to scare him. Rainy carefully set the paper, image side up, on the table between them.

"The time has come to tell me what's going on."

Terry's lips locked and pursed together. He sank farther into the couch as if trying to gain distance from her. Nathan leaned forward and prepared to relay the facts.

Disappointment had her inwardly sighing. The man who had occupied her every thought would not be the one to reveal the events. Refusing to show how deeply Terry's actions affected her, Rainy drew on inner strength and straightened her back. *So be it.*

"The monster in the picture has been haunting Terry's home since we started the move. That thing, whatever it is, is responsible for everything from changing his personality, to doing its level best to divide us. Hell, that thing had Terry by the throat and almost killed him today."

It's no wonder he wigged out so bad. With clarity now shed on Terry's actions, she knew it would be useless to try and engage him. Fear was a powerful weapon, and something or someone had used it flawlessly against Terry. Terror had taken root deep within the man, she couldn't help but love, and currently controlled him. She'd have to address his best friend instead. Rainy stared deeply into Nathan's eyes. "I'm assuming, by Terry's reaction, that you found a pentagram somewhere on the property." Nathan conceded with a grave nod.

"Tell me, where was it, and what direction was the pentagram pointing?"

Unable to control himself any longer, Terry angrily retorted, "What the fuck does *that* have to do with anything? Who the hell cares what direction it's pointing? I want to know why you have the same symbol in your home that's been the cause of all my problems since I moved in."

"Terry!" Nathan's sharp voice abruptly put a stop to his angry rant.

"Thank you, Nathan, but Terry has a right to know about the pentagram. It's misinformation that fuels his anger. Before we go any farther, I'd like to explain the symbol so he has a better understanding of what's happening."

Continuing his hold on Terry, Nathan relaxed and sat back.

"Terry, I'm assuming you're a Christian. Is that correct?"

Doing everything in his power to close himself off Terry folded his arms tightly against his chest. No longer speaking, his only answer was a single hard bob of the head.

"A symbol of your religion is a cross, correct?"

This time the nod was a little less angry.

"A pentagram is a symbol of the Wiccan religion. It's also known as a pentacle. Let me ask you this—are you aware that people practicing black magic or even

Satanism use your Christian cross in their ceremony? They invert it. An upside down cross is a powerful tool in their religious rites. Does that mean that all crosses are evil?" Her hand waved the notion off. "Of course not. Only when in the wrong hands can it be a symbol of darkness and wickedness. The same holds true for a pentagram."

The symbol that offered her so much peace flashed in her mind. Jumping up, Rainy ran across the room to retrieve a necklace. Placing the jewelry between them, she leaned forward. "Please, take a look at this. I'm going to start with the very basics so you can understand what this symbol means to me. There are five points. Each one symbolizes the five essentials for life's sustenance—fire, water, air, earth, and spirit. The circle surrounding the star represents the Universe.

"This is going to be hard to understand, but contrary to popular myth, whether inverted or not, the pentagram does not represent good versus evil. In my religion, the pentagram points up when we perform rituals, and reflects working with the higher power. The symbol also offers protection as does the cross for Christians. When we use the pentagram inverted, it is to ground our energy or life force which had been elevated through ritual. It helps level our body and spirit.

"When a Satanist or even a layperson playing around calls on the dark arts using our symbol, the pentagram will always be inverted just as your cross is inverted. In those instances, the pentacle is being used to bring and fulfill the baser and materialistic whims of the castor. Those people are only concerned with themselves. We call this black magic, and it is extremely harmful. Generally speaking, the castor is soliciting dark influences—what you'd call the devil, a demon, or even a trickster—for something materialistic such as fame or fortune. Sometimes, it's worse. Maybe they want to hurt or influence another person. There are as many reasons why people do this as there are stars in the sky. If you see a pentagram permanently drawn on any surface such as a floor or wall and it is pointing South or down, then it has been used in conjunction with black magic. Doing so, even if by a layperson, can and most likely will cause many problems for the environment where the ritual took place. You can think of this phenomenon as a sort of payment to a dark lord. The evil is stamped on the surroundings and will linger to cause as much damage as possible.

"As for the Wiccan religion, we hold ourselves responsible for everything we do. There is no higher deity to forgive us or blame for our actions. We believe all souls are connected. If we cause harm to anyone or anything, that harm will come back to us threefold. True practitioners of the Wiccan religion do not seek to injure anyone or anything. It goes against everything we're taught and believe. Using the broadest strokes, we are nurturers by nature and practice with light and love in our hearts."

Picking up the paper, she focused on every aspect of the drawing. "I guarantee you that whomever or whatever penned this drawing, was not a member of the Wiccan community."

Terry held his hand up to stop her. "You've said before that you couldn't read me. How did you know I did not sketch this?"

While allowing a slight smile to cross her features, the gesture was meant to convey a sense of tranquility.

There was no sign of cheerfulness in her expression. "I know you had nothing to do with this because I have deep feelings for you. Even though I can't read you, I know you are not capable of this kind of hatred. I wouldn't be able to love you if you were."

The turmoil perceptible in Terry's features was excruciating to witness. She'd believed in him even though he hadn't been able to believe in her and that truth was eating at him. The fact he thought her capable of such an atrocity was unbearable. Doing what she could to protect herself from the pain of that wound, Rainy's focus turned back to Nathan. "If you would allow me, I'd like to see exactly what has been happening. All you have to do is relax the walls you've put up and take my hand. By doing so, I'll get a complete picture instead of a second-hand telling of the events."

Nathan's hand shot out before she'd even finished.

Terry pushed Nathan's arm away. "Here, use my hand instead."

Was that an apology in his voice? She wanted to believe so. Doing her best to hide the heartbreak he'd caused, she shook her head in the negative and looked away. "Don't you remember? Even if you want me to, I can't read you. I need to do this with Nathan."

Not knowing what to expect, Rainy crossed the room to the mantle stepping over what was left of her beautiful pentagram and removed a ritual athame from a wooden box.

Excited to finally get this information off his chest, Nathan was ready to jump right in. "Before we start, do you need me to do anything special?"

"If you will come and stand in front of me, I'm

going to invoke a prayer of protection before we begin. I have no idea what we are dealing with, so I want to make sure we're safe.

"Terry, it's important that you join us." Knowing she wouldn't be able to continue unless he agreed, Rainy closed her eyes and waited until she heard him move to stand by Nathan's side.

"Thank you." To clear her mind from any negative thoughts, she breathed in and out three times. Holding the ritual athame above her head, Rainy started the protection prayer and visualized the knife point alive with flame.

"I call on the five wise Elements for protection."

The athame slashed through the air downward and toward her right leg. Her mind's eye captured the movement in a trail of bright white flame. "I call on the Fire Element to provide us three with the energy and passion needed for the task before us."

The athame moved upward and pointed out past Rainy's left shoulder. "I call on the Air Element to provide us with wisdom and answers to our questions."

The athame cut through the air and pointed straight out from Rainy's right shoulder. "I call on the Water Element to unite and bind us with love and compassion for all that we do not understand."

The athame ripped through the air in a downward motion toward her left foot. "I call on the Earth Element to provide us three with practical knowledge of what we are about to face."

To complete the pentagram the knife moved upward above her head where it had originated. "I ask that the Spirit Element surround us and provide wisdom in the dangerous task before us. I ask for your protection for the three standing here now."

With the pentagram complete, the athame moved in a circle enclosing the protection spell. "I call on the Universe to connect all Elements and keep us three within the circle safe from all that would do harm. In Love and Light. So mote it be."

Rainy extended her hand to the sofa. "Please be seated." Sitting next to Nathan on the couch, they joined hands. "We three are protected. Nothing can hurt us. Lean back and get comfortable. Just think about the first time you noticed a problem, no matter how slight. Run the events through your mind like you're watching a movie. We'll start at the beginning and move on to everything else." She gently touched Nathan's temple. "You'll feel me. I promise not to wander in your mind. I'll just get the information I need and be out as fast as possible."

Nathan shocked Rainy by tenderly touching her cheek and smiling. "I trust you."

The gesture caused tears to pool in her eyes, but she kept them from falling—barely. "Thank you."

Clutching his right hand with both of hers, she pulled their joined hands to her heart and opened her mind. Nathan didn't hold back. Now mentally joined, he shared every experience they'd had since Terry had moved in without saying a word.

By the time she'd viewed the final attack Rainy was spent. She broke contact and leaned back unable to utter a sound. It was now clear that with everything the two men had been through, Terry's main objective had always been to protect her.

A damp cloth wiping her forehead brought her out of the stupor. Her eyes met Terry's worried gaze as he tenderly cared for her. "Thank you, Terry. I'm okay."

Intense affection washed over the face of the man she loved. "I'm so sorry I ever doubted you. Can you find it in your heart to forgive me?"

Rainy's spirit soared. She wanted this moment to go on forever, but Nathan interrupted. *Couldn't he have waited just a bit longer?*

"Did it work? Were you able to see that thing? Do you have any idea what Shadow Man is? Do you think you can get rid of him?" Nathan's rapid fire questions flew so fast she didn't have a chance to answer before the next one shot out.

Terry's features turned stern. His head whipped to the side. "Are you kidding me? I'm not letting her anywhere near that place. Look at her. She's exhausted just by seeing it in her mind. It's not safe." He protectively pulled her into his arms and held tight.

His manic mood changes where she was concerned made her dizzy. But under the circumstances, forgiving him was easy. Squeezing tight one last time, Rainy finally found the strength to let go. "By everything you've shown me, I have a good idea what the problem is. I'm going to have to call in reinforcements, though. We will fight this thing during the day. The night is its sanctuary. It feels most comfortable in the shadows of darkness. So, I'd like to meet at Terry's house around ten in the morning. That should give me time to bring the appropriate people in to help. I don't want anyone venturing inside that property line until we're ready. It's not safe."

Terry waved the grotesque picture of her brutalized body in the air. "*No.* I'm not going to take a chance that this thing will hurt you. Shadow Man told me he would kill you if you stepped foot on the property."

Rainy managed a smile and grabbed the paper as it flew past her head. "That's very kind of you, but I don't expect this to happen. Please don't misunderstand what I'm saying. I'm not being cocky. It's afraid of me. It knows I can see its secrets and can figure a way to get rid of it. That's why the entity drew this. That thing wanted you to keep me away. I'm a threat that it doesn't want to deal with."

To help ease Terry's ramped up fear, she peered at the rendering one more time and giggled. "Look at this drawing, Terry. This image is *not* real. I'll have you know that my breasts are much better than how they're depicted here." Before the men's shocked looks fell, she moved to her three-wick candle and lit the edge on fire. The dreaded drawing flashed in an instant and was gone leaving no ash in its place. Rainy smiled. "Do you understand now? You can't believe anything you see, hear, or feel that's done in the trickster's name. Nothing's real or as it seems.

"I'm not going to lie to you. At best, black magic is hard to fight. But in the end, I have faith that good will prevail just as the blessed candle destroyed that repulsive drawing and left no trace."

There was still some question as to what exactly this thing was. Rainy wouldn't know for sure until entering the property. The primary concern right this minute was Terry's safety. He was the one in grave danger. He just didn't understand that. She'd protect him with her life if need be.

"Now, I'm not sure about you fellas, but I'm starving. If you'll excuse me, I'll go and turn the oven on and put my enchiladas in to warm up. Nathan, please take a seat and get comfortable. We're going to enjoy the rest of our evening. Terry, would you join me in the kitchen to pour the margaritas?" He answered with a broad grin and bow. "At your service, ma'am."

As soon as they were out of sight, they were in each other's arms. Terry's forehead connected with hers. "My God. I don't even know where to begin. I can't explain what came over me. I never even gave you a chance." Heartache over his behavior became apparent as his breathing hitched making it difficult for him to continue. "There are no words to convey just how sorry I am. I'll never be able to make it up to you."

"I'm only human, Terry. Your words and actions hurt me. You destroyed something tonight that held great sentimental value for me. While I forgive you, that doesn't lessen the pain. It will take some time for the sting to go away completely."

Her fingers tangled in the hair at his neck. "That being said, I understand the why of it. You have no idea the danger you're in. This dark manifestation you've been dealing with used your fear to separate us. Whether you know it or not, the entity is manipulating you even when you're away from home. This thing is in your head. I refuse to let something so vile into my life, and I'm certainly not going to let its actions dictate how I react to you.

"You're a good man, Terry. I can't explain why or how I know that, but I do. If I were to allow the incident tonight to come between us, that thing wins, and we both lose. I'm not going to let that happen. As long as the negative is allowed to stay in your environment, it has a hold on you. The entity can and will use you to fulfill whatever it desires, and that pisses me off more than anything. I promise you that we'll work through this."

When their lips met, the fervor behind her words solidified as their bodies molded together. All the hurt slipped away.

Chapter Eighteen

Nathan patted his belly and offered a satisfied sigh. "Thank you so much for having me over tonight. Supper was delicious. I hope I'll be able to convince you to share the recipe with me, Rainy."

"You cook too? How did I get so lucky to find a man that not only creates restaurant quality food but also has a best friend who knows his way around a kitchen? If I play my cards right, I may never have to slave over a stove again." The sincere, joyful quality of Rainy's giggle reminded Terry of a little girl. "Of course I'll give you my recipe. I love to see someone enjoy their meal as much as you did."

Not willing to let a jest handed to him on a silver platter go by, Terry grunted and added his two cents. "In other words, you ate her out of house and home."

Rainy's lighthearted slap to the arm warmed his heart. The woman's cheerfulness radiated through the room and could lift the spirits of a dying man. "You're terrible. That's not what I meant at all." In the snap of the fingers, her attention was focused on Nathan again. "I've got a little surprise for you. I made an extra two dozen enchiladas. I'd like you to take them home, so you have a nice little midnight snack."

Dramatically patting the space above his heart, Nathan's face went all soft and dreamy. If Terry didn't know any better, he'd think the man was smitten. "Oh,

Rainy, I think I'm in love. What do you say? Let's dump this jerk. I can make you so much happier than he can."

Terry's laughter died. *Wait. What?* His jaw fell open from the shock of being thrown under the bus.

"Shut your mouth, Runt. I'm just joking. I'd love to take some leftovers home with me." Pulling his phone out, Nathan groaned as he checked the time. "It's getting late. I guess I should get going. We've got a big day ahead of us tomorrow." Terry crossed his arms over his chest and scowled. *Damn straight you should be moving on.*

"Terry drove separately so you two could have some time alone. But if you'd rather I cart his sorry ass off, just say the word. I'll be happy to oblige."

Not sure when this turned into the bash Terry hour, his heart melted when Rainy flashed a hundred watt smile as she started for the kitchen. "That's sweet, but if it's all the same to you, I'd like to keep him. Just give me a minute, and I'll have a doggie bag ready to go."

Unable to take his eyes off of Rainy's retreating form, the sway of her hips left Terry mesmerized. He couldn't wait to get his hands on her.

Nathan closed the distance between them and fisted Terry's shirt to yank him close. There was no jest in the action. The unexpected hostile gesture left him off balance. Doing his best to release the aggressive hold, Terry grabbed his friend's huge hand and squeezed. Not sure what he'd done to rate this kind of treatment and not wanting to alarm Rainy, Terry tried to put some force behind his whisper. "Hey! What the hell are you doing?"

Nathan leaned down and murmured in his ear—

well, more like growled. Apparently, he didn't want Rainy to hear either. "Don't you dare screw this up, Runt. I know you're not blind. That is a good woman, and you two are *meant* for each other. With everything you put her through tonight, she's forgiven your sorry ass. I don't know how or why, but you've got a second chance. Rainy's the type of woman that can make a man happy. She's smart, sexy…"

Put off by the fact that it appeared his best friend was trying to move in on his territory, Terry objected while all but dangling from Nathan's grasp. "Hey! Watch yourself."

Ignoring the venom in Terry's verbal backlash, Nathan's grip grew tighter. "She's beautiful, and holy shit can she cook! I'll also add that if you hurt her again or she decides to kick your ass out, *I'm* taking a shot with her. Do you understand what I'm saying? It's just blind luck someone hasn't snatched her up already. Don't do anything boneheaded. Don't. Fuck. This. Up. You've got a chance at real happiness here." Knuckles cracked against Terry's skull to emphasize the point. "You better think before you speak, so something stupid doesn't come out of that mouth of yours. I'm giving you fair warning."

Not so sure he wasn't serious about having a go at his girl, Terry shoved at Nathan's chest but still wasn't able to break free. "Whoa! Wait just a damn…"

"Here you go. I also put some flan in the bag for you."

Abruptly releasing him, Nathan patted Terry's head like he was a four-year-old and crossed the room to take the food. "I sure appreciate this." Terry had to bite his lip when his best friend embraced Rainy. The ass had the balls to look over her shoulder and smirk. *Did he seriously just kiss my woman on the top of her head?*

There wasn't a sneer fierce enough to brandish the nonverbal warning of just how pissed he was by these intrusive actions. Nathan had crossed a line, and Terry wouldn't stand for it. *Oh, hell, no!* He plopped himself down on the couch. Terry penned a mental note to let his so called best friend know exactly how he felt about *that* little maneuver.

As if embracing weren't enough, the two of them walked arm and arm to the door, laughing and carrying on like they were the only two people in the room. *Yep. I'm going to nip that in the bud as soon as I see his sorry ass again.*

Only when the door clicked shut leaving Nathan securely on the outside, was Terry able to relax again.

"Can I get you something else to drink while I'm up?"

Finally, they were alone. Without being too obvious, Terry did his best to tamp out the jealousy. He'd already committed enough reprehensible acts today to last a lifetime and didn't want to add to the heap. Patting the couch, he hoped his smile conveyed nothing but an easy contentedness. "No, thank you. Please, come and sit down. I've wanted to get you alone ever since I got here."

Her lips curled in a seductive grin. "Really? I'm a little disappointed. I've wanted to get you alone since our kiss at the guest house." Terry's heart thudded. The damn muscle pounded so hard he could hear the blood as it rushed from his head to just below the belt.

As Rainy crossed the room, he couldn't help but notice the sexy sway of her hips was just as good coming as it was going. Watching this incredible woman in motion was like poetry to the eyes and stirred a deep longing. Gliding, instead of merely walking, each movement was fluid and graceful and so damn feminine. *Damn, this woman is smoldering hot.*

Terry didn't want to, but he had to put on the brakes at least for a while. Before the evening could progress any further, he'd have to control his physical reactions long enough to broach the subject of his earlier bad deeds. Even though she'd forgiven him, Terry just couldn't let it go. It was only right to address that moment of insanity one last time before he could allow anything sexual to happen between them. He needed her trust more than he cared to admit.

Rainy worked with battered women for God's sake. Knowing the signs of an abuser, she must be having reservations about him or at the very least his actions. He hated the thought that he'd opened the door to any misgivings she might have, when, in reality, there was no foundation for them at all. *But how the hell is she supposed to know that? She's not.* Those thoughts twisted his guts into knots. Never before had he displayed anger in such a brutal physical way. Somewhere under the surface, she must be worried that I'm some kind of maniac.

The guilt over destroying something so precious to anyone—let alone Rainy—ate him alive inside. His heart told him that there weren't enough words in the English language to make up for the profoundly egregious way he'd behaved. And he always followed his heart.

During dinner, an idea had finally materialized in his thick skull. Instead of just *saying* he was sorry,

Terry would remedy the situation by *showing* her just how sincere he was. Actions always spoke louder than words.

"Rainy, about earlier. I…" Her hand cradled his, and their fingers intertwined creating a sweet sense of tenderness between them. His senses picked up on her soft, feminine scent. The light perfume had teased him all night long. Being a guy, he was never one to identify flowers or their aroma. Truth be told, he'd never cared for perfume. But there was something so familiar about the floral scent she wore that it struck a sentimental chord. Inhaling deeply, the familiarity that he'd struggled to identify finally hit him like a quick jab to the solar plexus.

"Gillyflowers." Lightheadedness enveloped him as a long forgotten memory sparked deep emotions. Rubbing his eyes, he couldn't believe the coincidence that Rainy wore his beloved mother's favorite flower scent. Out of all the flowers in the world what were the chances?

"Did you say Gillyflowers? How on earth did you know that name? Most people call them Stock."

Lifting her hand to his mouth, Terry pressed a gentle kiss to Rainy's wrist. "My mother used to garden. Being a practical woman, she focused on fruits and vegetables. But Mom had one weakness. Gillyflowers. She had a whole bed devoted to them, mixing multiple colors which resulted in a striking patchwork of color every spring. The bed was so pretty that she refused to take any cuttings. She'd say that it would be a travesty to deprive the hummingbirds and butterflies of such a fine meal." The childhood memory evoked a smile.

As an afterthought, he added, "The pink blooms were her favorite. My mother was a good woman. She was strong and kept the family going even when times were lean. Mom wasn't an overly emotional woman and rarely showed her feelings. But she loved Dad and me and worked her fingers to the bone so that we'd be fed and comfortable.

"The day of my father's funeral, my mother dropped the stoicism and filled our home with Gillyflowers. There wasn't a single bloom left in the garden. That was the only time I ever saw her cry. She walked around the house from vase to vase arranging and rearranging the flowers. I couldn't understand what she was doing. We should've been on our way to the funeral home, but she couldn't seem to leave the house until those flowers were just exactly right.

"When I tried to nudge her out of the door, she broke down and told me, *'I've been hard on you over the years, but you're my treasure. I may not have always shown my love, but these flowers represent everything good in life that I've experienced with you and your dad.'* I was fourteen years old, and it was the first time she'd ever spoken to me as a man."

This newfound correlation between Rainy and his mother deeply touched him. *Gillyflowers. Out of all the scents in the world, that's the one my Rainy wears.*

"Oh, Terry, that's a beautiful memory. I've been drawn to Gillyflowers since I was a young girl. I don't use perfume, but every year I make a tincture and add the scent to my lotion. The smell calms me." Rainy kissed his forehead. "Did you know that particular flower symbolizes a contented existence? You and your father must have been your mother's pride and joy."

There was something mystical about the connection between Rainy and himself. But Terry wasn't looking for an explanation, nor did he care if one was forthcoming. He liked the mystery of not knowing why she affected him the way she did and enjoyed discovering the ties like the one with his mother.

While in Rainy's presence, their spirits somehow commingled and made him feel whole. He didn't care if that notion sounded corny, even to his own ears. He wanted *more*. The mystery between them was empowering. Never would he consider breaking the connection. Every muscle relaxed when he inhaled another deep whiff of her scent. Every worry disappeared. He was exactly where he wanted to be. And when all was said and done that was all that mattered.

As his emotions solidified, it became even more necessary to repair the damage from his earlier outburst. "I'm sorry. I got a little sidetracked. I want to talk about what happened earlier."

"Let's not go over it again. All's forgiven, Terry. I understand why you were so angry. It's all right. Really. It is."

Rainy's eyes reflected the truth of her words. She'd forgiven him the unforgivable. He'd defiled an extremely personal object in a fit of rage. It would be understandable, even expected, if she had kicked him out of the door never wanting to see him again. But she hadn't. *Gillyflowers. Contented existence. She feels the connection too.*

Both arms rose to entice Rainy into his embrace. "Can I hold you?"

241

His heart rate sped when that sexy smile lit her face. In one swift movement, she was practically sitting on his lap. Encouraged, Terry held on as tight as he could. "If it's all right with you, I'd like to help you fix the pentagram."

"Oh, Terry, I'd love that. The idea that you're willing to take the time to repair it means the world to me. *That* particular pentagram is dear to my heart, as are you."

He could get lost in her eyes. Now that he had stated his peace, he needed the sensual pleasure of her touch. Terry wanted to start the rest of their evening off slowly with a gentle kiss. But all reasonable thought flew out the window when their lips touched. A deep burning fire erupted in his groin when she groaned his name into their joined mouths. He all but tumbled into madness.

Somehow, she'd gotten the upper hand and had his back prone on the couch. As the kiss deepened, dreams of fulfilling her every sexual desire surfaced. Those thoughts provoked a feral drive to take over. The kiss turned savage. Hands flew across bodies. Moans became passionate growls. A deep primal need urgently thrummed through his core demanding that he have her naked body beneath him.

Breaking the embrace, Rainy shifted her weight until she straddled him. Bucking and rocking across his clothed length produced bright stars that all but blinded him. "Too many clothes," he cried, his voice ragged and breathless. "Too many clothes." If they didn't get naked fast, he was all but certain his jeans would spontaneously combust.

The atmosphere around them came alive. Electrical

charges pricked Terry's skin—awakening an arousal the likes of which he'd never known with any other woman.

All motion between them suddenly ceased. Time seemed to stop as Terry looked up at Rainy's flushed face. An urgent desire coursed through his body, begging for her to continue. His breathing became labored as he battled for control. Still sitting astride him, Rainy rose and fell with each inhale and exhale. Squeczing her hips, he ground his erection into her center. Her body quaked and shuttered with wild abandon and left him utterly intoxicated on lust.

Reaching out, Rainy took her time unbuttoning his shirt. Her fingernails grazed and scratched his skin as she slowly made her way down his chest. The vixen derived a great deal of pleasure out of driving him crazy.

Her sensual gaze bored into him. "Will you stay the night with me?"

Heart racing, Terry savored the moment by kissing each of her fingertips. "There's no other place in this world I'd rather be."

Rainy leaned back and rested her elbows on his knees. Staring down at him, she offered a wicked grin. Her fingers twined in the coarse hair above his belt. His erection pounded with the need to be freed. As a fingernail scraped down the length of his zipper, he almost bucked her off.

Knowing just how to soothe, Rainy quieted him with kisses and an exploring tongue from his navel to his nipples.

A whoosh of breath escaped from his burning lungs when her attention moved to her blouse. Craving every inch of Rainy had him salivating as the first button between her breasts unfastened. Teasing him, she spread the shirt just a wee bit wider. The siren had only exposed the top of her voluptuous cleavage. "You're special, Terry." She ran a finger over the curve of her breast. "I feel as though I've been waiting for you a lifetime."

The next button released. Unable to hold out a moment longer, Terry yanked at her blouse—tearing the rest of the buttons off. Fanning the shirt away from her shoulders gave his fingers access to trace those gorgeous curves. The scent of gillyflowers consumed him, reminding him of two of the most elusive sensations in the world—unconditional love and a fresh spring drizzle in the Arizona desert. Rainy's soft, moist skin shimmered, creating a play of light resembling an ethereal halo surrounding her exposed flesh.

As if begging for attention, her breasts all but spilled over the top of the bra. Reaching up, Terry fidgeted with the clasp until every inch of those beautiful breasts spilled into his hands.

Rainy's lust coupled with Terry's desire to explore her body sparked an agonizing tension in his erection. The longing became painful. The need to sink himself deep within her drove him on. Without that release, he'd explode. She groaned and threw her head back.

"My God, you're the most beautiful woman I've ever seen. You're my very own angel."

He lightened his touch, skimming the palms of his hands from her throat to the tips of her hard nipples. Goosebumps covered her flesh as he toyed with the rosy buds. Every impassioned signal spurred him on. Sitting up, he buried his face between those lush womanly curves. Turning his head, he licked the underside of her breast causing Rainy to squirm on his lap. His tongue made a slow journey over her ample bosom and latched onto her nipple—sucking and squeezing until he could stand it no longer. The desire to have all of her burned him up. Unable to control the impulse, he bit down, gently at first, until she screamed. "Yes! Harder!"

Rainy's hands cradled his head to urge him on. "I'm yours. I'll never refuse you. More. I need more, Terry."

Having difficulty maintaining any amount of control, he increased the pressure of his bite until her body vibrated with its first orgasm. The sound of her screaming his name was all it took for any remaining reasonable thought to vanish. Yearning to hear that squeal again and again drove him on. He was out of his mind. Grabbing hold of her back, he flipped them onto the floor as her partially clothed body continued to quake from his touch.

Seams ripped, and the zipper broke as he jerked at her pants. Throwing what was left of her clothing aside, he stood over her and looked his fill. *She's a goddess. My goddess.* His woman was full-figured, and the most beautiful sight he'd ever seen.

Rainy's back arched and those beautiful round breasts beckoned him. His erection, hard and ready, stood at attention once he'd freed it from the confining clothing.

Terry all but screamed in agony when his pants refused to go any lower down his right leg. Lost in a sexual haze, he couldn't understand what the problem was. Jerking and twisting, he tried to force the pant leg off. The sound of her giggle turning into outright laughter stopped him short.

Clearing her throat, she gestured to his leg. "Your knee must be feeling better. You forgot your brace." Her hand flew to her mouth to stifle another snicker.

Oh shit! The brace. She'd had him so hot and bothered, he'd forgotten all about the damn thing. Balancing on his good leg, he pulled his pants up far enough to tear at the straps and Velcro. His movements so jerky and balance precarious at best, failed him altogether. Before he could steady himself, he tilted sideways like a tree about to be felled. Unable to stop the momentum, his body hit the chair as he tumbled over. A thud sounded when he crumpled onto the floor with a choice curse word or two for good measure. He'd never survive this embarrassment.

Now in a prone position, he took the upper hand in this ridiculous situation. The brace flew across the room without a second thought. Finally able to get to his feet, he kicked the pants off. Rainy's laughter stopped him short. Tears streamed down her cheeks.

Perturbed at himself for screwing this moment up, he stood over her with hands propped on his hips. Her laughter died, and all movement came to a standstill as she stared at his naked form. His erection jumped, begging for attention as that luscious tongue swiped at her lips. Her leg rose, and her foot gently touched his erection. Barely able to wheeze in a breath, the contact nearly sent him over the edge. He leaned forward for more. Closing his eyes, he threw his head back and relished in the erotic way she stroked him. His heart all but stopped when he felt her tongue slide up the length of his arousal. Each breath now audible, he watched as she took him into her mouth. The sensation was rapture and torture all at the same time. She must have sensed how close he was because with one final nibble, she reclined back on the floor.

Kneeling beside her, Terry straddled Rainy's leg, kissing every inch as he moved toward her center. She liked his teeth, so he used them. His erection glided along her silky thigh while pounding with the urgency of release. Opening herself to him, she clamped her free leg around his back. "Make love to me, Terry. I want to feel your orgasm while you're deep inside of me."

He parted her center and licked the length of her just as she had done for him. He moved slowly, enjoying every twitch and contraction. Increasing pressure when he reached her nub, she exploded in his mouth. Her body lunged, and her breathing accelerated to the point of panting. Intensifying the orgasm, he sucked her sex into his mouth and rode the high with her.

As Rainy recovered from his ministrations, Terry knelt over her proud and ready. Putting on a show, he grabbed the tip of his erection and slid the length through his palm. His core tightened, and everything inside him threatened to release. Absorbed in the show her body started to shudder as he sheathed himself with a condom. Caressing the inside of her thighs, she lifted her knees. "Come into me now."

He kissed the curve of each foot before placing them on his shoulders. Lifting her butt, he almost fainted with pleasure as he watched while entering her inch by inch. Slowly at first, his hips rotated until she screamed his name. Enthralled, he was mesmerized by the way her core contracted around him. Finding her nub, he squeezed, and Rainey bucked against his hand. Unable to hold out any longer, he plunged into her one last time and laid his heart wide open.

Chapter Nineteen

Tiptoeing into the bedroom, Rainy placed a piping hot cup of coffee on the bedside table. The sight of Terry in her bed all but stopped her heart. Images of the previous evening's carnal endeavors popped into her mind and curled her toes.

Typical for a person that didn't share a bed, Terry was sprawled out on his stomach, spread eagle, and took up every spare inch of the mattress. She'd hated leaving him in the middle of the night, but as soon as he'd fallen asleep Rainy had slipped out of the room. Calls had to be made, and she needed the time to prepare herself for today's house cleansing. So, in the end, his bed hogging ways hadn't been a problem.

Pushing the covers aside, she playfully nipped at Terry's shoulder and kissed his ear. Having no luck rousing him, she resorted to more mischievous ways. She smacked him on the bare ass and cooed, "Wake up, sunshine. It's time to rise and shine."

Before Rainy could blink, he had her on the bed beneath him. Terry's waking reflexes were sharper than she could have ever imagined. Nibbling at her neck, he made quick work of her buttons and had her bra undone in mere moments. His mouth clamped onto her breast and turned her brain to mush. *Oh Goddess, what I wouldn't do with an extra half hour this morning.*

A round of boisterous laughter rang out from the

living area. Terry's head popped up, and an almost imperceptible curse left his mouth. "Who's here? God, it's the butt crack of dawn. Don't they know it's too early for a house call?"

Before she could answer, Nathan's rowdy voice chimed in. "I'm taking bets! The runt has never been a morning person. I give him a full hour before he finally makes an appearance. Who's in?"

Genuinely confused, Terry sat up. "What the hell is Nathan doing here? I thought we were meeting him at the house. Who are all those people out there?"

"*Those people* you are referring to have gathered here at an ungodly hour to get rid of your nuisance house guest. When I called everyone last night, they thought it would be more productive if we met here before going to your home. I'd put my pants on and get moving if I were you. Everyone's getting hungry. I don't think I'll be able to keep them out of the food much longer."

She grabbed his face and plopped a juicy kiss on his mouth. "Like I said, rise and shine. Here's some coffee to help you wake up. I've got shampoo and conditioner in the shower. Feel free to use whatever you need."

Terry tenderly touched her lips. "You called *everyone* last night? When did you sleep? Why didn't you wake me? I would've helped you."

Nipping at his fingers, she quipped, "It was evident you hadn't gotten much sleep over the last week. You were exhausted. You need your strength today. Now get up and let's do this."

Redressing while sashaying across the room, Rainy wiggled her butt at him. "And Terry? Don't make any plans for later. We *will* be resuming this tonight."

****

Clean and shaven, Terry peered down at his clothes that Rainy had picked up from the living room. It hadn't occurred to him last night to make the trip out to his car to retrieve the overnight bag. "Dirty clothes it is. At least they're not wrinkled."

Not only had the ruckus in the other room continued to grow, but the smell of fresh cooked bacon and eggs gnawed at his empty stomach. Dressing quickly, he grabbed the coffee cup and took a gulp. Forcing a smile, he prepared himself for the walk of shame. His mood brightened when he glanced at the clock on the wall. It had only taken fifteen minutes to shower and get dressed. "At least Nathan won't win the pool. That's something."

Sheepishly entering the dining area of the apartment, Terry was greeted with raucous applause and cat calls. Everyone, even those he didn't know, seemed to be having a ball at his expense. There were four women and a child mingling around the table. The only one he recognized was Cheryl, Rainy's assistant.

Nathan and Jursic were stealing bacon from the platter. *Jursic?* He should have guessed the guy would help out. He'd been a true friend throughout the move. There was another man he'd never seen before who sported a wide, knowing grin while sipping his coffee.

Rainy slipped through the crowd to Terry's side and offered a hug and kiss. "I can see you're stunned. I'll make the introductions in a minute, but there are a couple of people here that are *really* pissed at you. I think you should probably deal with them first." Leaning in, she whispered, "Tread carefully. She's so angry that tears have been threatening since she got here." His face scrunched with confusion. Throwing him to the wolves, Rainy nudged him to turn around and glance into the living room.

Rainy took the coffee cup from Terry's hand as Jody scrambled into his arms. They clung to each other as though it had been months since they'd last seen each other. Throughout his lifetime, he'd depended on Jody and Nathan to get him through any disaster life threw his way. A calming sensation immediately overtook Terry. *Everything's going to be all right now.* That blissful feeling lasted all of five seconds until he looked up and saw Jared glaring at him. *Oh shit.*

Removing himself from Jody's embrace proved impossible. Terry ended up crossing the room to his best friend's brand new husband as she clung to his side.

"Jared, I'm sorry. I had no idea Rainy was going to call you two. I would never have allowed her to interrupt your honeymoon."

Out of the blue, Jody punched Terry in the stomach. The unexpected blow left him bent over and wheezing to catch his breath. "Is that so? What do you think of that, Jared? Apparently, Terry doesn't need us."

Jared grazed the side of Terry's head with the palm of his hand. "*You* should have been the one to call us, you idiot. We're family. When Rainy told us about what's been going on, Jody was beside herself. *You* broke her heart." The tone of his voice lowered with an added menacing edge. "Let me make this clear. I don't like it when someone makes my woman cry."

"Jared, Jody, this thing is dangerous. I didn't call

because of Jody's history with spirit communications. I'm terrified about what might happen to the two of you if you were to step foot on the property. Please, I'm begging you. Keep Jody away. I'd never forgive myself if she got hurt because of me." Jody's lip quivered. *Oh shit.* "How dare you think I wouldn't be here when you need me. It wasn't that long ago that I was in trouble and wrecked the most important evening in your life. Do you remember? It was the night of your very first art show, and I was in dire straits. You dropped everything for me. Do you seriously think I wouldn't do the same for you?"

Pulling her into his arms, he held on for dear life. "Jody, this thing, it's…"

"I know exactly how bad the situation is thanks to Rainy and Nathan. Since you were being such a jerk and wanted to exclude Jared and me, *they* filled us in on the situation."

"But you were on your honeymoon." No amount of whining or pleading was going to get him out of this mess. He'd royally screwed up. The only response forthcoming were tears. Knowing it wasn't just anger that fueled them made him feel even worse. He'd hurt her badly and felt like a real prick.

Jared intervened by tucking Jody into his side. "Terry, we were on a boat a few hours away. It's not like we were across the world. We can get back to Lake Powell once you're safe."

Before the lecture continued, Jared trapped Terry with a threatening gaze. It would have been impossible to look away. *Oh shit. I'm about to have my ass handed to me.* "You've known Jody a lifetime. In the short time I've known her, she's taught me how important family is. Let me ask you this—do you think so little of Jody now that she's married to me? In the future, if my wife ever needs you, can we ascertain by your actions that if you're busy, she won't be able to call on you for help? Is that what the relationship between the two of you has come down to now that you're not the only man in her life—we can only call for help when it's convenient? You have broken Jody's heart, and you damn well better to do some quick talking to make it right."

Terry would have preferred an ass kicking to the bite of that stinging statement. What made the situation worse was the fact he couldn't argue. He *should* have called.

Trying to smooth out the hurt feelings, Terry ran his hand down Jody's arm. "Of course I don't feel that way. You're right. I should have called you immediately. I'm sorry. I wasn't thinking straight. Just ask Rainy. I've been a real dick lately."

Nathan—the asshole—raised his arm and chimed in. "I can attest to that."

Jared gently shoved Terry's shoulder. The gesture was meant as a temporary cease-fire. The anger and misunderstandings would be put on hold *for now*. He had no misgivings. This conversation would come up again once this nasty business with the house had finally been put to rest. "Rainy already told us. Consider this your *only* warning. Do *not* hurt my wife again. In the future, if you need us, call. Jody and I are here for you and Nathan anytime. I hope the reverse is true as well."

Terry planted a kiss on Jody's cheek.

Rainy cleared her throat. "All right, enough of this. Come on. I've got a few people to introduce you to, and then we can sit down and eat while we work out some details."

Terry settled his arm around Rainy's waist as she guided him back to the table. "You've talked to Cheryl, my assistant, on the phone." The pixie woman smiled and nodded her head. "Yes. It's nice to meet you, Cheryl. I'm sorry it has to be under such difficult circumstances."

"This is Father Eric Gaines. He's the chaplain at the Flagstaff hospital and also works with the Flagstaff police department. Over the years, we've become good friends and have worked together several times." By his appearance, Terry never would have guessed this man was a priest. There's a story there that he'd like to take more time to explore. The man looked more like a Navy Seal. Muscles bulged beneath the bright red polo shirt and military tattoos decorated his arms. *No offense to my favorite preacher boy, but—booyah! This man personified the kind of strength that he was looking for in a battle against Shadow Man!* Shaking the priest's extended hand, Terry couldn't contain his grin. *We're going to kick some demon ass today.* "Thank you for coming. I really appreciate any help you can give."

"This is Sarah and Camille. They're members of the Circle of the Pines Coven. They drove down to the valley with Eric and brought everything we should need to cleanse your home." The two women were identical twins. Somehow, under the circumstances, that added a creepy vibe to their presence. "It's a pleasure to meet you," they both chimed in at the same time. Unnerved, he tried to hide his discomfort. "It's nice to meet you too. Thank you for helping me."

"This is Amy, and the little munchkin covered in

syrup is Marcus. She won't be coming along with us today. Since it's her first day in the Phoenix area, I wanted to let her meet some new friends and offer up a proper breakfast."

Amy must be the woman Rainy transported from Flagstaff. Knowing a little of what she'd gone through, Terry made sure to move slowly and tried his best to relay kindness. "It's a pleasure to meet you and Marcus. You're going to like living in the Valley."

"And, of course, you know Nathan and Peter."

"Who?"

Rainy giggled and slapped his arm. "Very funny."

Unable to contain his smirk, Terry stared at Jursic. *"Peter?* I've known you for months. I feel gypped just thinking of all the times I could've had a little fun with that name. I have to say that I expected your first name to have a bit more badass behind it." Enjoying the normalcy of the banter, Terry reached for a slice of bacon and popped it into his mouth. "You know, something like Thor or Angus."

Like a kid, Jursic beamed at the off-handed compliment. "Dude, careful where you tread. Peter is a family name. By the way, I'm down with you calling me Thor."

Between the bacon and the laughter Terry choked.

Rainy chimed in. "Peter—*Jursic*—isn't going with us today. He will be staying with Amy to help her get settled. Since I needed Cheryl, Nathan thought he'd be the perfect person to help out." There was something Rainy wasn't saying. Then it struck him. Jursic was going to be Amy's bodyguard today. The woman's thoughtfulness melted his heart. *She has everyone's best interest at heart and somehow manages to think of everything.*

Nathan tapped Terry on the shoulder. "I talked to Dave to see if he could join us, but he was called out of town. His mother is ill and it's not looking like she's going to make it. I told him we'd keep him updated."

"I'm sorry to hear that. I hope she recovers." Preacher boy's magical sword Terry had imagined crossed Terry's mind. "He's a good man. I'm sorry he won't be here to see this to the end."

Rainy waved a hand over the loaded table. "Now, why don't we all sit down and have a nice breakfast together? I'll go over everything I know. Nathan and Terry can add any missing details, and we can discuss a plan of attack."

Chapter Twenty

There are moments in every lifetime that stand out above all others. The first impression of Terry's home would stay with Rainy for the rest of her days. Pure, undiffused malevolence the likes of which she'd never experienced before resided here and had for many years. A black hole existed in the middle of this beautiful neighborhood—its sole purpose, to suck the joy and ultimately the life out of anyone who dared to enter.

Standing on the sidewalk and looking at the house gave Rainy the chills. Crawling tingles swept over her scalp. Furiously scratching at the crown of her head did nothing to stop the creepy sensation. The spider web impression was so intense that she wanted to rip each hair out by its root. The fear this place provoked was shocking. *Mother Goddess, help me get it together.*

With trembling hands, she clutched the pentagram around her neck. Now that she was here, Rainy refused to back down. Setting her mindset, she stood her ground to assess the situation and ascertain what exactly they were up against.

Taking three deep breaths to calm her nerves, Rainy opened her senses to get a better view. Withdrawing into her second sight, an otherwise imperceptible sphere over the property became noticeable. Inside the bubble, the house, barely visible, rested in an oppressive shroud of mist. Vile things had been done in the name of evil at this location—leaving the land scarred permanently. If it were up to her, she'd level this place and condemn it for eternity.

With danger all around, Rainy wasn't willing to take her eyes off the house. She addressed the team who'd assembled around her. "The situation is far worse than I initially suspected. Black magic was conjured at this location. There are powerful wards in place. The fortification will make the extraction challenging and dangerous."

Terry inched closer to Rainy. The awed hush of his voice revealed the depth of his fear. "What's a ward?"

"A ward is a magical structure that creates unseen boundaries of protection. It's the reason your chaplain had a difficult time entering the studio. His strong faith gained him entry, but the breach took so much of his energy that the powerful resources needed to exercise the entity had dwindled exponentially.

"From what I can tell, the wards were not originally placed around the home and property in its entirety, but only around the structure in the back. So much time has passed without intervention that the influence behind the protective wards shifted and grew to encompass the house and property. Because the evil trickled out from behind the walls of the warded barriers, the protective magic is far weaker in those areas. The outlying reach of the spell is meant to scare off anyone who poses a threat and dares to cross the property line.

"Talismans have been used to create the protection magic around the studio. Once the main house has been cleansed, our priorities will shift to finding those objects. We will not be able to enter the studio and purify it until we have confiscated those items."

Holding her hand out, she signaled for Jody and Jared to approach. "Jody, as far as I've been able to ascertain, we are dealing with the spirit of a man whose greed drove him to make a pact with dark forces. He committed unspeakable acts of sacrificial offerings while performing black magic. I do not currently sense anything remotely human remaining of the man's spirit in this location.

"I'm telling you this because the fact that he *was* human at one time makes *you,* and your abilities, particularly vulnerable. The entity doesn't know it yet, but having that information also makes *him* vulnerable to us. If we can somehow separate the soul of the man from the evil, *that* will weaken the entity. During the walk, you may be able to garner information about this man and his lifetime on earth that can help humanize him again. If so, we will use that against the dark forces at work here.

"Maintain close collaboration with Jared. Give him any impressions that you perceive no matter how inconsequential they may seem. We need every piece of information we can get our hands on to fight this thing. Don't stray. Don't let it trick you. This thing will lie to you. It will say things that will hurt you. It's all a smokescreen. Stay strong in your faith and stay strong in the connection you share with Jared. Those two things are unshakable and unbreakable.

"While we are all in danger, Terry is the primary target. This thing, whatever it is, believes he is a kindred spirit and has been calling to him since he was a child. Nathan, I expect you to stay by his side and yell out if you see something you don't like or understand. One of us will come running."

Nathan stepped beside Terry and took his arm. "This little runt means a lot to me. I'll keep him safe. I'll stick to him like glue."

Rainy nodded her approval. "Evil has been invited here. It has been allowed to persist and flourish for decades. It will *not* go willingly. Anything is possible. If we—no—*when* we get the upper hand, don't get cocky. Doing so gives the entity an advantage. We, as individuals, cannot remove the evil. Only the convictions of our beliefs can do that. We must all stay strong in our faith.

"I do not expect much of a fight for the main house. We may see some opposition, but that part of the property has nowhere near the coverage of protection that the outbuilding has. I anticipate seeing some frightening things. Objects may be thrown. Water may turn on and off. Lights may flicker and worse. Just remember, they're all parlor tricks meant to cast fear into your hearts, so you turn tail and run. We must stand strong and united.

"I have prepared a protection amulet for each of you. The personalized talismans contain black salt, a pentagram, various herbs, and several agates and crystals. These amulets should protect you from a physical attack. Wear these charms around your neck at all times. If something goes wrong and you do get scratched or pushed or hit, yell out immediately. Until either Cheryl or I can get to you, use the Holy Water that Father Eric has provided."

Rainy faced Eric. "Father, I know that powerful protection surrounds you. Even so, it would mean a lot to me if you wore this protective charm. I made it specifically for you."

The priest offered a gentle smile and dipped his head allowing Rainy to place the amulet around his neck.

"I too have brought protection for you, Rainy. I would be honored if you'd allow me to place this blessed crucifix around your neck."

His thoughtfulness brought tears to Rainy's eyes. "Blessed be. I would be *exceedingly* honored, sir. Thank you."

To ensure the crucifix remained around her neck, Rainy slipped it beneath her shirt. "Once we start, we must finish this. Every time a negative energy cleansing is unsuccessful, the malevolent spirit is granted more strength from its master. The entity gains strength each moment it is allowed to stay.

"Cheryl has prepared and given everyone a vessel of burning white sage. While in the main house, we will stay together. Once a room has been thoroughly smudged, Father Eric will say a prayer and anoint the doors and windows.

"The Father is fluent in Latin. He has chosen to speak the ancient language to add credence to the prayers. You may not understand what he is saying, but I guarantee you will feel the power behind his words.

"Sarah and Camille will follow behind and spread black salt throughout each room. They will then wash the walls with a potent saline solution brewed with black salt. When those steps are complete, the area will no longer be compatible with *any* spirit, good or bad.

"I will be vocal about what I'm seeing and uncovering. At the same time, Father Eric will be stating prayers in Latin. It may get loud and confusing, but try to stay within range of our voices. The Father asks that you say the Lord's Prayer aloud as we walk through the house.

"I can't emphasize this enough—*never* separate from your partner. Without them, you are an easy target. Consider that person your lifeline.

"That's about it. Is everyone ready to get this done?"

The mood was somber, but everyone sported their fiercest game face. *Mother Goddess, please keep them all safe from harm.*

Rainy turned and faced Father Eric. Their hands clasped in a show of unity. She reached up and kissed his cheek. "Let us begin."

They converged on the house as a united front. Intense emotion can generate a tremendous amount of energy, something akin to a sonic boom. Upon reaching the door, a concussive wave of malignant rage undulated on the air and thrashed out at their bodies. Inhuman growls shrieked from just beyond the door. The moment Rainy grabbed the knob, the thud of heavy footsteps from within the house stopped her cold. A loud crash sounded from the other side as something rammed the door. The frame bowed, but the barrier held. The sheer force of the hit left the ground beneath their feet shaking.

Rainy shouted to calm everyone. "This dramatic show is nothing more than a scare tactic to keep us out. Let's all keep our wits about us."

Father Eric sprayed the entry with holy water and shouted his intention to enter. Rainy placed her palm on the door. Focusing, she imagined her energy as a solid mass and pushed the entity away. Deafening noises of large objects hitting walls and breaking apart sounded as the darkness fled the room.

As they entered the home, Terry's gasp was audible. There wasn't a single piece of furniture left intact. The entity had destroyed everything in its wake. She wrapped her arms around him to offer strength. "I'm sorry, Terry. I know this is difficult, but we have to remain focused."

He laid his head on her shoulder and nodded. "You're right."

"Let's continue. Shadow Man has fled to its sanctuary in the back yard. Let's proceed with cleansing all negative energy from the house. We will start at the far northern room and work our way through the rest of the house."

Entering Terry's bedroom proved to be a chore. They had to climb over debris to get to the center. Speaking in Latin, Father Eric started his prayers. Cheryl opened the windows and doors so the smudging process could begin. Everyone stood in a circle back to back and held their burning sage aloft as Rainy moved throughout the room.

"All negative energy and impurities must vacate these premises immediately. You are not welcome. I demand that you leave. Only love and light shall remain." She repeated this chant several times while moving through the room. When finished, Rainy carefully made her way back to the rest of the group. Father Eric anointed the windows and doors. When it was evident the prayer had concluded, Rainy stated, "Blessed be." As the last person left the room, Sarah and Camille entered with buckets and washcloths.

They continued this process throughout the house without any sign of opposition. The moment they stepped onto the back porch, everything changed. Peering across the yard, Rainy got her first physical glimpse of the studio. Since the walls were glass, the inside of the building should have been visible. Instead, a thick, roiling black mist churned within obliterating the area. As if the gates of hell had just opened up, an oppressive rumbling sounded within the protected boundary. Another explosive vibration concussion hit them, and it carried the weight of outright aggression in its wake. An overwhelming sense of impending doom laced the atmosphere. It took every ounce of control for Rainy not to double over and lose her breakfast.

Father Eric held his Bible up and yelled in Latin. Rainy closed her eyes and envisioned his words striking the studio and penetrating any weak spots. The powerful thrum continued, but the shock wave ceased enough to allow them to move forward unimpeded.

I have to find those talismans.

Holding her hands out, she closed everything out of her mind. "Mother Goddess, lead me with your light, take me to the talismans that provides evil its blight." Trembles coursed through her body as she placed one foot in front of the other. Rainy gave herself up to the love and light that flowed through her. There was no telling where she'd end up. Much like a living divining rod, the magnetic sensation guided her forward.

In an instant, a powerful tug changed her direction drawing her to the side of the studio. Taking her time, she kept her hands outstretched as a beacon for the potent talisman. She crouched, and her fingers trailed through the grass until the pull of energy was at its strongest. Rainy had located the first talisman. Marking the spot with a black tourmaline, she continued the process until all four charms were found—one at each corner of the structure. "Blessed be.

"I've located all of the buried charms. A black stone marks their placement. We must remove these to break the protective force before we can enter.

"Terry, do you have any shovels?"

"I think there's two on the side of the house. I'll go get them." He whipped around and started to leave.

"Wait! Take Nathan with you. I don't want you to go by yourself." Nathan scurried after him without being asked.

"Cheryl, while we're doing this, please go to the car and get a wooden box. You'll also find strips of silk. Bring those as well. I need you to bless the silk and then have Father Eric to do the same.

"I'd like each of us to take a corner and expose the talisman at the same time. They're not buried deep. I believe we are looking for a coin of some kind—a gold coin. Do *not* touch it. Just unearth the coins. I will collect each talisman when they are all exposed and terminate their power."

"Rainy! Come here! Quick. Something's happening with Jody." The terror in Jared's voice shattered the air.

Rainy rounded the corner and found Jody crouched on the ground a few feet from the northern most wall of the studio. Her face was shrouded in an unreadable mask as her hands pounded the ground. Jared grasping her shoulders and holding on tight looked up with an expression verging on madness. "I can't get through to her!"

Rainy dropped to her knees and ran her hands through the grass.

Struggling to speak, Jody stuttered, "There's a body buried here."

"You're right. I feel it too."

Jared gained the upper hand and yanked Jody into his protective arms. "I've got you, babe. Distance yourself from the emotion." He turned his steely gaze to Rainy. "Is this body of the man who practiced the black magic? Or do you think he went so far over the ledge that he sacrificed a person?"

Shivering at the thought, Rainy closed her eyes and focused on the bones beneath her. "Talk to me. Show me why your remains are here."

Flashes of moments in a man's life filtered through her mind. *An artist down on his luck—standing at an easel inside the studio painting—sitting on the floor burning a candle—a knife plunging into a cat.*

Witnessing the barbaric act shook her to the core. "I command you in the name of all that is righteous, show me how you ended up in this grave."

Fear threatened to strangle Rainy as more images become visible. *Two men argued, angry voices bellowed. A knife slashed through the air.* A high pitched scream ripped through Rainy's head and threatened to deafen her. *'I'll not allow you to desecrate the land me and my wife have worked so hard for. To hell with you and all of your evil ways.' The knife, now crimson with blood, plunged into the artist again and again.*

Horrified, Rainy crumpled to the ground.

Jody broke free from Jared and wrapped her arms around Rainy. "What did you see?"

"You've found the remains of the man that cast the spells. In a nutshell, he frightened the landlord, and they argued. The property owner murdered the artist for delving into the black arts."

Rainy kissed Jody on the forehead. "I think that you've just found what we need to get rid of the negative entity.

"Jared, please get Nathan and Terry to help you dig. We need to uncover this body. The grave is not consecrated, so you are not in danger of disturbing hallowed ground.

"Jody, while they are digging, keep focusing on the man. Get whatever you can from him. Every little piece of information will help."

A loud bang shook the ground. The shockwave rattled the windows of the studio. *Yes. This body is the key.*

As the men worked to unearth the bones, Rainy, Father Eric and the twins had no problem uncovering the protective talismans. The charmed coins were only buried a few inches beneath the surface. *Thank goodness.* They collected each gold charm and individually wrapped them in blessed silk that had been saturated with holy water. Once they were bound, the packages were secured in a wooden box effectively rendering them powerless. Rainy poured a line of black salt all the way around the studio trapping the entity within.

The evil mass emitted a piercing scream. Father Eric stood in front of the door and resumed his prayers. Holy water hit the windows and sizzled. There was still a good bit of fight left, in the entity, but they now had the upper hand.

Rainy cupped Terry's face and kissed his nose. "Terry, you must enter the studio with us. This is *your* property. *You* need to stand your ground and take it back."

Standing behind Father Eric, they joined hands. In one swift movement, the priest flung the door open and ran inside. Dragging Terry behind, Rainy threw herself into the black fog and was pleased to find no resistance as they entered.

The protective wards were broken, but the enemy still resided within the space and was pissed. Losing contact with Terry, unseen hands pulled at Rainy's hair and scratched at her face. A bird like claw with massive talons came out of nowhere, grabbed her arm and threw her off balance. Crouching down, she was forced to feel her way along the floor. She wondered at the sound of glass grinding beneath her feet. Something sharp sliced into her fingertips and pain radiated throughout her hand. It was only then that she'd remembered Nathan's visions of the mirror exploding. *I can't worry about that now.* Pursing her lips to offset the sting, she continued to run her hands along the floor ignoring each new gash the best she could. Before long, the floor became sticky with her blood.

She almost sighed with relief when her fingers grazed the pentagram painted on the floor all those years ago. Springing into action, she retracted her bloody hand and threw fistfuls of black salt over the pentacle to disrupt whatever influence remained. At first, there was only a slight shift in air pressure. Father Eric's voice seemed to amplify as he continued the ear-piercing phrases in Latin. The black mist undulated in a rhythmic motion. The pulsing action reminded Rainy of a heartbeat. With each rolling boil, the entity tried to retreat. No longer black, the mist surrounding them had lightened to the color of campfire smoke. In some places, the haze was even lighter. *Progress.*

Terry screamed, and the sound all but stopped her heart. Ready to do battle for the man she loved, Rainy stood and pivoted to find the entity had him in its grasp. This man that had become so dear to her heart hung above the floor by the neck—his attacker unseen.

The creature, still concealed within the fading mist, felt the wrath of Father Eric as Holy water flew through the air around Terry.

"Stop spewing me with that piss! I'll kill him first, and then I'll slaughter the witch. I'll leave you for last so you can witness and fear my power." The demonic hiss lashed out at the priest, as the creature continued to hold Terry tight.

Grasping Terry's legs, Rainy shouted. "This man is mine! He is under *my* protection. Release him this minute." Terry toppled to the floor but was unconscious. Nathan ran to his side and held him. Rainy circled them in a protective barrier with black salt. "Stay here with him and no matter what you see or hear, *do not* break this circle."

Father Eric confronted the demon in English, a sure sign the entity was weakening. "In the name of all that is holy, what is your name?"

The cackle in the room was both gravelly and horribly menacing. *"I don't have to tell you my name. I was invited here. I'm not leaving. It is you that has trespassed, and I demand that you leave."*

In response, the priest shouted the Archangel Michael's prayer. In what must surely, she hoped be the last act of rage it committed, the evil one turned the brunt of its force onto Rainy. Claws came out of the mist and swiped at her midsection—leaving bloody scratches in their wake.

Fury fueled her. Brandishing her ceremonial athame, Rainy thrust her arm forward and demanded her intentions be heard. "I call on the man that invited you. Free yourself from the bindings of this creature."

Her throat closed, cutting off her air. The monster was suffocating Rainy to silence her. The shadow man dug its claws deep into her neck. The gutless coward! The pressure burned her eyes. Her throat was ablaze with pain.

"Stephen Cutler! I beseech you. Speak with me. I can release you!" Jody's voice rang through the room while holding the skull above her head. Hope blossomed within Rainy.

Ripples of intense fear cascaded through the beast. A low buzz sounded in her ears, and the tight grip on her throat released.

"I demand to speak with Stephen Cutler. Release him!" Without warning, Jody hurled the skull deep into the mist leaving an open chasm in its wake. The spirit of a man spewed from the abyss and landed at Rainy's feet. The tortured condition of his soul broke Rainy's heart. He was emaciated. Deep gouging wounds covered what was left of his ethereal body. Working quickly, Rainy encircled the spirit in a protective barrier of black salt.

As the prize was wrenched from its clutches, Shadow Man howled. The mist heaved and lurched as if being torn apart from the inside out.

The remnants of the man's soul tried to stand, but

weakness won out. Instead, he held his arm out for Rainy to grasp his hand. *"Help me. I'm begging you. Don't send me back there."* His mewling plea plundered Rainy's emotions. It was evident that the tortured soul's transgressions had subjected his spirit to decades of indescribable cruelty and anguish. Unable to bear another's pain a moment longer, Rainy faced off with the dark force. "This man is now under my protection. You must leave him."

"No! I will not give him up. He's mine! Through magic he invited me."

"Help me," the spirit wailed. *"Please."*

"Father Eric, this man has practiced the dark arts. He's begging for help. Are you willing to send him to the light and have him answer to God for his offenses?"

Without hesitation, the priest moved to the edge of the circle and started to state the Last Rites. The dark creature growled, but its weakened state had taken much of the fight out of the beast.

Rainy knelt beside the circle and spoke in soft tones. "You can leave. You're no longer chained to the demon."

"I'm afraid. I've done too many bad things to be forgiven."

"Go through the light. All will be well." Concluding the Last Rites, Father Eric looked to Rainy. "Is the soul still within your circle?"

"Yes. He's afraid he will not be accepted in the light."

He nodded. "My son, God is good and willing to forgive if you are repentant. You are one of his children. Give yourself over to Him."

A beam of light steadily growing stronger engulfed

what was left of the tortured man. A choir of cherubs sang their acceptance. Spirits in the form of orbs beckoned him. Still unable to stand, angels carefully lifted the spirit of Stephen Cutler and carried him safely to the other side.

Within the now empty circle, Rainy found a large piece of mirror. Knowing it was only a matter of moments before it would be needed, she picked the shard up and watched as Father Eric took the upper hand. "Tell me your name! I demand it in the name of all that is holy!"

No longer able to hide behind the mist, the mass crumpled in on itself revealing the true demon form. Weakened, it fell to the floor. All but defeated the entity lifted its head and growled, "My name is Mammon."

Shivers of relief ran through Rainy's body. The entity had succumbed. By announcing its name at Father Eric's request, the demon had just given all authority and power over to the priest.

Holding the mirror high, Rainy cast her spell. "Into this mirror flows darkness." The demon disappeared with a loud whoosh, escaping into the shard. "To forever depart this place and remain harmless. Blessed be. In love and light. So mote it be."

Father Eric wrapped the mirror in a piece of blessed silk and bound it for good. He placed the shard inside the wooden box and secured the top. "I'll take this with me to ensure its proper disposal."

Chapter Twenty-One

Rainy took a sip of champagne and studied each of the smiling faces around the table. As her attention turned to Terry, he winked and pulled her in for an affectionate embrace. He kissed her ear and whispered, "We did it." It was hard to comprehend that just this morning this group of people had set out to battle evil. Not only had they been successful, but a misguided soul was saved from an eternity of torture and anguish. Today was a good day.

Nathan, jovial as always, sloshed his margarita as he whooped it up and hollered over their success. Jody and Jared leaned close together smiling and sharing tender glances. Their experience in the supernatural realm had proved invaluable. Without Jody's quick thinking today, there's no telling what the outcome would have been.

Mother Goddess, thank you for blessing me with these friends.

"You guys kicked some serious butt today. I wish everyone could have joined us tonight for this celebration.

"Jody, I've got to ask you, how in the world did you know to throw the skull into the mist? That was brilliant!"

The open praise caused her friend's face to flush with embarrassment. "Over the last several months, you've drilled into me that I need to think with my heart instead of my head. To listen to what my inner self is telling me. It's hard to explain, but when Jared unearthed the skull, it spoke to me. Thank goodness it worked."

Terry raised his beer and toasted his friends. "If it weren't for you guys, I wouldn't have a home."

"*A home?* Dude, without us, you wouldn't have a *soul*," Nathan quipped to the delight of everyone at the table.

"Touché. Every one of you put your lives in danger for me. I don't know how I can ever repay you."

Nathan smirked. "You're not going to cry, are you? I hate it when you cry."

Raking his hand through his hair, Terry snapped, "I know you don't like anyone to acknowledge their appreciation, but would you just let me finish, please? I'm trying to be serious here." Sentiment shaded Terry's expression as he scanned his friend's faces. "I love all of you."

Glasses clinked around the table, and Jared piped in. "To family."

"Yes. To family.

Turning his attention back to Nathan, Terry queried, "I'm confused about something. Since you were in law enforcement, maybe you could explain it to me? I don't understand why it's going to take the police so long to clear my home as a crime scene. Detective March said the property could be closed up for almost three weeks while they investigate. If you ask me, the guy acted like a real dick. Did you hear the 'tude in his voice when he was speaking to me?"

"Pfft. You're kidding, right?" Nathan shot back.

Genuinely perplexed, Terry responded with a shrug.

"Okay. I've got an idea. I think this will help you understand Detective March's mindset. Close your eyes." Pouting over Nathan's request, Terry just stared. "Why?"

"Jeez, Runt. For once in your life, just do what I ask."

"Fine."

"Thank you. Now, imagine, if you will, being outside of our little group and hearing this: Detective, thanks for stopping by. Me, the priest, the witch, a few coven members, and a few friends were just randomly digging in my back yard and happened to find skeletal remains. And the reason the head is in the outbuilding is because this sweet little woman, here, tore the skull from the spine and tossed it like a softball into the studio. So your CSI group will probably find her fingerprints all over it."

Terry opened his mouth to interrupt, but Nathan held his hand out. "Let me finish.

"You say you'd like to search the house? Sure. No problem. And, oh, by the way, you might have a difficult time with that because the place has been completely trashed. We've been fighting a demon for the better part of six hours, and he didn't want to go. Funny thing, he broke every piece of furniture I had so you're going to have a hell of a job sifting through the carnage."

Jody's hand flew to her mouth. "Uh-oh." Her cheeks turned crimson. "I forgot. On my way from the grave to the studio, I bumped into Cheryl, and another idea popped into my mind. I asked her for a piece of malachite and wedged it inside the skull for a little extra added oomph. I can't imagine what that detective is going to think when that beautiful stone is recovered from inside the skull."

Nathan threw his head back and laughed. "You see what I mean? Come on, give the guy a break. With the crowd we had there, he probably believes there are more bodies to be found. It's going to take the cops awhile to sift through that mess at your house. You should be happy they want a thorough investigation. It means the cops are doing their jobs.

"If I were you, I'd expect a little extra attention from the Tempe PD over the next year or so. Take it from me, after answering that particular call, they're going to keep you on their radar."

Terry gulped his beer. "Yep. Okay. You're right. That explains all the dirty looks and snide remarks.

"I just don't know what I'm going to do. My old apartment is already leased out to someone else. Where am I going to stay until I can get back into my home?"

Jody extended her arm across the table and intertwined fingers with Terry. "Jared and I were hoping that the three of you would join us on the houseboat at Lake Powell. After what we've been through, we all deserve a vacation." Everyone at the table perked up.

"We could go kayaking, jet skiing, hiking. If you want to fish, all you have to do is crack a beer open and throw a worm over the side of the boat, kick back and relax. Jared and I discussed this, and we'd love the company.

"Since both Rainy and Terry are self-employed, and Nathan works with Jared, there's no problem with any of you taking the time off. When the police tell Terry he can return to his home, the helicopter can fly the three of you back. The arrangements can be handled with a single phone call. No muss. No fuss.

"Please say you'll join us. We'll have such a good time."

Before anyone could accept, Rainy objected. "That's such a generous offer, but this is your honeymoon."

Jared patted her hand. "Our plan has always been to leisurely explore the lake. We fully expect to be gone for two or three more months. When we left the boat to help out, we'd only made it about twenty miles up the lake. Every day or two, we pick up stakes and move a little farther down. By my calculations, we still have another hundred and seventy miles or so to go before we get to the far end of the lake.

"Believe me when I say that you've never seen a sunset until you've been on Lake Powell. Jody and I eat dinner in the open air on the top deck of the boat. Every night the sunset is more spectacular than the last." Leaning back and tucking his wife into his side, Jared kissed the top of Jody's head. "The views are breathtaking. We explore new territory every day. We'd love to share that with the three of you."

Nathan raised his beer. "Count me in. It's been way too long since I've been fishing."

Terry grinned at Rainy. "Let's do it."

"It sounds too good to pass up. I'm in too." Rainy cupped Terry's face and kissed him.

Jody's dreamy sigh was so loud that it was heard over the background music. "I'm so happy for you two. Love looks good on you both."

Turning her focus to Nathan, the mother hen in her took over. "So when are you going to do something about Bright Flower?" She tapped her wrist and grinned. "Tick tock."

Aghast, Nathan choked on his drink. "*What?* Why would you think anything would need to be done?"

Jody's exaggerated eye roll had Terry in stitches. "I was there at the wedding, remember? Every time you looked at that woman, your expression softened."

"Oh, please. Give me a break. You don't know what you're talking about."

"Is that so? Well, I also noticed that every time you walked near her, that sweet woman's whole demeanor brightened. And when you refused to talk to her, or even look at her, her shoulders slumped with disappointment."

Nathan's brow furrowed, a dead giveaway that his focus had turned inward. "I'm sure you're just exaggerating. She didn't even notice me. I tried to catch her attention, but she always dropped her gaze when I came close."

"Of course she did, you idiot. She's more or less Navajo Indian royalty. What did you expect her to do in front of all those people? Chase you down?"

Nathan abruptly stood and lifted his empty margarita glass. "I need another drink. Does anyone want anything?"

"Or for God's sake, I'll shut up. Don't run off. Let's change the subject to what everyone will need to bring for the lake trip."

****

The night was cool, the moon full, and the water was still as glass. Terry and Rainy had located an isolated beach on their evening excursion. It was the perfect spot to be alone and enjoy each other's company. The final night on the lake had been one to remember. Their lovemaking had lasted for hours leaving both of them exhausted.

Terry pulled Rainy tighter into his side. "Can you believe this view? This lake is an oasis paradise in the desert. I've never seen a more beautiful place." He pointed to a mountain in the distance. "Before we leave tomorrow, I'd like to take some pictures of you in front of that landscape. I have these incredible visions in my mind that would make a beautiful portrait. This place is so inspiring that I might do a whole series of Lake Powell paintings."

His enthusiasm went unanswered, so he believed she'd fallen asleep in his arms. "I love you, Rainy. I want to spend my life with you. Is it too soon to ask you to marry me?"

He jumped when she lifted her head. "What?" Not having the guts to pursue this discussion right this minute, Rainy's groggy response offered some hope that she hadn't actually heard his little speech.

"What?"

"Did you just ask me to marry you?"

"I thought you were sleeping."

"Nope. Wide awake. *Well?*"

"Well, hypothetically, if I were to ask you to marry me, what do you think your answer might be?"

"*Are* you asking me to marry you?"

"I don't want you to feel rushed. Do you think it's too soon to ask?"

"Terry, I've already told you that I've been waiting for you a lifetime. From my perspective, it's taken you over a quarter of a century to ask me—that is, if you *are* asking me. In my book, that makes you slow as molasses."

"Then—hypothetically—I guess I'm asking you, provided you say yes."

"Maybe you could ask me without the word hypothetically thrown in. What do you think?"

Sitting alongside Rainy, Terry gazed into her eyes. "These last few weeks with you have been the happiest of my life. I don't want to go back to being alone. I want you in my life every day. Rainy Stratton, will you marry me?"

"What are your thoughts on living arrangements?"

"I thought you were going to say yes?"

"Before we get to that, there are some things we need to discuss. We're two adults living in two different cities. I don't even know if you want children. Do you want children?"

"I want a whole herd of children."

"That's a good answer. Where do you want to live?"

Over the last two weeks, he'd often thought about future living arrangements. "I've just bought the house of my dreams. I've fought a life or death battle to keep it. I'm not too keen on giving it up just yet. Also, since Jody is living in Flagstaff, Nathan doesn't have any family left in town but me. I'd feel like I was abandoning him if I moved to Flagstaff.

"On the other hand, you have a business in Flagstaff, and then there's that whole coven thing." They both laughed. "I would never expect you to pick up and leave that behind. I think I'd like living in Flagstaff. Jody and Jared love it there. I'm an artist. I can work from anywhere as long as I have space."

"It's a quandary."

"Yep."

Rainy tugged Terry close and squeezed. "What if we lived in both places?"

"Both places?"

"We could commute. One or two weeks in Phoenix, and one or two weeks in Flagstaff. That way, Nathan wouldn't be orphaned, you wouldn't have to give up your house, I wouldn't have to give up my business and coven, and Jody and Jared would be close. What do you think?"

"I love that idea!"

"My Flagstaff home has a huge sun room that looks out over Lake Mary. The lighting is breathtaking, and the elk come out to graze every day. If you like the space, you could use that as your studio.

"Your new house has four bedrooms, one for us, one for Nathan when he stays over, and I'm hoping you'll consider letting me have one for an office."

"The best of both worlds."

"Yep. Ask me again. I'm ready to answer now."

He nipped at her lip. "Will you marry me, Rainy Stratton?"

"Yes."

A word from the author…

I've been an avid reader for years. To my husband's dismay, I have bookshelves full of books, rooms full of books, boxes full of books. My cars have books in them. I just can't seem to get rid of them after I read them. You just never know when you will want to read it again, right? When my husband bought me a Kindle, it cut down on our need for storage, but it opened me up to books that I might never have experienced otherwise.

The biggest transition in my relationship with books occurred, however, when I, much to my surprise, became an author. I had started having dreams about people I didn't know. I started looking forward to my dreams every night. Then I realized that I was daydreaming about these people as well. I'd just be sitting there, and these people and their antics would pop into my mind. Finally, I gave in and began writing their stories down.

My books invariably feature strong women. My husband, Michael, and I have raised two strong daughters, Pilar and Shandelle, and they inspire the characters in my stories.

I've had fun with the books I've written. Inserting real events, things that have actually happened in my family's lives, is like having a private joke.

My romance novels always contain a paranormal twist. I imagine my future writings will always contain romance with strong women and men of character, influenced by events that reach beyond what we consider normal, and perhaps seasoned with a little touch of whimsy.

http://sandywolters.weebly.com/

Thank you for purchasing
this publication of The Wild Rose Press, Inc.

If you enjoyed the story, we would appreciate your
letting others know by leaving a review.

For other wonderful stories,
please visit our on-line bookstore at
www.thewildrosepress.com.

For questions or more information
contact us at
info@thewildrosepress.com.

The Wild Rose Press, Inc.
www.thewildrosepress.com

Stay current with The Wild Rose Press, Inc.

Like us on Facebook

https://www.facebook.com/TheWildRosePress

And Follow us on Twitter
https://twitter.com/WildRosePress

www.ingramcontent.com/pod-product-compliance
Lightning Source LLC
Chambersburg PA
CBHW060519260626
47161CB00003B/709